This Is All Your Fault

WITHDRAWN

WITHDRAWN

This Is All Your Fault

Aminah Mae Safi

Feiwel and Friends
New York

SQUARE
FISH

SQUARE
FISH

An imprint of Macmillan Publishing Group, LLC
120 Broadway, New York, NY 10271
fiercereads.com

Copyright © 2020 by Aminah Mae Safi
All rights reserved.

Square Fish and the Square Fish logo are trademarks of Macmillan and are used
by Feiwel and Friends under license from Macmillan.

Our books may be purchased in bulk for promotional, educational, or business
use. Please contact your local bookseller or the Macmillan Corporate and
Premium Sales Department at (800) 221-7945 ext. 5442 or by email at
MacmillanSpecialMarkets@macmillan.com.

Library of Congress Control Number: 2019948801

Originally published in the United States by Feiwel and Friends
First Square Fish edition, 2022
Book designed by Liz Dresner
Square Fish logo designed by Filomena Tuosto
Printed in the United States of America.

ISBN 978-1-250-79194-8 (paperback)
10 9 8 7 6 5 4 3 2 1

LEXILE: HL720L

For my baba,
who taught me to never give up the fight

This is the story of the day that Wild Nights
Bookstore and Emporium closed down.

I'd say sorry, but I don't feel that I need to explain my art to you.

TUESDAY EVENING

AN HOUR AFTER CLOSING

PROLOGUE

There Is No Sinner Like a Young Saint

Eli

Eli had never been certain of much. His most defining belief so far was that he could get through life with a wink on hand, a smile at the ready, and a lighter in his pocket. But here was one thing—a suddenly new thing—he believed without question: Wild Nights Bookstore and Emporium was going under.

Eli had seen the signs. The dwindling customer base. The fewer and fewer repeat booklovers coming to the sell counter. The way their online reviews had stagnated. The fact that the number of authors who came to do signings anymore was next to none.

What Eli didn't understand was *why*.

Bookstores were supposed to be making a comeback. Actual paper books were, according to all those experts on the internet, crushing digital sales.

But for some reason none of those trends had touched Wild Nights. It was as though the store had been left behind to rot among the ashes of the book resurgence. It didn't make sense.

The store had the right vibe and the right location and somehow it was still floundering. Still sinking under the weight of its inventory.

There were really only three things left for Eli to do.

1. Root through the store's records to find the proof of their imminent demise.
2. See if there was a way to save Wild Nights Bookstore and Emporium.
3. Kick back and smoke a disposable pen from Jo's bag of vapes, because there probably wasn't a way to save the store and doom was almost always inevitable, as far as Eli was concerned.

Eli should have done the first thing first and saved the smoking for last, but Eli had never been much for rules, even if they were of his own invention. He embraced his doom as he sat at the desk in the back office of the bookstore, typing the store's daily totals with his left hand, because his right was occupied with one of the disposable vapes Jo had stashed away in her bottom desk drawer. Jo was the manager at Wild Nights, and she bought the variety packs of vapes from the local corner store because they were cheaper and she suspected her employees dug into her stash while she wasn't looking.

She was correct.

Besides, Eli would have to be a saint to keep his hands off them as he closed the store alone and did *math*.

Eli was not a saint.

He was just a sucker for that heady buzz that came from smoking one of these. It was bad for him. But Eli was, in general, into things that were bad for him. He'd figured this out years ago, and, contrary to what all the adults around him said, he hadn't grown out of it. Everything Eli touched turned to shit no matter what he did. He might as well go for the kind of stuff that would destroy him, rather than the other way around.

Eli took another puff. He didn't like counting inventory on the old tape calculator. He had tried to do it the way Danny had shown him, but he was no natural at math, the way she was. It was slow going and would have been so much faster if he could have tallied the daily totals on the laptop, with a proper keyboard. And a spreadsheet.

Instead, he was using a calculator the size of a book. Not only was it enormous, the ancient machine actually printed out the numbers onto a roll of paper like the old-school register they kept up front. Every time Eli typed, the calculator made a scratching *chut chut* against the paper and spat out even more numbers. And then he was supposed to tally these numbers in a black, leather-bound notebook that held all the records of Wild Nights since the beginning of time. Danny usually closed and was the one typically entrusted with this job. But she'd been given the night off, and, despite his reputation, Eli didn't want to mess up this job if he didn't have to. He was going to tally the day's totals and then get to the bottom of Wild Nights' financial records.

But the more Eli totaled numbers, the more he thought about the process—it was super strange that the store's owner, Archer Hunt Junior, hadn't switched to any kind of digital records. Eli didn't typically care about answers to impossible questions. But he couldn't stop asking himself what was going on here. His mind couldn't stop whirling with possibilities.

Where were the records, anyway? Why hadn't Hunt Junior invested any energy into bringing new customers into the store? Why didn't Hunt Junior even come down to the store anymore at all?

A pulsing blue glow caught the corner of Eli's eye.

Jo had left her laptop in the office.

Eli hesitated for a fraction of a second. He really *shouldn't* go rooting through other people's laptops. Especially not people he respected. It was just, laptops could double-check Eli's math. Laptops could be used to make a digital archive of what was currently only ink and paper. Without anyone else on-site, all of Eli's suspicions were really only guesses. A feeling that had grown unavoidable to Eli. A truth he knew but couldn't quite prove.

Eli had been blindsided enough in his life to know when it was happening, and he *knew* it was happening now. He just had to figure out *how*. And he had to figure out how without getting *caught*.

Besides, if Jo hadn't wanted Eli to use the old black brick of a laptop, she ought to have made her password more secure than *thebatman* in all lowercase. She was always going off that "the Batman" was the least interesting part of any of the comics. It wasn't hard to guess that she used the phrase as a catchall key to all her digital castles. She used it for the Wi-Fi password, too. And Eli had seen *Hackers* enough on TV to know that people reused their passwords. It didn't matter how many times people were warned that they shouldn't. They just did. Jo hadn't even bothered to add a number combination at the back end to throw off the average, prank-level hack.

Though, to be honest, Eli probably could have guessed the number combination at the back end of Jo's passwords, too. She was predictable, and Eli knew her well enough after working under her at the bookstore for the last couple of years. He knew her birthday and the date her mom had died. If you paid attention, you could really see people when they weren't taking notice of themselves.

The login screen accepted Eli's password and, in an instant, he was in.

Except Jo's desktop was pristine.

Nothing but her hard drive and a shortcut to her email.

Eli knew that, next to going through someone's search history or maybe looking through their messages, clicking on another person's email was one of the most invasive things that he could do. But Eli wanted *answers*, and adults, even adults like Jo, were never going to give straight answers. Adults were always saying they were *protecting* you, but Eli knew that was just a fancy way of saying *lying*.

So Eli clicked the lone desktop shortcut and into Jo's email he went.

Wild Nights property sale: PENDING

That was the only message in her inbox. Eli should have stopped there. Should have closed down the mail client and shut down the laptop. It was very obvious, really, what Eli should have done next. *Don't open your boss's email*. Especially the boss who hired you when you still had a juvenile record. It was one of those things that went without saying, really.

Eli clicked open the email.

Of course, once he'd opened the message, Eli wished he'd never seen it. Wished he'd actually listened to Jo and not touched her laptop in the first place. Wished he'd let the adults protect him from the truth instead of going out searching for it like a real asshole. As he read, the pit in Eli's stomach grew until it formed the kind of chasm that he didn't know how to climb his way out of.

NOTICE

This is a notice that the sale of the property, plant, and equipment—Wild Nights Bookstore building and lot—is

under consideration with the West Garden Property Group
and will likely be finalized in the next fourteen days. Please
consider yourself advised.

Regards,
Archer Hunt Jr.
Owner, Hunt Properties, LLC
Tempus Fugit . . .

Leave it to Archer Hunt to not even put a greeting at the top of
a message that told his oldest and most senior employee that she
was going to be without a job and out on her ass in two weeks.
Attached to the email was a series of documents—unsigned—
but all looking like pretty official contracts. The valuation of the
property that the bookstore sat on was blacked over. Like Jo
deserved to be given two weeks' notice to find a new job but not
to understand the basic underlying numbers and monetary value
of what she was being sold out for.

It wasn't right. It wasn't fair.

Eli was used to this by now. He was under no illusions that the
world was a fair place. He had accepted that as true and real for as
long as he could remember. The world was an unholy and random
dumpster fire, so stick it to the man as much as you can.

The problem was, Eli realized, that he kind of *was* the man.
Or, at least, he very easily could become the man in, like, twenty
years. He had all the traits that could boost him into that vaunted
position. Fair hair and the kind of chubby-cheeked smile that—
combined with the fact that he was a straight white dude—meant
people just *believed* him, without really trying. Meant that people
honestly wanted to *help* him, in whatever his endeavors were.
Remove roadblocks rather than set them up in his way. Hell,

courtesy of his eighteenth birthday, his petty criminal record had been wiped clean. Nobody in Chicago had even considered trying a fourteen-year-old white boy with curly blond hair as an adult for a string of grocery and convenience store beer thefts. He was just a boy to them, being a boy. And while maybe he deserved a little reprimand, he didn't really deserve a permanent record.

That was how Eli knew that life wasn't fair. It had never been fair to him. It had been unreasonably kind to him. He had to make up for that somehow.

Eli put down the vape pen. Playtime was over. Really, he had two choices now.

1. Help Jo make a case for what Wild Nights Bookstore was worth.
2. Give up and go back to being as complacent as he'd ever been.

That was it. Help out the person who had given him a real chance—back when Eli's record was still a thing that kept him from being hired—or give up now. He could easily go back to being the kid who thought stealing six-packs was the best way to show the world that he saw it for what it was.

Or he could save the day. Like the real Batman.

Eli started searching for commercial property values in Wicker Park. He whistled when he saw how many zeros gentrification added to a purchasing price. Eli wasn't sure how to compete with that. But maybe if he could make a case for a strong, sustainable business, Archer Hunt wouldn't want to sell.

Eli started searching through the office, looking for old invoices. He found them—daily takes stretching back to the nineties—in a series of binders on the bookshelf behind the desk. All the numbers were down, year over year. For decades. Not that these were exact data. But he could see the downward trend as he looked. The worst of it was recent, too. Almost a year ago to the date, the numbers started to really and truly spiral downward. The more Eli flipped through, the more he realized that there wasn't a real case for Wild Nights staying open. If Eli just took the last twelve months of data, he'd probably make an excellent case for closing the store down permanently.

Eli had been right. Wild Nights Bookstore and Emporium *was* going under.

He went back to the laptop. Maybe Jo had found more info than he had. She must have put together her own case of what the business was worth, or at least what the finances looked like. Maybe she had found something that Eli had missed.

Eli opened up Jo's calendar on the web browser. He looked over the week. Jo had, in all her anal-retentive glory, made a note on her calendar for this Friday—

last day of full staff.

It was such a simple note. No caps lock. No exclamation points. Just a direct statement of fact marked into her calendar.

Here was the thing—Jo had taken Eli in and given him a chance when nobody else would. She'd hired a kid with a record, and instead of yelling at Eli and lecturing him, she had handed him responsibility and told him to step up to the plate. She'd made this space—Wild Nights—a place for the art kids like AJ and the book nerds like Rinn and the angry girls like Imogen. Even Daniella Korres didn't mind working at Wild Nights, and Danny was disdainful of nearly everything. She rolled her eyes whenever Eli called her Danny. True, when he'd started calling her that, it was kind of a joke. But by now, he couldn't help it. She had white-blond hair and a heart made out of stone. If anyone could have been a real-life Mother of Dragons, it was Daniella Korres. But she was also more than a fictional queen, so Eli elongated her name when he said it, made sure it sounded like he'd added an extra *n* and made the nickname her own.

And Jo, she had made the bookstore a haven. She had made it *theirs*, even though none of them were at all alike, except for the fact that some piece of them didn't fit in anywhere else. Wild Nights couldn't just close. Staff couldn't be let go on Friday, without warning. Jo couldn't suddenly *not have a job*. It wasn't right.

Eli opened a new tab on the browser and started searching. The patron saints of the internet had to tell him something useful.

Because *what* to do was tough to say.

The first problem was—Eli didn't have any money.

And he didn't come from money. And even if he had, given how much trouble he'd gotten into in the past, he doubted his mom would have forked over any funds, no matter how legitimate Eli's reasons. After her last desperate bid to take Eli back to church had failed to produce any results, Eli's mom had largely washed her hands of him. That was the problem with being found out as a good liar—people couldn't trust that Eli was telling the truth rather than telling a good lie in a true-sounding way.

Eli started typing the names of large banking institutions into the browser bar of a series of new tabs. It was a desperate bid for information and resources. Usually the accounts logged you out. *Usually.*

But Jo—oh God, Jo—had left herself signed into her password manager. Eli could practically envision her clicking *Trust This Device* and not giving it a second thought. He found an account where two-step verification hadn't been turned on and he was, miraculously, in. It was a petty-cash account, but Eli had money to play with now. He had resources.

He cracked his knuckles. He opened a new tab.

What could he do with nine thousand dollars?

As he searched, he found a staggering number of pyramid schemes. Weight-loss supplements. Protein powders. Laxative teas. Tupperware. Makeup. The inventory was irrelevant, really. But the key was to buy volume and then trick someone else into buying more volume.

Eli wanted to get rich quick with a low-capital investment here. Not get stuck with massive overhead costs. The more he searched, the more he saw that all those multilevel marketing schemes cost people money. Besides, if he was going to buy inventory, it had to look like something the bookstore could legitimately sell. Nobody came to Wild Nights looking for detox-laxative tea. At least not intentionally.

He needed a way to flip the cash in this account into more cash. If he could do that successfully, maybe he could help Jo get enough to buy a stake in the bookstore.

There had to be another way to flip the money.

Maybe gambling?

There was online poker, but it was difficult to wire the cash now that gambling online was illegal. There was no good way to funnel the bookstore's funds into the online accounts.

Not good enough.

Maybe he could buy into some kind of cryptocurrency. But it would take days to figure out how to transfer the cash, then another few weeks at least of growth, if it even went up at all.

Eli didn't have that kind of time.

Friday. He had until Friday.

It was nearly 1:00 A.M. when Eli found the inventory of Jordans.

They were older and more rare, the kind that could really go for something. The photos looked good. Eli noticed a couple of potentially super-unique items—a retro Air Jordan IV and a pair of kicks that looked like they could have been those Nike Mags—the *Back to the Future II* ones.

The price was low enough to account for the fact that the seller wanted to off-load them, but not so low as to ring alarm bells. And the total inventory was priced around the nine-thousand-dollar mark. The sale of the individual items all together was worth at least eighteen to twenty-one thousand, though. That was what Eli had gotten from googling all the shoes he could ID and seeing what they were going for.

Eli was interested but still cautious. He messaged the seller. *Whats up with the Jordans*

nothing, man, the seller wrote back pretty quickly. *I just need to move into a smaller storefront and I've got to let this older merchandise go.*

That made sense. Eli cracked his knuckles again. There were two paths forward.

1. Do something for someone else for once in his life.
2. Sit back and watch the bookstore close and enjoy the rest of his vape.

This was it. He either did something, here and now. Or he gave up. Went back to tallying the day's totals. Went back to accepting the status quo. Went back to being the kind of person who rebelled against the system when it was most convenient to himself but sat by and watched when shit was really hitting the fan. Let Jo lose her job and let the bookstore close without doing a damned thing about it.

Eli made a decision.

alright lets do it, and Eli put the payment through on the vendor website—because he knew better than to give away a billing address and a bank account to a stranger on the internet—and watched as the available funds drained out of the account.

He'd done it. Or at least, half of it.

Eli took the photos that were already on the seller page and asked for copies, double-checking that those were images of the actual product. The seller assured Eli that they were and sent along the photos as a measure of good faith. The overnight tracking number arrived quickly in Jo's inbox after that. The merchandise would arrive *tomorrow*. The timing was perfect.

Eli had his first pair of Jordans listed by 2:00 A.M.

Ping. He had a hit. Already. Eli let out a sigh of relief. He was really doing it. He was really saving the bookstore.

These photos of the actual merchandise? That was from the buyer.

Eli assured the buyer that they were.

no good

But that didn't make any sense to Eli. Having photos of the actual merchandise was always helpful. *No good?*

The response was almost immediate. *Nah, man. these are fake af.*

Fake??? Eli had trouble breathing. He'd been managing just fine before. But he struggled to inhale now. There was no way—*no way*—these were fake. They were real. They had to be real.

Didn't you know?

No, typed Eli. Because this wasn't happening. This couldn't be happening.

But the person on the other end was relentless. *The lightning bolt in the back isn't right. The tongue doesn't say Be Like Mike. dont mess with me man. you gotta know they're fake.*

Eli felt a pang in his chest. But now was not the time to panic.

Sure, the money was out of the account. But he could message the original seller and see what was up. He could definitely get a refund. Definitely. He had *not* made the problem worse. He would check in with the original seller and he would fix this. And then get back to saving the bookstore.

yo someone said these are fake. i'd like a refund if they are

The original seller messaged back immediately. *You buy the merchandise it's yours. I already shipped it out, man.*

Eli typed so that he hit every key with precision. He hit a hard return. *I. want. my. money. back.*

You snooze you lose, kid. And then the original seller logged off.

Eli went back, trying to use the buyer protection plan on the vendor website. But it was too late. The money was gone. The banks could possibly work it out, but the account wasn't his. If he reported this to real authorities, Eli would be the one on the hook for stealing the bookstore's money to begin with. Especially since Eli had wanted to use the money to help Jo buy a stake in the store from its actual owner, Archer Hunt Junior.

It looked like fraud. Eli didn't have to be good at math to know that.

Eli logged out of the bank account. He logged out of the vendor website. He scrubbed any email evidence of the purchases out of Jo's inbox. Eli scrubbed and scrubbed and scrubbed, so that there was nothing left. No trace of what he'd done.

Of course, there was nine thousand dollars missing. So that was a trace.

But Eli kept scrubbing anyway, as best he could for as long as he was able. He couldn't look at any of it anymore. Couldn't clear his mind of what he'd done. He'd lost more than nine grand. Over a bunch of fake Air Jordans. The store would be lucky if it could operate past tomorrow. The petty cash was gone.

Gone.

Eli closed Jo's laptop. Put it back exactly in the spot where he'd found it.

And then he finished closing, as though nothing had happened. He tallied the totals on the calculator. He input them into the account ledger, just like Danny had shown him. Then he stood, locked up Wild Nights Bookstore, and went out into the muggy, early Chicago morning. He started walking, not sure of where he was headed. He heard the vape fall out of his pocket, but he didn't stop to pick it up. He had to keep moving, keep going.

Then he got out his phone and he messaged Danny. *Wild Nights is closing down. Top secret. Cover for me until I get to work tomorrow.*

She'd understand. If he could explain in person, at least Danny would get it. And even if she didn't, she was probably out tonight and wouldn't see the message until the morning anyway. Eli had at least six more hours to magically come up with nine thousand dollars.

Sure, he'd read fantasy books with less fantastical premises. But Eli wasn't giving up yet.

Eventually, the hammer would come down on Eli. But right now, he'd go for a walk and he'd figure this out. He had six hours and he could do this—he *could.*

Because Eli knew that *eventually* wasn't some undefined date in the future.

Eventually was very likely tomorrow morning.

WEDNESDAY MORNING

8:00 a.m.—11:59 a.m.

1

A Variety of Beginnings

8:17 A.M., Wednesday
Daniella

Daniella pulled up to the parking lot of Wild Nights Bookstore and Emporium with her music as loud as she could possibly take before nine in the morning.

Daniella was not, as a rule, a morning person.

It hadn't helped that she had gotten a message from Eli the night before while she was out, and, in the aftermath, had gone from sociably drinking to basically annihilated by tequila.

Wild Nights Bookstore and Emporium was closing.

She parked on a street that was three blocks back from the store, because she liked that walk from her car to the door. The distance between her own space and her work life. She didn't like to park close. She liked to transition, to ease into the role. It didn't matter to Daniella that the air was sticky with early-morning humidity; she took her time gathering her stuff out of her passenger seat. She drove an old Mustang from the seventies that she'd managed to pick up from a graduating senior girl for a song. She didn't even need more than liability insurance on the thing because it was made of solid Detroit steel and either she was going to go out in a blaze of glory or she was going to take out whatever car she hit like a tank.

She'd been teaching herself how to fix up the old boy. It had vinyl seats and a big boat wheel. The radio was a dial with buttons that jumped the red notch down the line when she selected one of the preprogrammed buttons. The engine rumbled as she drove, and the whomping mess of a car made her feel like she had a space that was hers and that would always be hers.

Which she needed right now, because she'd just found out one of her favorite ways to get out of the house was closing down and there was nothing that she could do about it. Daniella pulled up the emergency brake and shifted the gear into first before turning off the throaty, muscly engine. Daniella started thinking how she liked her cars the way she liked her boys, but that felt like too obvious a piece of humor this early in the morning, so she buried the joke down deep and didn't laugh.

Daniella pulled the strap to her tan leather satchel over her shoulder and pulled the bag and herself out of the car. The bag snagged for a moment on the gearbox and then the e-brake, but Daniella kept pulling, kept using momentum to get everything out in one solid swing.

The satchel came to an abrupt stop against Daniella's hip, but she wasn't thrown off balance by it. The thwack against her leg was grounding, if anything. She was here, in this body, in this incomprehensible life.

Daniella took a deep breath, trying to keep a wave of nausea at bay. She'd thrown on a pair of cutoff black denim shorts, some Docs, and a worn-in, soft T-shirt that read *Visit Crete*, complete with a cartoon of a minotaur on it. And this wasn't from a quick road trip through Crete, Illinois. This was from actual international travel. Yia-yia had brought it back for Daniella when she and Mom went back to the motherland for a trip without Daniella or any of her siblings.

These were her favorite, threadbare clothes, and she needed that when she had to deal with a hangover. She opened the front flap of her bag and began digging through, past her notebook—her secret notebook, leather-bound in black—trying to find her keys to the front door of Wild Nights Bookstore and Emporium. She was the only high school employee with her own set. And they were nearly all high school employees. For reasons that were beyond Daniella's comprehension, the only employee at Wild Nights who was an adult with a master's degree was the manager, Jo.

Actually, Jo was the only adult, full stop.

Even Rinn Olivera didn't get a set of keys. At least Daniella would always have that.

Wild Nights Bookstore was still closing, though. Daniella took another deep breath because she was not going to throw up and she was *not* going to cry. She was also *not* going to tell anyone. She'd promised Eli she wouldn't.

She was going to handle herself, and she was going to open the damned store.

But her mind was still screaming. *Wild Nights was closing, was closing, was closing.*

Daniella didn't know how she was going to make it through the morning without telling anyone. Luckily, she was opening the store, which typically gave her time to think.

Daniella was supposed to get to the store right at eight, even seven, on a morning that she opened so that she could set up the bookstore right. But nobody ever came into the store directly at opening at nine—which, now that Daniella thought about it, really *wasn't* a good sign, as far as business went. And, anyway, Daniella was usually the one closing at night, so she often got everything organized then—that way it would take her the least amount of time to open the next morning. She was lucky that she never really had to take opening shift while there was school, but, then again, that also meant most of her day was taken up by school.

Summers were different, though. They always had been. So much more time to fill. So much more creativity required to get out of the house and stay out.

Daniella's jet-black aviator sunglasses slipped down her nose, and she squinted for a moment due to the pain of the sun against her eyes. The air was that heavy kind of humidity that permeated the entire area as soon as April rolled into May. They were into June now, so when she inhaled, Daniella got a taste of her own car's vintage exhaust and the kind of fumes that only came out of buses or trucks. Industrial-grade smog. A real Chicagoland smell. Daniella pushed her sunglasses back up, unused to having a hangover, much less a workday one. She swatted at a mosquito she felt prickling at her leg.

Normally, Daniella led a carefully segmented life. Weekdays were filled with school. Evenings filled with work. Saturdays were workdays, too. But Saturday evenings were for going out. Sundays were for recovery, while her mom went to church and Daniella claimed she had too much schoolwork to catch up on.

But Daniella typically did her homework in class. Sundays were mostly for Daniella to devote to her own church of sorts— her poetry. Daniella wrote while her mind was still fuzzy and impressionable from the night before. When she didn't have the energy to censor herself or overthink her words. When she could just write and believe in her words enough to not stop every other word, wondering if she'd gotten it right, wondering if she had done enough. She'd post it throughout the week. Photos of what she'd written on paper. Sometimes she'd doodle. But mostly it was her words scrawled across a page.

The spins overtook Daniella for a moment. She reached out, steadying herself on a nearby parked car. It took two counts for the spinning to stop again. Daniella reached back into her bag and mercifully found the store keys, despite the fact that her sunglasses blocked her ability to see any real depth into her purse. She'd been searching by feel and had grabbed at her notebook more times than she cared to in a public setting. Nobody knew about Daniella's poetry, and she was planning on keeping it that way.

She hadn't figured out how to compartmentalize her life for nothing.

Daniella crossed the narrow, flat street, under the speckled shade of the big, circular buckthorn trees. She rounded the corner and made it to the front door of Wild Nights Bookstore and Emporium.

AJ Park was sitting against the curb. AJ was one of those devastatingly handsome artistic boys, with hair that flopped into his eyes and clothes that were perfectly worn in. He looked like the kind of kid who could reveal the mysteries of the universe in his deep, dark eyes.

Daniella preferred boys who held no mysteries and carried no depth. They were the kind of boys who were good for one thing and one thing only. The kind of boys who a girl only needed liability insurance for. Destroy or be destroyed. AJ was too thoughtful to be the kind of boy that drew Daniella's interest. And AJ seemed to see nothing in Daniella but another one of his three sisters. They could be friends in perfect safety.

But even AJ didn't know about Daniella's writing.

Daniella hadn't meant to become a great secret keeper. But she had learned early that information was not just power—it was safety. So she kept from AJ, too, that Wild Nights Bookstore was about to close.

According to Eli, at least.

Daniella had to assume that she could trust Eli, that he wasn't exaggerating for effect or lying by omission, but that wasn't an assumption made lightly or easily by Daniella. Ever.

"What's up?" AJ stood; he brushed some of the asphalt rubble from the back of his pants.

Daniella shrugged. All she had to do was compartmentalize this one thing. Just one more segmented section of her life. *Easy.* "The same."

"You close last night?" asked AJ.

"No, didn't you hear? Jo trusted *Eli* to close. Alone. Told me I could have the evening off. I guess she decided to trust him. Or try out trusting him." Daniella hoped her worry didn't show on her face. Eli was a hell-raiser, but he was basically harmless. He liked to give Jo shit and then do everything that Jo asked. Or at least, that's what Daniella had always assumed. She'd hate to give him the benefit of the doubt now, at the end of things, when he didn't deserve it.

A troubled expression crossed AJ's face. "Shouldn't he be here, though?"

Daniella shoved the key into the lock, but it was old and it got stuck as she tried to turn it.

Stuck. *Typical.*

Daniella almost had the door unlocked and she'd almost made it through this conversation with AJ. She just had to hold on to this secret for a little while longer. She just had to finesse the key and—*there it was*—the tumblers would turn and she could shove the door open.

Daniella breathed a sigh of relief as she walked into the store and the bell that hung on the door jingled. She flipped the sign at the front from CLOSED to OPEN. Everything in Wild Nights was still manually operated. "If he closed last night, I don't mind him coming in a little late. It's not only me in here. You made it on time."

"And if I hadn't, you'd probably be more mad at me than at him."

Daniella laughed. "True. But I expect more of you."

"And why is that?"

"Because you're much more handsome than he is." Daniella winked.

AJ laughed. "Thanks, that makes me feel all warm and fuzzy inside."

Daniella was glad he was laughing and distracted. "Like you don't know you're gorgeous."

AJ rolled his eyes, like he really never had thought about it. Like his looks were something beyond his own power and therefore beyond his notice.

Daniella had nearly used that in a poem a thousand times—the beautiful boy who wore his extraordinary looks like an everyday pair of jeans and an old T-shirt—but every time, she had come to the conclusion that the irony was too clean and too simple, and she rejected clean and simple literary devices outright.

She liked old language and old forms. Purple prose, that's what her English teacher had called it. And she certainly didn't want to write poetry that could one day be studied in school and picked apart and dissected like a dead frog in a science lab.

Daniella *liked* purple prose. Mr. Fischer could go choke on his copies of Hemingway.

The bell jangled again, reminding Daniella which plane of reality she needed to be on right now.

"Hey, guys—I'm here." It was Rinn Olivera—a girl who was moderately internet famous, at least in the bookish corner of the universe. She had a mass of curls on her head, but they weren't the wild kind. These were the kind of curls that had been curly method–ed into perfect, submissive ringlets. They bounced as Rinn walked and added to Rinn's otherwise insufferable level of perfection. She wore one of those annoyingly pressed tennis skirts and a polo, like that was how actual humans dressed or something. All she needed was a ribbon in her hair and Daniella could have gagged on command.

Rinn was a walking, talking reminder that nobody was perfect, except for people who spent their days filming themselves for *content*. Rinn bounced up to them—because it wasn't enough to be a straight-A student and have an enormous, bookish following on the internet. She had to be all smiles and springing ringlets, too. "Hi, Daniella. Hi, AJ."

This last part Rinn said a little bit breathlessly, because, as was obvious to everyone in the store and potentially on planet Earth, Rinn had an enormous crush on AJ.

Well, obvious to everyone but AJ.

"Oh, hey, Rinn." AJ smiled his devastating but standard smile, and Daniella had to watch Rinn melt where she stood.

It was revolting.

Daniella's stomach lurched. She was so not in the mood to deal with Rinn's attempts at flirting. Daniella was not, on the whole, into love. And Rinn's doe-eyed, fairy-tale kind of expression only made Daniella want to shake the girl and tell her that gallant knights were a thing the Victorians made up and to toughen up already because no matter who you loved, they were more likely than not to smash your heart into a million pieces.

But Daniella didn't know Rinn well enough to tell her this.

And anyway, that morning, Daniella was barely in the mood to deal with anything other than a bottle of Pedialyte and a double dose of Pepto-Bismol. If she told Rinn that love was dead, she might end up telling her the bookstore was closing, too.

Daniella ignored Rinn and dug the Pepto out of her purse and popped the chewable into her mouth. Each spin was getting worse than the last. But she'd made Eli a promise and she was sticking to it, hangover or no hangover. Maybe there was something salvageable in the books that Eli hadn't seen. Daniella had been tracking Wild Nights' book sales for the past year. She knew them inside and out.

She couldn't believe she'd missed something so huge.

"Okay, I'm going to go into the back and deal with some inventory. One of you take the floor, and the other one take the register." But then Daniella realized that Rinn would take the floor just to try to hang around and flirt with AJ as he took the register, so she amended. "Actually, Rinn, could you take the register? You do *such* a good job."

There. That would give AJ some space, for the morning at least. He never directly *said* he hated the cash register, but Daniella could tell that AJ enjoyed having the floor and time to himself in the mornings. Too much customer interaction too early really wore AJ out.

Daniella understood that—she hated most people. Her problem was, she needed them. She gained her own kind of boundless energy from being around other humans, even if they irritated her. There was a kind of poetic irony in being the kind of person who recharged around others but who resented having to recharge around them in the first place.

AJ shrugged and said something that sounded like *sure* as he walked off, receding into the safety of the unilluminated corners of the store.

Rinn's face fell for a moment. Daniella wasn't trying to thwart Rinn's love story. She just didn't care enough to help it along, either. Daniella felt a small lump in her throat, which she tried to swallow along with her mildly guilty conscience.

But then—in the road—a terrible screeching sounded. In Daniella's experience, that could only mean one thing.

Imogen was here.

2

Thrown with Great Force

8:32 A.M.
Imogen

Imogen Azar screeched to a halt.

Her back tire skidded in protest, but the rest of her scooter stayed upright. She had misjudged the distance to the curb by a good five feet. She'd had to pull up on the brakes hard in order to not accidentally crash through the window of the bookstore where she worked.

Typical. Just typical.

Imogen swung her leg over the moped. It wasn't even a real bike. Just a dinky old Kawasaki that got the job done. Got her from point A to point B. Though, in the summer, it got her to point B with considerably more sweat on her body than she would have wanted. She left it there, on the sidewalk. Chicago PD could give her a ticket for all she cared. Imogen wasn't going to spend another second outside in this heat.

She could feel the sweat already trickling down her armpits. Everything was wet and slick and disgusting here in the summer. The store was situated in Wicker Park, beyond the northwest edge of downtown Chicago, where the heat from the bigger sky-scrapers just baked into the whole area and where they were too far inland from the lake to get much of a wind to clear any of the heat out. But Imogen wore a leather jacket, weather be damned. Because no matter how disgustingly hot she was feeling, road rash was on her list of hard nopes for the entire rest of her life. She'd gotten it once while she was learning to ride her scooter and that was one time too many.

Imogen didn't bother taking off her helmet. She grabbed her bag out of the stash compartment in the scooter, then headed into work. She slammed the door behind her and saw that Little Miss Perfect, the self-appointed Coolest Girl in the World, and Brooding Art Boy were all already there. All three of them were staring at her.

All of this was still typical.

Cool Girl—whose real name Imogen had always thought ought to have been something like Skylar or Brooklyn or Indie, because Daniella was just such an *ordinary* name for such an extraordinary girl—spoke up first.

"Imogen. How wonderful to have you gracing us with your presence. Are you going to wear the helmet during work hours to prevent scaring away the customers with all of that sunshine that you bring to the job?" Cool Girl smirked, her north-suburb staccato especially prominent when she was giving someone else hell.

Little Miss Perfect gave Cool Girl a gentle, correcting tap on the arm. "Hi, Imogen," said Little Miss Perfect in her most appeasing, brightest voice, because Little Miss Perfect was never not trying. "Hot outside, huh?"

It fascinated Imogen to look at the contrast between the two girls. Little Miss Perfect had dark hair, controlled curls. She was pretty and femme and everything about her was a little bit soft—big eyes, wide nose, full lips.

And then there was Cool Girl, with last night's eyeliner and her hair bleached and frizzy. Cool Girl was *not* pretty in any sense of the word. She was electric—and occasionally bordering on stunning—but nothing so palatable or socially acceptable as pretty. She had a proud nose that jutted out from her face and eyebrows that punctuated her angular features. Like somebody crossed Maria Callas with Debbie Harry and gave her a worse attitude than the two of them combined.

And Brooding Art Boy, he just stared at Imogen. For a second, Imogen stared right back.

It was strange that Imogen felt so at home in a place where she had so little in common with her coworkers. But the facts were the facts, and Imogen had stopped questioning the truth of them a long, long time ago. Wild Nights was better than home, for reasons that would always remain a little mysterious to Imogen. There was love at home. Here, there was none.

She would rather be here.

Imogen committed herself to ignoring them all and kept on walking. One step after the other, the heels of her heavy boots digging and clomping against the old wood floor. The back of the store got darker and darker as she moved away from the storefront facade and into the spaces where the light from the windows didn't reach that well.

Imogen didn't stop until she got to the employee bathroom in the back. It was off the side of the break room, where they kept Wild Nights' boxes of surplus inventory that didn't fit in the storeroom, along with all the staff lockers and the two sad, worn cozy chairs that looked like they hadn't even been new when *The Golden Girls* had gone off the air.

Imogen slammed the bathroom door shut.

Slamming felt good. Felt like a way to wake up. To make noise. To make something out of that awful nothing that was swallowing her whole, that was invading her chest. That nothing that made her numb everywhere.

Imogen finally took off her helmet. She slammed that on the dresser that Jo—Wild Nights' manager—had put inside the bathroom, next to the sink. She dropped her bag onto the floor. It landed with a satisfying *thud*.

Imogen needed all these noises, all these sounds. Because aside from the everlasting nothing that was invading her body, there was also a string of thoughts running through her mind. Telling her to give up. Telling her to give in. Telling her nothing was worth it anyway. Imogen needed the noise to break the sound inside her head. She needed the noise to know there was feeling, honestly any sensation outside of herself.

For a moment, Imogen couldn't look at herself in the bathroom mirror. All she could do was hang on to both sides of the sink, propping herself up with the support of the cool porcelain. And then Imogen looked up, into the mirror. She saw her face, looked into her own eyes, assessing the resolve she saw there. She nodded at herself.

She needed this. Needed a clean break. Needed something new, something different.

She needed to feel cleansed, and there was only one thing she thought would work. And there, in the bathroom of the break room at Wild Nights, was the only place where Imogen could even imagine it would work.

Imogen picked her backpack up off the aged tile floor and leaned it against the yellowing porcelain sink. She dug into the bag and found the hair clippers—the ones she'd taken out of her father's drawer, the ones that he used to trim his beard—and she stood back up, grabbing a handful of her dark hair in one hand and holding the clippers with no guard on in the other. She turned them on, feeling the weight of them, the buzzing vibration in her hand. They were heavier than she thought they would be. And for the first time, she felt something in her hands that wasn't cold or numb. She felt cool plastic and a humming motor. She felt her hands shaking into life. As though the clippers could resuscitate her, could give her back what she thought she'd already lost for good.

Then she took a deep breath and began to shave her head.

She took smaller, half-inch-size chunks at first. But then she grew in confidence with every stroke of the clippers, and she began to shave larger clumps of hair. Every clip of hair that came off was a weight. A memory. A wince and then a piece of relief. That relief grew stronger, grew bolder. It took hold of the nothing inside her chest and made a tiny, tiny spark.

Imogen had plugs all over her head now. She took the clippers and was so much more careful this time, so much more methodical. She let the shaver hum across her head, smoothing out the rough patches. Her fingers prickled against the freshly shorn hair. The clippers themselves were marvelous, efficient, almost magic in their work. The vibrations that Imogen had felt along her hands now reverberated across her scalp. Pinpricks of soothing feeling coming back at the very root of her hairs. Because that was all that was left now, the roots of her hair.

Eventually, she was done.

Imogen looked in the mirror, this fresh reflection looking back at her. She felt her head again, the feeling smooth and soft and fuzzy across the palm of her hand.

She felt new, fresh. She felt cleansed. From all the loathing that had been welling up inside of her. From the slow creep into the darkness.

Wild Nights had saved her. Again.

Imogen grabbed the enormous pile of hair that had accumulated in the sink. There was so much of it. Thick and black and shining. It was the kind of hair she was supposed to pride herself on. Black as midnight and gleaming like the moon. That's what the Arabic poets used to say. Persian ones, too. She had the beautiful hair of the beloved, and the relief she felt as she dumped it into the trash and did her best to dust the hair off of her clothes was a feeling unparalleled in her entire life. Her scalp was so pale compared to the rest of her skin, having been blocked from the sun by that carpet of thick, black hair.

Luckily, all of her clothes were black, so she didn't have to worry about how much hair she got all over herself in this process. She looked back at herself. At the girl looking directly at her in the mirror. That wasn't an Imogen she knew quite yet, but she was better than the Imogen who had come before, that much was certain. Imogen locked her backpack away in the employee lockers. She was ready to step back onto the ground floor of the bookstore.

She just hoped this new haircut wasn't a fireable offense.

3

Bright Star

8:37 A.M.
Rinn

AJ Park was the most beautiful boy in the entire world.

From her spot by the register, Rinn could see him shelving books back by the historicals section, and the sight made her dizzy and warm all over. Like the sun finally peeking out from behind the cloud cover of winter. He had soulful, deep eyes and long, deft fingers and an intense focus on whatever he was doing.

He had that kind of Keanu Reeves–in-the-nineties vibe, except more tan and more Korean. He had hair that was short in the back but somehow too long and constantly falling into his eyes in the front. He had to regularly run his hands through it, pushing his dark locks out of his face. He was forever in motion, too. The only time he ever sat still was to sketch, and even then, his hands were flickering back and forth across a page.

But, anyway, that's what AJ looked like.

Like a dark-haired Apollo. Like a young god.

Like a boy who ought to have been a model but was instead an artist.

He was *perfect*.

Rinn sighed. It was hopeless. The only thing AJ talked to Rinn about was work and old murder mysteries. Still, she kept AJ in her line of sight, hopeful that he might come over to the register and chat. It was the first official day of summer, and Rinn had read enough to know that summer was peak romance.

Anything could happen on midsummer. Even AJ Park could fall in love with *her*.

Rinn knew that she was a modern woman and she ought to go and talk to him on her own. It was just that whenever Rinn thought about talking to AJ about anything other than books, her breathing got all shallow, like when she was filming one of her daily vlogs and she started sweating in places she didn't know a person could sweat. Rinn had been to therapy. She knew the word for that. *Panic.* And she knew the cure, too.

Go do it. Go say hi.

Rinn nodded to herself, smoothed down the front of her skirt, and took one step out from behind the register. She could do this. She could definitely go talk to AJ. He's a person. She's a person. They could be two people who just said hello and then maybe fell in love forever.

And that was when Imogen Azar came out of the staff room and all hell froze over.

Nobody moved for a solid minute. Not Imogen. Not AJ. Not even Daniella. Rinn could barely *breathe*. And Imogen, she seemed to be waiting to see what everyone else was going to do, waiting to see how everyone was going to react.

Rinn didn't mean to stare. Not *stare* stare. But Imogen had walked into the break room wearing a helmet and—Rinn was pretty sure—all of her hair. Imogen walked out of the break room with a shaved head. Which was no hair whatsoever, save for the tiny quarter inch of stubble that was left. Rinn simply couldn't compute what to say to that. She'd never seen a person lose all of their hair in five minutes flat.

Everything else about Imogen was the same. The short motor-cycle boots. The faded black T-shirt and the worn red leather jacket. The baggy, ripped-up, baby-blue jeans were still cuffed to her ankles. Her face was still angular and proud. Her skin still deep olive. And her dark, brooding eyes were still dramatically framed with full black eyebrows.

Just no hair on her head.

Daniella was the first to break the silence. "Are you kidding me right now, Azar? Did you hear there was an award for most misguided youth at the store today, or did you just decide to get a fresh summer cut?"

"¿Por qué no los dos?" Imogen gave one of those smiles that looked like she actually wanted to give Daniella the finger but couldn't, because they were all at work and there would be cus-tomers in the store soon.

"Cute," said Daniella. "Do you always make a joke of the state of your mental health? Because shaving your entire head is like one of the hallmarks of depression, Azar."

Rinn knew Daniella didn't intend to be mean. Not *mean* mean. Daniella was just one of those people who dealt with uncom-fortable situations with sarcasm and bitingly direct language. Typically, she used poetic levels of pop-culture-laced sarcasm. But it was still humor-as-a-defense-mechanism. Rinn had grown up in between her father's Mexican American culture and her mother's German one. She was used to looking at a thing from all angles before drawing absolute conclusions.

And in general, Rinn had trouble drawing any absolute conclusions.

It's what made her so nervous, really. That the world was full of shades of gray. That she could see one thing but reality could be another. That she could be in love with AJ and he could maybe want nothing to do with her beyond friendly coworker chatter.

Rinn still didn't know how Imogen could withstand the level of hostility thrown her way by Daniella, though.

Because rather than getting upset, Imogen just shrugged, somehow unperturbed by both Daniella's commanding demeanor and all of them staring at her. "I'm not depressed. I'm taking the floor."

And then she walked off.

Daniella looked like she really was going to throw something at Imogen's head, regardless of the fact that Imogen was no longer wearing her helmet. Rinn hated being caught between their near-constant power struggles, but she also couldn't stand by and do nothing.

"Do you need help with inventory?" asked Rinn, honestly wanting to help. "Isn't that what you said you were about to go do?"

Daniella rolled her eyes. "Stuff it, Olivera. You can't kiss up to me the way you do Jo."

Rinn was about to argue that she *wasn't* kissing up, and that she honestly was never trying to, when the phone—a putty-colored landline with a cord and everything—trilled into the silent store. Rinn did her best not to jump, but she flinched at the noise, it was so unexpected.

Briiiing.

  Briiiing.

    BRIIIIIIIIING.

Rinn stared at the phone. She was *not* picking it up. She looked at Daniella. From the look on her face, Daniella was also *not* picking it up. Neither of them moved as the phone continued to rattle and ring.

They waited until the answering machine clicked over, echoing scratchy feedback for a moment before the caller left a message. "Hello—Josephine, this is Mr. Hunt. I was calling to check in with you about last night's sales numbers, but I'm concerned that you're not already in the office—"

At that, Rinn caved and picked up. "Hello, Mr. Hunt!"

"Josephine, is that you?" Archer Hunt Junior had one of those deep, smoothed-out Midwestern accents that people from places like Ohio liked to brag about—the kind of accent that every newscaster in America was taught to adopt because it was considered neutral.

It disturbed Rinn to hear a voice so proudly scrubbed of any location markers. It also disturbed her that Archer Hunt Junior had employed Jo for five or six years and he couldn't remember that her name was Joelle.

Daniella reached out her hand, ready to take over the phone now that she knew it was the boss. Except, Rinn was *not* about to hand over the phone to Daniella. She didn't cave that easily under pressure.

"No, sir, this is Rinn Olivera. One of the employees. Just made it to the phone."

Daniella held her hand out more insistently and more in Rinn's face. Rinn swatted Daniella's hand away. She would not be intimidated by Daniella and her cool bleached-blond hair and her ability to show up to work in an outfit that Rinn wouldn't even be able to wear to the convenience store with confidence.

"Was nobody manning the register?" Archer barked back.

"Sir?" Rinn didn't understand the question. Of course nobody was at the register. The store wasn't open yet. Why had her heartbeat kicked up a notch? Rinn knew she wasn't wrong. She looked around, double-checking herself. No customers were there yet.

"I *said*—was nobody manning the register? How could you have possibly been so far from the phone? I made sure the phone was installed right by the cash register." He was so insistent, so sure of himself, that for a moment Rinn faltered.

Daniella took the opportunity to snatch the phone out from Rinn's hands. "Hello, Mr. Hunt! Apologies, Rinn is one of our newer employees; she's a little slow on the uptake."

Rinn bugged her eyes at Daniella; Daniella stuck out her tongue.

Rinn could still hear Hunt Junior through the receiver, even though it was up to Daniella's ear. "Josephine, is that you?"

"It's Joelle, sir. But yes. What can I do for you?" Daniella didn't miss a beat.

Rinn shook her head. *You can't just impersonate our manager.*

Daniella narrowed her eyes, like she was saying, *Watch me.*

"Why weren't you at the register already?" That was Hunt Junior again.

"Sir, the store isn't open yet, and I was just double-checking the takes from last night in the office. Otherwise, we've been setting up the store for opening, which is why such a junior employee had to answer the phone." Daniella gave an honestly impressive stink eye in Rinn's direction.

Rinn straightened her spine. She would *not* be intimidated by Daniella or her rudeness.

"Fine. Call me as soon as you've got final numbers. It's *important*." Leave it to Mr. Hunt to sound miffed and mollified all at once.

"Will do, sir."

Mr. Hunt couldn't see it, but Daniella did a little mock salute and hung up the phone.

Despite everything, Rinn had to stifle a laugh.

Daniella, however, was not amused. "Do you understand what you nearly did?"

"Answer the phone?" Rinn couldn't imagine what she'd done to upset Daniella this early in the day.

Daniella scoffed. "You've got to be joking. You nearly got Jo fired."

"Why would Mr. Hunt fire her for not being at the register before we're even open?"

Daniella put her hand on her hip. She gave Rinn a good long stare. Her smudgy eyeliner lent her expression a feral quality. And then she pointed to the store around them. "Do you think everything is just *peachy keen* around here? You think that the store is just *doing swell*? Because it isn't. The store is *dying*. Of course Hunt Junior would be worried about her manning the register. Don't you know anything? Don't you have eyes?"

Rinn frowned. "I know there aren't customers. How many times does somebody have to say it? *The store is closed right now.*"

"You know, for such a smart girl, you can be so stupid." And then Daniella was off, clearly unwilling to explain further.

And that left Rinn with one thought, one idea rattling around in her head. She couldn't believe it. She didn't want to believe it.

Wild Nights Bookstore and Emporium was dying?

She looked at the store from her vantage point nearly in the middle of the ground floor. The entire bookstore had this amazing almost gothic vibe going on—from the dark walls to the lack of windows in the back. It was authentic and moody. The kind of place where even if they stood in the same spot, no two people would get the same picture or even see the same thing. The dark walls shifted from black to slate gray to deep navy, depending on where you stood. Rinn still couldn't say what color they really were.

It was also one of those old City Beautiful buildings. It had Roman-style coffers in the ceiling that created this rad three-dimensional pattern of square woodwork when you looked up. It had old, classical-style columns that ran from floor to ceiling—gigantic, fluted white pillars that were the only source of brightness in the entire space. And the second floor was a loft with a balcony, meaning that the entire first floor of the building was effectively two stories high. The second-story balcony was covered in fairy lights. And on the main floor, all the bookshelves were offset and formed this stunning radial pattern across the floor. The only right angles in the place were where the walls or the balconies met.

They even still sold penny candy and taffy and fancy, felt-tip pens by the register.

It couldn't just *close. Where would all the books go?*

And Archer Hunt Junior—who owned the place—well, his dad had put up these wild art installations all around the place. There was a headless statue of a girl in roller skates installed so that she was hanging from the ceiling, over a set of stairs. And there was a tunnel of books, pinwheeling out from one of the walls. And somehow, he'd gotten an old bank-vault door up to the second story and put all the crime resale books in a vault. *A vault.*

This place was magical, and nobody really seemed to know about it anymore. Rinn didn't understand it. Old Mr. Hunt, the current Mr. Hunt's father, he had stipulated in his will that the bookstore was to remain a bookstore in perpetuity. It was supposed to stay in business for the community. Unless, of course, it was really becoming a hardship to keep open. As long as there were customers, Wild Nights was meant to stay open as a bookstore, and no sale of the land was allowed. Jo had told Rinn that once, right after she'd been hired.

And there was business, wasn't there?

Rinn looked up at the balcony on the second floor. It was beautiful and haunted in the way that a space that holds worn, resale books can be—but was so often empty, when it should have been full of people snapping photos and giggling and picking up books and reading detective fiction in a freaking vault.

Rinn couldn't believe it. That all of this could be gone soon.

She didn't want to believe it.

Don't just tell me a problem, give me solutions. That's what Papa was always saying. And that's what Rinn had inevitably learned to do.

That's why she'd started her books account. She wanted to encourage reading. She wanted to take photos of what she was reading and share them with others. She wanted to celebrate books. She even had built a reading counter onto her website that people could add their books to.

And this was the wild part: she'd gotten nearly ten thousand people to pick up a new book.

She hadn't cried when she saw the abysmal statistics online about how little Americans read, and she wasn't going to cry now. She was going to make a plan, and she was going to help.

Rinn Olivera was *not* going to let Wild Nights Bookstore go under.

She believed deep in her soul if she could get ten thousand people to read a new book, then she could definitely get a few hundred more to come into the store and buy one.

Rinn could do it—she could help. She just needed to be given the opportunity.

No, she needed to find a way to *make* the opportunity. That's what Papa would say. That she would have to make her own opportunities in this world. Nobody would hand her anything.

Rinn looked around her. Nobody else was around.

She pulled her phone out of her back pocket.

What was the point of having all these followers if she didn't reach out to them to help an actual struggling independent bookstore?

Rinn didn't dare get out her selfie stick, in case Jo came into work soon. It was way easier to stash a phone than one attached to a long, telescopic arm. Rinn had already figured that one out the hard way. Her phone had been immediately confiscated, and she'd been given a lecture on the "no photography, no phones" policy at Wild Nights.

All the employees here had their phones taken at some point. Well, except for Daniella. She had managed to escape detection so far. Rinn still hadn't figured out how Daniella had gotten away with it.

Rinn moved away from the cash register. She unpinned her name tag. When she filmed, she didn't want to look like one of the store's employees. She might be open about herself and her reading habits on the internet, but she wasn't totally reckless with her personal life, either.

Rinn hesitated for a moment.

If she did save Wild Nights this way, she might have to quit her job here. If people started showing up to the store because of her posts. If people started tagging her every time they came in. She'd be always looking over her shoulder when she got into work.

But either way, Rinn was likely losing one of her favorite haunts. The store could close, or the store could become a place

Rinn couldn't work at regularly. She had to make the decision she could live with. Rinn took a deep breath. She knew what choice she'd make. She might as well save it for everyone else, even if she couldn't save it for herself.

Rinn smiled and then she hit record. "Greetings, people of Earth—Rinn here. Guess who made it to the bookstore early? I'm not tagging my location—yet—but know that this bookstore is *where. it. is. at.*"

Rinn panned around the room slightly. She could, from where she stood, catch a glimpse of the roller-skating girl's feet hanging precipitously over the back staircase. She could even catch a few of the ribbons of words that cascaded around the roller girl's feet. But then the time ran out, and she couldn't get any more of the store into the shot.

It was so much easier shooting video of the store than shooting video of herself.

Rinn uploaded the video—it would make a good intro—and began shooting the next. If she twisted, she could maybe get the whole roller girl into the shot, and she *knew* people would have a lot of questions in the DMs about that.

Rinn swallowed her nerves. She was fine. Filming was fine. She was going to save this bookstore. Sometimes, Rinn wanted to thank God herself for selfie mode.

Rinn offered up a silent prayer and did her best to smile for the camera. But then she tilted her head and the lighting changed on her.

Oof, not a good angle.

Rinn moved her head back to its original position. She held on tight to that smile. But even she could see it—the edge that crept into her face. The way her eyes looked overly bright and her smile seemed totally pasted on.

Rinn took another deep breath. Hit record. "I know there's going to be a reading, followed by a Q and A, and a signing. But I think there might be some special prizes in store for a few lucky readers. I can tell you that this store is about to start setting up for the signing. I cannot wait to see what they do to the place."

Okay, Rinn was getting aboard her own hype train, since she was the one who'd planned out the decorations herself. But her viewers didn't necessarily *need* to know this. All they needed was to start getting excited for the Brock Harvey signing. Because then maybe a few more people would show up to the store.

Rinn looked through the stickers, trying to find a way to add a geotag to the location. But it came up empty. She couldn't believe it. Rinn clicked a few more times, because that had to be a mistake. It wasn't, though. Wild Nights Bookstore wasn't even on the map anymore. Then Rinn felt a tug as her phone was snatched out neatly from her hand. She whipped around.

Jo had her hand on her hip and her eyebrow raised. "How many times do I have to tell you—no filming in the store?"

Rinn stretched out her smile in an exaggerated nervous expression. She wasn't faking it, per se. But she did hope that exaggerating the look on her face could at least be comedically winning. "Always once more?"

"Nice try." Jo rolled her eyes. "I'm confiscating this."

"But, Jo—" Oh my God she couldn't *take* Rinn's phone. Jo wasn't a principal or a teacher. As much as the whole staff liked to rag on Jo for being old, she couldn't have been more than ten years older than Rinn, really.

"No *buts,*" said Jo. "Now is not the time to piss off Hunt Junior, trust me on this. And given how much you love Brock Harvey, I'm not leaving your self-control in your own hands on this one.

You can have this back at the end of the day. *After* the signing."

Then Jo stuck Rinn's phone into her back pocket and walked off.

But Rinn didn't lose at anything if she could help it.

She was going to save Wild Nights all by herself if she had to.

And the first order of business was putting it back on the map.

4

Eternity in an Hour

Daniella

Why had she told Rinn Olivera that the store was going under?

That totally had not been Daniella's intention. Not that she had any intentions other than to get to the bathroom as quick as humanly possible. A wave of nausea had come over Daniella so fast and so furious, she had felt like she was in the middle of a Tokyo drift. Mercifully, she had reached the bathroom in time. She was going to lay her face on the cold tile and then the wave of nausea would pass.

That was, of course, when Daniella spotted all the hair. Little bits and pieces of it. Small dustings of short clippings. Imogen had cleaned up most of the big chunks that she had shaved off, but nothing short of a broom or a vacuum was going to get the stuff that now clung to all the crevices of the bathroom.

The urge to vomit intensified, and Daniella was forced into a dilemma—stay in the bathroom and definitely throw up but have an excellent receptacle (i.e., the toilet), or leave the bathroom and *maybe don't vomit*, but lack a proper receptacle if she did.

To puke or not to puke, that was the question.

Daniella fled the bathroom.

For a little while, all she could do was lie on the floor and wait for the Pepto-Bismol that she had taken on her arrival to kick in. Eventually, she was able to sit up and take in her surroundings. It was only the break room, but it helped that she knew the layout so well.

There were the two worn-out chairs covered in a floral print that had to have been the ugliest fabric Daniella had ever seen. She stared at the chairs, willing the spinning that was overtaking her head to stop.

After a few minutes of sitting, Daniella crawled over to the mini fridge that Jo stashed under her desk. It was full of Diet Snapple and Big Red. But Daniella would not be deterred by Jo's horrendous taste in beverages. She was digging toward the back, hopeful. Daniella pulled back a few red cans and tan bottles until she saw the glimmer of purple.

Saints be praised.

There it was—a lone can of grape soda. Daniella cracked it open with a satisfying pop and reveled in the overly carbonated sugar as she took her first sip. If anything was going to bring her back, it was going to be this purple stuff.

Daniella belched properly in the empty room and—*Oh my God*—she could finally sit up and breathe without feeling like the world was going to end. Like the world was spinning out into eternity. It was one thing to know that the planet was hurtling thousands of miles an hour through space and infinitely spinning. It was another to have your body feel like it was hurtling thousands of miles an hour through space and she would keel over before the spinning stopped.

Daniella drank some more soda and, for a moment, believed that there was some good in the world. The next thing Daniella did was pull her bag down out of her locker, get out her phone, and switch from her personal account to her poetry account.

Daniella never left her poetry account open—ever.

Same way she didn't let anyone see her notebook or touch her phone. Her safeguards were all in place for a reason. They were why she'd never gotten caught writing her poetry by anyone in her life. Not even her mother. Her personal account was DaniellaDaze, which was innocuous and perfect and what everyone would think her handle ought to be. It was the cool-girl-that-smokes-weed-and-drives-muscle-cars identity that she had willingly carved out for herself to get through the four years of hell that high school was. But her poetry account was something else.

Her poetry was anachronisticblonde, and that was perfect, too, but for entirely different reasons. It was a literary term, and Daniella loved those. A word for out of its own time. She liked to revisit the old forms. The sonnets, the odes. Maybe even one day a real epic. But it was also a wink at the blond—the DaniellaDaze—that she had created. A girl out of her own time. That part was perfect for her alone. Daniella dug in her bag to find her notebook and flipped through her work. Nothing caught her eye.

She'd have to make something new.

A warm-up. That's what she'd post. She didn't have the mental space to write a whole piece. But she could handle a fragment. She put her knees up and balanced her notebook on them. She bit on the end of her pen to free her hands as she flipped until she found a blank page. She took the pen in hand and sketched circles, thinking about the spinning. Thinking about the world. A makeshift globe, moving and spinning. A rock hurtling around through space, held together by invisible forces beyond its control.

And as she drew that, she knew what she would write.

In truth the sun does not rise, but Earth
Spins with all her might to bear creation

It was a bit maudlin. But it felt right, given how intense Daniella's spins had been not a moment before. "Ode to a Hungover Girl," she might call it. "Lament of the Wild Night," even. But the title would come later—it wasn't a full poem, yet. It was still in its infancy, still simply a fragment, with the potential for anything. A bit that might eventually grow into a sonnet. But now it was simply a couplet with a little doodle.

It always felt good to create.

Daniella took a photo of the page. She hit post, and she tucked her phone back into her bag. Now that she had found a little bit of steadiness and a bit of poetry, Daniella really did need to double-check the books.

They were over on the desk where Jo kept the old calculator. Daniella took the hefty calculator in hand and sat, back against the desk and legs akimbo for a solid minute. She reached back up and grabbed the black leather-bound notebook that kept the financial ledgers off the desk.

She was going to double-check her sales record.

Daniella hoped Eli was wrong. Hoped she had unwittingly lied to Rinn Freaking-Stick-of-Sunshine-Up-My-Butt Olivera about the store closing.

Ugh.

Daniella's stomach nearly revolted again, but she took a deep breath and stuck her head between her knees for a moment and, eventually, the feeling passed. She took another sip of the grape soda, and she knew that would hold her over until the Pepto kicked in—which should be at any moment now.

Daniella scanned another line of sales. She'd been keeping the books for a while. She had a copy that she sent in for Archer Junior's review and she had the copy that was kept in this notebook in the break room. She started with this year's numbers, and even in six months, things were not looking good. But they weren't the worst sales she'd ever seen. Along the margins, there were the little notes Imogen had written by hand.

Customer requested When We Were Us. That was dated from just a few months ago.

Eight customers were looking for books by Jonathan Gold. That had just been last week, Daniella remembered seeing it. At the time she had guessed that everyone had read the same think piece or posthumous profile. It was too much of a coincidence otherwise.

Customer returned asking for When We Were Us update.

There was something about these requests, the simple human annotation of them among all the numbers. Daniella couldn't believe the store was closing.

But numbers didn't lie. And the numbers were down. Daniella was just disappointed that she hadn't figured it out herself. Math was one of those things—like poetry. Once she got into a flow, Daniella could practically keep going until infinity. It didn't make sense that she'd miss something so huge.

Daniella pulled her own notebook out from under the ledger. She didn't normally do this, but she wanted to check something. She started scribbling the distribution curve. Started seeing where the pattern fell. It took a minute, but everything checked out. Everything seemed normal. There were rules about the way that numbers were supposed to be distributed in groups. Rules that a person couldn't fake, not really. Those were holding with basic numeric distribution principles.

What had happened?

The sales were down, overall, but not dire. Just a steady, slow slide. Daniella looked around the room. Behind Jo's desk was a whole set of shelves. In the middle of the shelves was a row of binders. In front of her was Jo's laptop, whirring quietly, its blinking light beckoning her in.

Daniella knew she wasn't supposed to touch the laptop. But she also knew that she needed answers and that was the fastest likely route to them. She typed in *thebatman* as the password, because that had to be Jo's password. Jo complained about "the Batman" being the focus of the "Batfam" comics at least once a week. Also, it was the Wi-Fi password. There wasn't another master password that Jo could possibly use.

The password was correct. But all that there was on Jo's desktop was a shortcut to her email. Daniella clicked around for a bit, trying to find a document file that might provide her answers, but there was nothing. Not even in the documents folder.

Jo hadn't just kept her desktop scrubbed clean. She'd kept her whole machine nearly pristine. *Unnervingly clean.*

That meant that the only record of what Daniella was looking for had to be a paper copy. Daniella turned around, started looking through the shelves again. Row after row of those binders were labeled as *Inventory*, by year.

Bingo.

Daniella flipped through the binder labeled *Inventory: 2017–2020*. Everything looked fine. Mostly normal. But the systematic nature of the numbers she had in her sales ledger bothered her for some reason. They were random, in a way, but they were also tracking downward so steadily, so *perfectly*.

She looked at the distribution graph in her personal notebook. But she still didn't buy it. She started plotting some of the most recent sales. Again. This time just the numbers over time. They were down, but they weren't down exponentially the way they should have been. They should have looked like a hockey stick, sliding down until they hit a tipping point of no return. Instead, they were just down, down, down, like a perfect little escalator.

Daniella got up, found another binder. This one was from five years ago.

Holy pickles, Batman.

The sales were down because *the inventory* was down.

By a lot.

Archer Hunt Junior was buying about half of what he used to just five years ago. And Daniella knew it was Archer because he was such a control freak, he refused to hire a book buyer for the store. He did all the buying personally.

Daniella went back to the sales ledger, noting the places where Imogen had left those little notes in the margins about buying copies. She checked that against the actual inventory that the store had bought. Nothing. They'd bought none of the customer requests. Nothing new, either. Just a slowing trickle of classics and bestsellers.

Archer Hunt Junior was unwittingly hampering the sales with what he was buying.

But why?

A new wave of nausea hit. And this one had nothing to do with the hangover.

She went back to the laptop. But instead of looking for answers on the computer, Daniella clicked through to the browser, trying to see if she could find any records of the actual accounts online.

And Jo, God bless her, had left herself logged into her password manager.

Daniella suddenly had access to nearly everything. She went looking for the petty cash first, knowing that was the easiest thing to fudge, the easiest thing to fake.

And that's when she saw it—an inventory transaction for over nine thousand dollars in the account. Daniella looked over the business-expense totals in the binder again. She had records up until the last week. So unless the transaction happened literally last night, there was nine thousand dollars that went *missing*, somehow. But that didn't make any sense at all. Nobody just misplaced nearly ten grand. Not overnight.

She needed to talk to Eli. No—first, she needed to talk to Imogen. Because Imogen handled all of the weekly shipments coming *into* the store. That's why she was the one who made annotations about customer requests in the sales ledger.

Daniella reached for the call button that sounded the PA system over the whole store. She tipped the metal microphone toward herself and it balanced precariously along its front edge. "Imogen. Will you please get your bald, depressed butt in here and explain something to me."

Yelling at Imogen felt good. Took the edge off. Made Daniella feel in control. The store might be closing. Archer Junior might be committing some kind of fraud. She might be a nauseous blob, but she was a nauseous blob in charge of somebody else for the moment, and that made all the difference in the world.

"No," came Imogen's one-word reply. She'd shouted it from the bookstore floor.

"Immmoogeennn." This time Daniella had tried a singsong approach. She knew it would grate on Imogen's ears, if she knew anything at all. Besides, there weren't customers until the store opened officially at nine.

"I'm not bald, and I'm not depressed," Imogen shouted back. "And I'm taking my five now."

"Imogen, I swear to God if you don't get in here right now I will use the tiny modicum of power that I do have to get you fired." Daniella hadn't bothered using the store intercom. If she could hear Imogen's shout, then Imogen could definitely hear hers.

Imogen appeared in the doorway pretty quickly after that. It was still shocking to see her missing her shoulder-length hair. Like a whole piece of the girl had suddenly gone missing. Plus, Daniella had always assumed that, under all her hair, Imogen had tons of hardware and piercings in her ears. But Imogen actually had none whatsoever. Daniella had never noticed, not with how thick Imogen's hair had been.

Imogen raised an eyebrow. "What do you need—money for a midmorning beer run?"

"No, but funny that you should mention that. We're missing about nine thousand dollars in inventory. I need help finding it. And you're our girl when it comes to inventory."

Imogen just rolled her eyes. "And you're our girl when it comes to selling out. I'm getting Eli to deal with your hangover mood."

Daniella felt a screech building up in the back of her throat. "I swear, Imogen. Help me figure out this discrepancy. Or, hand to God—"

"I know, you'll have me fired. The thing is, Jo doesn't fire anyone. And she sure as hell isn't starting with me. There hasn't been a delivery since last week. Which you clearly know because you're messing with me to make yourself feel better about your crappy decisions last night. So I'm getting Eli, and you can go find your chill now."

Daniella let out that screech. "I have *plenty* of chill."

"Sure you do." Imogen winked in what could only be described as a taunting manner.

"Get out of my sight. And go get me Eli." Daniella ought to have learned by now that trying to control Imogen would never work, but still, she felt a need to throw the force of her anger that way. "You better sweep in the bathroom when you get back because your new haircut is still all over the bathroom floor. Oh, and this counts for three minutes of your five."

Daniella felt good about that, until Imogen fired her parting shot.

"Like hell it does. I'm counting from when I find Eli." The break room door slammed behind Imogen.

And Daniella was left alone, wondering whether the bookstore was going under or if its owner was accidentally sabotaging the entire operation.

5

Lonely as a Cloud

9:27 A.M.
Imogen

There were times when Imogen wanted to punch the simpering smile off Daniella Korres's face.

To be honest, it was most of the time. That was why she'd left the break room. She didn't want to actually give in to her violent impulses.

As she moved through the stacks, Imogen walked by Little Miss Perfect, who was helping a customer check out at the register with her signature smile. She had let the customer in half an hour ago—early—because "they really need to get to work," and Little Miss Perfect had been so understanding about it that there was no way she was actually human. They weren't even a regular. And they had stayed in the store for half an hour. Nothing about the situation that the customer created had been reasonable. Rinn had been mind-bogglingly understanding about the whole thing.

How could anyone be in that good of a mood all the time? How could anyone's default mood just be set to happy like that?

Like, Rinn literally arrived to work, straight off the L train, in that kind of a mood. Like the crowds and the frustrations of public transit never got to her. Happy, cheerful, nonplussed. With two hundred thousand followers who wanted to hang on every word she said about her latest read.

Like Rinn had no idea what a struggle the day could be. Like she'd never had a bad mood in her entire life. Happiness was like breathing to Little Miss Perfect. An everyday kind of reflex. It was the kind of happiness that drew others to her. The kind of happiness that had to have prevented loneliness.

Imogen mostly ignored Little Miss Perfect. That way Imogen didn't go around hating her all the time, too. Hating Cool Girl took up enough of Imogen's energy already.

Luckily, Imogen had seen Eli come in, not half a minute before Cool Girl had been screaming like a banshee. Or a harpy. Or whatever other mythological creature went around screeching other people's names rather than talking to them like an actual human.

Not that Cool Girl thought of Imogen as an actual human. She didn't seem like the kind of girl who gave anyone the time of day but her own reflection in the mirror and maybe about ten minutes of consideration for whoever she was hooking up with.

That was the kind of person Cool Girl was. Imogen was sure of it.

"Eli." Imogen had seen him earlier, ducked behind the manga section in the back. She was moving through the YA section— which already had a WELCOME BACK, BROCK sign strung up across it—when she spotted him.

Eli jumped when he heard his name. Then his shoulders relaxed when he saw it was her. Eli was blond and thin, with a mass of curly hair on top of his head. He had one of those everyday kind of faces that made you forget what he looked like. It made sense that he'd have a face like that, to get away with as much theft as he had and only get a slap on the wrist. "Hey."

"You okay, E?" Not being okay herself, Imogen could easily recognize the signs in someone else. Eli was, well, *off*. That was for sure. He was jumpy, and Eli was never jumpy. He was tense, ready for some kind of attack, some kind of fight.

He hadn't even noticed her haircut.

"Yeah, sure," said Eli. "Of course. Everything's cool. Super. Fantastic. What's up?"

"The lady doth protest too much," was all Imogen could think in that moment. It was her mother's fault, really, that Imogen could quote Shakespeare on command. Mom had gone through a phase of his writing when she'd been pregnant with Imogen. That was how Imogen had been stuck with the *name* Imogen in the first place, instead of something normal like Layla or Zara or Amira. Mom couldn't even name her for a *normal* Shakespearean heroine. She had to go into some deep cuts and find a name out of *Cymbeline*, of all the plays.

Imogen stared at Eli. Trying to assess what he was hiding. How much he was hiding. "Daniella needs you in the back."

Imogen watched as Eli's whole body went rigid.

Something wasn't right.

"Cool. Cool. I'll just go. Yeah. I'll go check that out. Now." And then Eli disappeared around the corner from the stacks he had just been hiding in.

Imogen rubbed at her neck, thinking to brush away the hair there. But then she remembered she didn't have any hair anymore. That feeling was a phantom, a trace of what had been before. She rubbed her palm over the top of her head again, still in wonder at herself.

She'd shaved her head.

Somehow she'd nearly forgotten. Cool Girl might yell and screech and make fun, but there had been something about fighting with her that had distracted Imogen from the actual hell storm that she had created in the store not an hour ago. That moment when everyone had stopped and stared at her. Even Little Miss Perfect didn't have the right thing to say or a smile for the occasion. Instead, she'd had the expression of a goldfish— mouth dropped and eyes wide. Not a smile in sight.

"Now that's a haircut," said a voice from behind Imogen.

She turned. It was Charlene. She was one of the regulars at Wild Nights. She was an ex-zoologist and both her arms were covered in sleeves of tattoos. Animal tattoos, of course. She had retired early in her middle age and was usually in the bookstore for feminist theory or social history. Or both.

Imogen shrugged. "Felt like a change."

Charlene smiled, like she was more than willing to participate in the charade. "Oh, sure. Must be nice during the summer. Keeps the hair off your neck."

"Exactly," said Imogen, with a decisive nod.

"Kid?" said Charlene.

"Yeah?"

"Be careful," said Charlene, dropping her friendly front for a moment and letting true concern flash through her features. But the expression was gone just as quickly as it had appeared.

"Yeah." Imogen cleared her throat. "What do you need today, Ms. Charlene?"

A smile pulled at one side of Charlene's mouth. "I've been looking for this book I read about. *Daughters of the Sun*. Supposedly it's a take on Mughal history from the perspective of the women."

"Very cool," said Imogen. And she meant it, too. Feminist

revisionist history wasn't exactly something she sought out on her own, but she loved getting the highlights from people like Charlene. No reader could specialize in every genre. That's what Imogen loved so much about Wild Nights—that everyone was into their own thing and everyone could potentially find what they were looking for. It wasn't a guarantee, of course. But that they all could look and that they all could hope for themselves in the same space was what made bookstores so magic. "How was the last one?"

"*She-Wolves*? It was excellent. Conversational and not quite history-history. But fascinating to see the way women in power have always been treated."

"Rad," said Imogen. "All right, let's see if we can find the new one."

They found it, eventually. Not under history. Not under India. Someone had decided that it went under women's studies. Which, Imogen got. That wasn't *wrong* per se. But it wasn't exactly where you'd go looking for it, either. And it certainly wasn't where Imogen would have shelved the book.

Not for the first time did Imogen wonder who had originally shelved all the books. The system seemed to have gotten more chaotic as she worked there, rather than more refined. As though the inventory was being shelved in its third or fourth category, rather than its primary one.

But at least Charlene had found her book. She practically bounced when she made her way over to Little Miss Perfect at the register, and Charlene on the whole was not someone who bounced.

The bell on the front door jangled as it opened and then slammed shut. Myrna—Imogen didn't know her last name—was about eighty years old, carrying her usual homemade pastry in a brown bag that she reused for a whole week before she threw it out. She was carrying her one little luxury—a coffee from the café next door. She liked to come into the store and sit in different stacks. She would sit and then stand all across the store for an entire morning.

Imogen loved the ritual of it.

Plus, it made Imogen almost happy that Wild Nights was a place the little old lady went every day to get out of her house. "What is it today, Myrna?"

"Danish," said Myrna, waving her brown bag so that it made a rustling, crinkling sound. "Cheese Danish."

"You enjoy," said Imogen, enjoying the casual exchange herself.

"Always do." Myrna headed straight for the only chair in the gardening section.

There was such a vibe to the mornings at Wild Nights. It was a quiet kind of bustle. The people in the store really wanted to be there—either for the quiet as they browsed or to pick up a specific book—and there was something so calm and industrious about the store and its customers right around nine o'clock.

As she passed by the checkout stand, Little Miss Perfect called out to Imogen. "Are you all right?" She had one of those worried creases in the middle of her eyebrows, like she cared a lot and wanted to help.

Imogen didn't need her help, thank you very much. She didn't need anyone's help. And right now she was just floating around the store, making sure people were finding what they were looking for. "I'm fine."

But, of course, Little Miss Perfect couldn't just leave it at that. No, she *was committed* to rooting out uncomfortable truths. "Are you sure? I just know that Daniella can be, well—not always kind. And. I just thought I'd ask."

"You've asked," said Imogen.

"Oh," said Little Miss Perfect. The crease between her forehead fell along with her expression. "Did she *say* anything? When you were in the office, I mean."

Was that a trick question? "She said lots of things. Most of them not worth repeating."

But Little Miss Perfect was only half listening. Not like her at all, if Imogen thought about it. "But did she say anything else?"

"About what?" asked Imogen.

"About the store closing or about the numbers being fine after she checked them?"

Imogen stared for a full minute. She couldn't quite find the words. Eventually, she went with, "What?"

"Oh no, she didn't mention it. Look, I'm sure it's nothing. Daniella thought the store was closing. So she went to go check the numbers. I just thought, if she called you in, it's probably fine, right?"

Everything was so far from *fine* that Imogen did the only thing she could think of in the circumstance. She turned around and fled.

Imogen went to the side door by the manga section and kicked it open. She slapped at her neck, knowing a mosquito bite was imminent. Then Imogen pulled out her phone. She'd tucked it into her boots, all the better to hide it from Jo, who would confiscate their phones if she caught them on one during work.

It was the only way that being at work was worse than being at school.

Imogen opened up her feed and began scrolling. It was a compilation—friends and bands and a few robotics and history accounts. Oh, and the poetry accounts. Against her will, really, Imogen had inherited that from her mother—her love of verse.

Imogen devoured it all.

The newfangled stuff, the sketches and drawings. The empowered women of color. The sad faces with blackout text. The self-care poetry. The reposts of Mary Oliver quotes over stock photos and memes. But Imogen's favorite was anachronisticblonde. She did little doodles, like the new stuff, but she mostly did sonnets and odes and fragments of what could be a compiled epic. She wasn't the biggest or the most influential account that Imogen followed by a long shot, but there was something so raw and real about her work that Imogen thought it was only a matter of time before her account blew up.

The latest poem was at the top of her feed—*In truth the sun does not rise*—that was what Imogen needed. She felt it, down to her bones. Imogen hovered on that image, never *liking* anachronisticblonde's poems but always stopping to read. The algorithm must have known this about Imogen—that she was a grade A lurker.

Imogen couldn't believe that Wild Nights was closing. She didn't want to believe it. But she thought about Eli's jitters, and she thought about Cool Girl's extra snippiness, and Imogen just couldn't reassure herself on this point that she must have misunderstood or that Little Miss Perfect must have misunderstood.

And then other worries came rolling in. Where would Charlene get her regular feminist fix from? Where would Myrna go with her morning pastry? There were other regulars, too. The young mother—Imogen didn't know her name, but she had to be just out of college—who was sitting reading business books while her child read picture books out loud. Or the woman who came in every week looking for a selection for her book club.

It wasn't just that Imogen would be out of a job. It was that these people belonged here and they were about to be unceremoniously cut away from a place that they had each made a little bit their own.

That's when the side door to the alleyway opened and Jo came barging out of it. There was no getting out of this one. Imogen had no time to stuff her phone back into her boots.

"Oh, thank you so much. Love a new phone to add to my collection." Jo grabbed it out of Imogen's hands. "Nice haircut, by the way."

"Wait—" But it was too late. Any response that Imogen could have come up with was cut short by a truck driving through the back alley where they both stood, leaning against the outside wall. A delivery truck. Imogen thought it was going to rumble on through, but then she heard that horrible, squeaking brake sound that delivery trucks make, and she knew that they were going to drop off boxes.

Fantastic. Imogen hated having to do the heavy lifting part of her job. Everyone at the bookstore did. She was a *bookstore employee.* That had to be the literal definition of an indoor cat.

"Delivery for Jo Rivas?" The delivery driver had jumped out of the truck and was handing Jo one of those tablets that looked like an old graphing calculator, only these came with tiny plastic pens that never worked and were attached for recipients to sign across the window-box screen.

"It's not Tuesday." Jo shook her head, like she couldn't believe the delivery driver was standing there. "And I didn't order anything."

"Look, I got a delivery. Are you gonna take it or not?" The delivery driver put a hand on her hip.

Jo shook her head in resignation, then signed for the packages using the back of a pen that she took out of her pocket.

The delivery driver grabbed a box out of the truck and started stacking it onto a dolly. Once she had a good stack, she wheeled the packages into the store.

The puzzlement didn't leave Jo's face.

And that's when the gears in Imogen's mind started working. A shipment arrived that Jo didn't expect. Daniella was pissed about the discrepancy. And Eli was twitchy, nervous, and willing to go deal with Daniella when she was pissed. Imogen was starting to get a picture of what was happening, and not one bit of it looked good for Eli. Maybe Wild Nights Bookstore hadn't been closing.

Maybe Eli was the reason they were going under.

Jo looked up at Imogen. "Look, I better get in there and see what all of this is about. Daniella is probably running the numbers. I'm sure she'll get to the bottom of this in no time."

And for some reason—despite the fact that Eli had a record and the fact that Imogen hated Cool Girl and would have loved to watch her sweat under the pressure of Jo's potential interrogation—Imogen blurted out the one thing she knew would stop Jo cold in her tracks.

"Is Wild Nights really closing?"

Jo froze, the pen she'd used to sign for the delivery clattering to the ground in the alley.

Imogen ran a hand over her freshly cut hair. This was going to be a fun conversation.

6

Let Me Count the Ways

10:06 A.M.
Daniella

Daniella stared at Eli.

She had crossed her arms and was doing her best impersonation of her own mother when Daniella came home after curfew. Daniella had ample experience with this expression, so she was pretty positive that she was nailing the steely glare combined with that intractable forward lean.

Eli stared back at Daniella.

He was doing his best angelic face of innocence. And Eli had *quite* the cherubic features—curly dark blond hair, full and dimpled cheeks, and an absolutely guileless smile. When Daniella had first met Eli, she'd thought he was plain and unremarkable looking. But the more she looked, the more she noticed things about him—first those dimples on his cheeks, then a faint scar above his eyebrow, and lastly the way the sides of his eyes crinkled when he was trying to hide that he was up to no good.

Daniella didn't particularly *like* noticing so many things about him; she discovered a new set of freckles along his left cheekbone. Probably from the summer sun. But Daniella wasn't going to give up a staring contest without a fight.

This was a stalemate.

Luckily, Eli cracked first. "Funny running into you here."

Daniella closed her eyes for a moment. She took a deep breath before she reopened them. She was hungover. She was tired. Imogen had gotten her hair all over the bathroom. The way this day was going, Rinn would probably try to kiss AJ at some point and Daniella would end up having to *talk to both of them about it*. Eli, Daniella knew, had a secret. She could read it across that crinkle in his eyes, in the way that new dusting of fresh summer freckles jumped as she spoke.

"Can we skip the preamble and get down to the part where you tell me if you found this missing transaction for nine thousand dollars?"

"What?" asked Eli, as if he were as innocent as one of the seraphim.

Daniella knew deep in her bones that God never gave anybody dimples like that unless they were absolute hell-raisers. "Did you know about it?"

Eli glanced at Daniella, and then away again. "No."

Ah, guilt. She could hear it in his tone. See it in the way he stood—tensed and defensive. Ready for a fight. But Daniella couldn't say where the guilty conscious was coming from or why it was there. She just knew its presence, all its hallmarks greeting her like an old friend. Daniella took a guess. "How did you figure out the store was closing?"

Eli's guilt must have taken a determined turn, because he gritted his teeth and dug in his heels. "Everything just seemed off in the store. That's all."

"You had a *feeling*, so you just *decided to text me and start ringing alarm bells?"* Daniella tilted her head to really emphasize the point. It was vague enough to be believable, especially if you believed that Eli was a screwup. But Daniella didn't buy it.

"I didn't ring alarm bells. I told you that something was up. And I told you not to tell anyone. And I bet when you checked, you saw what I was talking about. You're just mad you didn't find the problem first." Eli raised an eyebrow like he'd made a real point there.

And unfortunately he had. She hated that she hadn't discovered this months ago. She took such pride in seeing numbers as they were. Numbers were honest. Numbers, theoretically, didn't lie.

"You're such a brat, do you know that?"

"I know." Eli gave a smug nod. "And I'm right. You *are* mad you didn't find the problem first, math nerd."

"Whatever," said Daniella. "Stop deflecting. I need you to tell me how you figured any of this out. For real."

"Make me." Eli smirked.

And even though he had just admitted to not telling the whole truth, even though Eli had definitely just conceded ground, Daniella's irritation flickered from low levels of radiation to a full-blown nuclear meltdown.

It was the smirk that had done it.

"You have five seconds, or I am going to call Jo in here and we're all going to sort this mess out together." She was typically the kind of person who said *Snitches get stitches*. But she needed to get Eli's attention. She needed to regain control of this impossible situation. She needed to stop watching the way his freckles danced across his face as his expressions shifted.

Eli didn't even bat one of his long eyelashes. Didn't miss a beat. His voice went soft and lyrical, like he was an old-fashioned muse. Like he could use that honeyed voice of his to get out of any and all trouble. "Come on, Danny."

"Don't you dare use that tone with me. You're not going to charm me out of getting an answer from you. What aren't you telling me?" Daniella uncrossed her arms and settled her hands on her hips.

Eli sighed. "I might have, just maybe, found an email saying that the store was closing and being sold."

"You what?" Daniella's voice went low. She had wanted to shout. But finely honed instincts had taught her that when she wanted to shout, she ought to whisper. "You just saw an email lying on the floor and thought, *Huh, I'll just pick that up—maybe somebody lost this electronic message and needs a hero like me to return it to him*? Nobody just *finds* emails, Eli."

Eli sighed another very put-upon sigh. But he didn't avoid her this time. "I went through Jo's email, and I found that there was a pending sale."

For a moment, all that Daniella could do was stare. And Eli stared back, his eyes full of earnestness and something else that Daniella couldn't place. Something Daniella could have easily mistaken for longing.

She blinked, fluttering some of the remnants of last night's mascara into her eyes. Daniella rubbed until the flakes were out of her eyes—probably fully entrenched under them by now. In an instant, she became conscious of what she looked like.

Daniella was still wearing the vestiges of last night's eyeliner. Though most of the mascara was probably now deposited under her eyes. And she kept reaching out for the nearest piece of furniture in order to get ahold of her body's delightful waves of nausea. Her peroxide-blond hair was fuzzy all over—the effects of having thick, wavy dark brown hair that had been bleached to hell and back. She usually smoothed oil or cream through her strands to keep them from fluffing out in all directions. But Daniella hadn't had time to do that this morning. She didn't know why she was so acutely aware of her hair right now. She could picture it—bleached and fried and pointing out in all directions, with no discernable wave pattern left. She was resisting the urge to smooth it out, to pull it down or back. Resisting the impulse to lick her fingers and wipe the makeup from under her eyes.

She was a hot mess that had cooled off, leaving behind ashes and sludge.

She wanted to look anywhere other than at Eli. Maybe the desk or the bookshelf or the piles and piles of boxes that were now all around them. She was talking about something serious, and he was avoiding giving her the truth. About the store closing. About the fact that he'd gone through Jo's emails and found out that Wild Nights was being sold out from under all of them, without so much as a notice until it was far too late.

She wanted to be mad. She wanted to yell. She wanted to shake him until he told her what the hell was going on.

But instead Daniella was staring at Eli, wondering why she couldn't look away. Wondering if she could just pull her hair off her neck and if this flushed, heated feeling would go away.

Somebody needed to turn up the air-conditioning.

Eli took a step forward. It was so soft and so gentle a step that Daniella wondered who he was worried about startling. And then the door to the break room slammed open and Daniella jumped, practically out of her own skin.

A delivery woman came in, toting boxes in on a dolly. "Where should I put these?"

Daniella stared for a moment. Her voice sounded a little far-away when she said, "Anywhere."

The delivery woman shrugged, then started unloading boxes close to the door. Daniella and Eli stood there as the woman carted boxes in and out.

It took an age. It took no time at all. Daniella couldn't have said, which was odd, because she normally had a very good sense of time. The delivery woman dropped the last box from her dolly, and she was off, out of the room, and probably back into her truck. She had been so quick with the delivery that it startled Daniella again that the woman was already done.

Daniella looked over to Eli. He still looked intractable—his smirk firmly in place and his arms decidedly folded across his chest—like getting the truth out of him would require a modern miracle.

"Get out of here, then. If you're not going to help or explain. Leave me to sort out whatever mess you've clearly made." Daniella turned away. She didn't want to look at Eli anymore. Didn't want to think about her own weakness in not going straight to Jo. Didn't even want to solve this problem that had landed on her today. All she wanted was to drink some grape soda and nurse her hangover and maybe post another poem on her account.

So, of course, that was when Eli decided to crack. "Okay, okay, I will tell you. But you have got to swear to not tell anyone. This is serious."

Daniella whipped around. "I cannot promise that. I have no idea what is going on. All I know is that nine thousand dollars has gone missing and you somehow went through Jo's work emails and found out that the store is being sold. Don't you get this? This isn't a prank. This isn't a whim. This is nine thousand dollars of bookstore funds that are missing on the ledger. This is all of our jobs and an entire store that is going under. You better start explaining, and you better start fast."

Eli swallowed hard. "See, I was closing up."

"Yes, I know. Jo gave you the keys. I left you alone. And now we have boxes and boxes of—" But Daniella had whacked her hand into a box and it had gone toppling over. She paused, for a moment, staring at the box. "That can't be books."

"Wait—" called Eli.

But Daniella was on a mission now. She pulled off the tape and ripped open the box. There, inside, were boxes of sneakers. Mostly Air Jordans from what Daniella could tell by the sheer number of black-and-red boxes.

Holy hell. No wonder the delivery woman had unloaded the delivery so quickly. They hadn't been heavy. Not the way their normal book deliveries were next to impossible to lift.

Daniella didn't have a witty repartee. She didn't have a comeback or a retort or any of the other fancy words for this kind of occasion. Namely the time and the place where a person showed that they cared more about themselves than for the place you thought that you both held sacred. She could only stare at Eli, then stare at the boxes of Jordans, and then stare at Eli again. Finally, she came up with the only thought that was in her mind. The one phrase that was repeating on an endless loop in her head. "You stole."

"No." Eli was shaking his head vigorously, like a fervent prayer.

Daniella nodded slowly, assuredly. "You did. You stole. From the bookstore."

"That's not what this is, Daniella, I swear. I know it looks like that, but I can prove it. I can prove it."

Daniella couldn't believe it. The bookstore was going under, and Eli had used it as an opportunity to steal. She said it again, her voice more steady this time. "You *stole*."

"No, no, no. They're not stolen, they're fake."

Daniella couldn't believe that was any better. "You took the money from the store, Eli. That's stealing."

Eli shook his head again, held up his hands. "Wait, no, please. Let me explain. Please let me explain."

"How could you possibly explain any of this?" Daniella knew Eli had gotten into trouble for stealing beer when he was a kid. But she never thought he'd do this. Go behind Jo's back—behind all of their backs—and steal from the one place they all loved.

The nausea came back. But this was nothing like her hangover. It was a sudden and swift roiling in her stomach. *Betrayal.* Daniella hadn't ever thought about it, but she realized then that she'd believed no matter who else she worked with, they were all loyal to this place. It was *theirs*, dammit. But Eli, he'd violated that. He'd destroyed her faith in something that Daniella hadn't even realized she'd believed in.

Shattered. Gone. A puff of smoke.

Daniella pushed past Eli, began walking to the door. She had to find Jo. Bookstores weren't exactly places that were flush with cash. If Eli had ordered this many shoes online, then it was likely to affect the entire store. She didn't have to tell on Eli, but she did need to tell Jo, and fast.

But Eli grabbed Daniella's arm. "Wait. Please. Wait. I was closing the store and I was checking the books and I didn't mean to look but her email was the only thing open on her computer and I saw an email from Hunt Junior on there and I had to do something."

"Had to do what? Blow money on a side hustle?"

"No. He's selling the store."

"Why should I believe you? You've been lying this whole time."

Eli reached out tentatively for her hand. Despite her best attempts to hold on to her anger and her frustration, she couldn't. Daniella took his hand.

He led her over to the laptop and opened up Jo's email. "Look. Archer Hunt Junior. He emailed Jo. We've got two weeks. Archer gave her two weeks' notice. The bookstore is closing. I was trying to save it. I didn't know the shoes were fake. I thought I could sell them; I could flip them and get Jo the money to invest back into the payroll. At least, buy some more time. I don't know. I swear to God, I was trying to help. I wasn't trying to make a quick buck. I mean, I was, but not for myself."

Daniella watched Eli. As far as bullshit stories went, it was not a good one. Daniella had to hope that if Eli was going to lie, he would have the decency to tell a better lie. But it all seemed so improbable to begin with.

Eli could tell Daniella was softening to his arguments, though. "Look. Just *look* at the email."

"Eli, we are *not supposed to touch the laptop.* That's like literally the only rule Jo has. She says not to touch her laptop or her vape pens, but she knows we find her vape pens, so all we literally have to do is not touch her laptop. What is *wrong* with you?"

But Daniella looked over Eli's shoulder as he clicked through and opened up the message.

Wild Nights Bookstore and lot—is under consideration with the West Garden Property Group . . .

Daniella didn't grab an errant box or the edge of the desk. It wasn't enough to support her. She sat down, directly on the floor. When that wasn't enough, she lay all the way down. "Holy shit."

"I don't know what to do, Danny."

Daniella stared. "You don't know what to do, but you did know how to steal nine thousand dollars of the bookstore's money?"

"Please, please, please don't go shouting it everywhere. I have to figure out what I'm going to do to get us out of this mess. I promise I will tell Jo once I figure out what I am supposed to do here."

Daniella watched Eli wring his hands. He was staring at all of those boxes. All the evidence of his poor decision-making. He was responsible, all right.

It was just that he had been trying, and that counted for something for Daniella, too.

Daniella stood up, grabbed the nearest box, and began stacking. "Give me a hand with this, will you?"

"What good will that do?" Eli was positively despondent. He looked like a vision of sad Romantic poetry about mortality and the fragility of humanity come to life. Morose, ready for tragedy to strike him at any time. He was slumped, and he was desperate.

Daniella was ready to take any action to keep him from breaking like that.

"First, it will keep the boxes in order. Second, it will keep anyone from digging too deeply into the boxes. Third, I'm going to need you to have a much better attitude here, prince of accidental larceny."

Eli groaned.

But Daniella wasn't finished yet. "Because after we stack the boxes, I'm going to tell you my plan to get us all out of this mess."

And for the first time since he walked in, Eli looked like maybe the sun would come out again.

7

All Mimsy

10:25 A.M.
Rinn

All Rinn wanted to do was get out her phone and start filming the bookstore.

The morning light was filtering into the room just right, and all the books looked like they had a magical glow. The store wouldn't look like this again until sunset. She liked to take advantage of the light whenever she could, for content's sake. But instead Rinn was stuck behind the register with no phone.

No. She wasn't stuck. She was only stuck if she believed she was stuck.

Rinn took a deep breath. There weren't any customers waiting to be helped. There was hardly anyone in the store. Just Myrna standing up and moving from her chair in the gardening section to the chair by the home organization section. No line at the register. Not even anyone casually browsing closer and closer to the checkout.

She could go get her phone. As long as Rinn returned her phone to the office by the end of the day, *Jo would never know.*

Rinn made a decision.

She worked her way through the stacks. She bobbed and wove her way through the sections. Philosophy to art. Art to cookbooks. Cookbooks to picture books. Picture books into chapters books into the YA section. Every store had its own flow, but this one—the one at Wild Nights—made intuitive sense to Rinn. It was an intellectual flow of ideas that was familiar and worn and well trod.

She made it to the break room in under a minute.

When she walked in, Rinn stopped short for a moment. Daniella and Eli were frozen, each of them with a box in their arms.

"What's going on?" Rinn couldn't put her finger on it. But something was off. She'd never seen two people just freeze up like that. Holding heavy boxes of books and looking as though they had been caught with their hands in the cookie jar. "You guys okay?"

"Peachy keen," said Daniella. But it wasn't with her usual sarcasm, as Rinn had expected. There was something overly bright and exaggerated in her tone—not undercutting and deprecating enough. Not laced with the usual level of bitterness. It was almost as if Daniella were panicked.

But before Rinn could think too much on *that*, Eli smiled bright and wide. It should have been charming, but it was just honestly concerning to look at Eli grinning with all teeth and no animation or expression in his eyes.

"Everything cool?" Rinn couldn't help but stare. *Something was going on here.*

"Fantastic, really super," said Eli. "Bordering on superb."

Had Rinn interrupted something? Rinn looked for clues that Eli and Daniella had been flirting or even hooking up. But nobody could kiss with two enormous boxes between them. Rinn ruled that out. Maybe they were—

"What are you doing here?" Daniella practically shouted the question. She was clearly trying to catch Rinn off guard, but she was still holding the box in her hands and still looking uncomfortable and overly cheery, and the shouting didn't land the way it ought to have.

Rinn, who was, by rights, the worst liar in the world, said the plain truth. "I'm getting my phone."

And then Rinn, who didn't want to either ask or answer another question, moved quickly over to Jo's desk, pulled her phone out of the drawer, and then brandished it for both Eli and Daniella to see. *See*, her movements said, *just getting my phone. Nothing to see here, either.* "Okay. I'll just be. Going now. You guys, good luck with. Whatever it is."

Rinn waved her hand over the general area of both of them. They were behaving *very* oddly. But then again, maybe so was Rinn.

"Thank you," said Daniella in that overly cheerful tone. It was especially disconcerting after the shouting.

Rinn stopped and stared for a moment. Eli smiled extra wide again, and Rinn decided she didn't want to know, not even a little bit.

Rinn breathed a sigh of relief when she exited the break room with her phone. *She'd done it. She'd gotten hold of her phone.* And at least Daniella hadn't been actively horrible to her, even if she'd been super weird the entire time.

It was content time.

Rinn looked around the store. This was her second favorite part of what she did—spotting the best light, setting up the shot, really seeing the space from a fresh point of view. The front of the store was lit up beautifully. But it was that middle ground that had the most interesting light. The shadows that were cropping up from the lack of light in the back combined with the sun that was shining through the front of the store.

Gothic in the best sense of the word.

Rinn ducked into the art history and criticism shelves. It wasn't the most interesting subject matter to her viewers, but she could definitely use this as a backdrop. She snapped a few photos for herself. Though she also wanted to film a quick video to see how the shot lined up.

But when she opened her app to film a quick story test, there they were—all of her notifications. All the messages. Flaring red and looking like they were screaming at her, shouting for her to take notice and to respond *immediately*.

Rinn turned her phone so that its screen was facedown and away from her for a moment. She took a deep breath. She could handle this. She had just stolen back her phone from the office. She was not beholden to all of her messages. Not right now. Right now, she was unstoppable.

And with that in mind, Rinn decided to take a slight detour on her way back to the register and find AJ.

He was shelving books in the history section. Rinn tapped him on the shoulder.

AJ turned around, smiling his quiet, devastating smile. Rinn felt her heartbeat all the way in her throat, and she didn't even mind that it was the kind of cliché she'd read about in countless contemporary romances, because the sensation was real and true and there weren't any other words for it.

"Hey," he said.

"Hi." Rinn tried her best to keep the breathlessness from her voice. Tried to sound measured.

"I found this in the dollar section in the back." AJ reached into the back pocket of his jeans and held out a book.

Rinn took the paperback and flipped it over directly. She tried not to stare as his hair flopped into his eyes. "Oh, the next Dorothy Sayers in the series. How did you know?"

"I saw that the last one was lying around in the break room. I assumed you had finished it."

"Oh." Rinn had hoped, secretly, that he'd watched one of her daily vlog videos and saw that she had finished it. That he'd read the caption on her post. Had read her words, had watched her tell a tale on the internet. But it hadn't been any of those things. It was just leaving a copy of the last one in the break room. Sure, he'd still noticed. But it wasn't the same as noticing someone on their accounts, watching what they were up to because he had no other way of knowing.

Not the way Rinn watched his updates when he posted his art online. Not the way she obsessively checked his web comic. But AJ, apparently, had no such need for her posts. Rinn wasn't sure why she cared so much. Her book account had transformed so long ago from something she did for herself to a business that she ought to have found it easy not to take it personally.

Rinn decided then and there not to be totally disheartened.

Unfortunately, what her brain decided and what her heart felt were two radically different things. "I really loved it—*Strong Poison*, I mean. It was really a phenomenal mystery."

"Yeah, and Harriet Vane is so good. Like she's so smart and so capable, even when she's accused of murder. And the two of them—her and Wimsey—their chemistry, they're one of those great ships. You have to wait for four more books. But it's worth it. I think."

Rinn sighed. At least he was talking about something romantic. "I need your help."

"With what?" AJ tilted his head.

"This is so embarrassing, but—" Rinn smiled, even though it hurt to look at AJ; he was so handsome. "Filming content?"

AJ didn't smile, but the sides of his eyes crinkled. "That's not embarrassing. Aren't you like a content master?"

Rinn nodded. "Something like that."

"All right, I'm game. What do you need?"

"A copy of *When We Were Us* and a steady hand," said Rinn with a nod. She could be authoritative. She could be commanding. She would not be embarrassed about the fact that she made money on the internet. She would not be embarrassed about filming in front of her crush. Even if she was used to filming most of her videos in the privacy of her own bedroom. Even if she was melting inside. That didn't mean that she had to *show* it. That didn't mean she had to *believe* it.

AJ left for a moment, but he was back in a flash with a copy of the book that Rinn had requested. "And what happens when Jo finds us?"

"She won't. I think I saw her just head outside. We've got a good ten minutes while the coast is clear."

For her posts, Rinn filmed higher-production stuff—the kind she used props and costumes and makeup and a whole editorial suite on her computer to get into good shape. The kind she actually got paid to do now, by publishing houses and book boxes and even the occasional lifestyle brand. But her followers also liked the daily updates on her stories, the rougher, less-pretty short videos as well.

What they saw as *the authentic stuff*.

Of course, Rinn still produced those as well, just to a different degree.

She handed AJ her phone. "Okay, I need you to film me as I talk about this book, and I need you to hold up a three-second warning with your fingers before my fifteen seconds are up. I'll nod when I'm ready for you to start filming."

This time AJ did crack a full smile. "I can handle that."

"Good."

Then she closed her eyes and took a deep breath. Because she didn't normally film with an audience. But this was for Wild Nights. She had to. Rinn opened her eyes. She looked directly at the phone—she had to pretend AJ was practically an inanimate object or a piece of furniture or anything other than an actual live human to get this done—and nodded.

"Hey, guys, Rinn here." Rinn smiled brighter, hoping that would make up for the fact that her original expression was, potentially, *noticeably* fake. These were supposed to be the real deal, these stories. If she started looking overly performative, Rinn would lose engagement and lose sponsorship and—but Rinn stopped herself. She took a deep breath in. Everything was *fine*. Hold that smile. She could do this. "Today is midsummer— aka the summer equinox, aka the first day of summer—aka a day for magic and peak summer vibes."

When she filmed by herself, Rinn liked to reference the other mini worlds of the internet—the front-facing makeup looks, the meme accounts, the poetry, the adorable kitten videos—and not just the book photos and posts that she did on the regular. She liked the idea that there were all of these various, significant kingdoms online. That really the spaces on her phone were like fantasy lands—constantly interacting and warring and conquering and trying to relate to one another. Separate but connected. And Rinn liked to draw on those connections.

"Let's talk about what I've been reading recently, because it's summer and I *love* summer reading. So, I know I tend to stay inside in this Chicago heat, but I like to imagine I'm by a pool, just to really give it that summer feel." Rinn caught sight of AJ holding up three fingers, then two, then one.

Deep breaths. You do this every morning. It's totally fine. Rinn took another deep inhale. "Just keep saving them. I'll post them after we film it all."

AJ nodded. "You're the boss."

Rinn nodded so that AJ would start filming again. "Whoo boy, I really need longer than fifteen seconds. Lol. I just did a reread of my favorite book of *all time*: *When We Were Us*. I'm so excited because I get to see author Brock Harvey *to-day*, and I literally cannot wait. I'm going to do what I can to film the lead-up to this momentous occasion. The bookstore that I will be seeing him at is definitely a huge stickler for *no social media*. But I am here now, and I am doing some stealth recon filming."

At home, Rinn had collected every version of *When We Were Us* that had come out since the book's release five years ago, and she had brought to work her most favorite, most worn, most beloved copy. She held it up, still on camera. "I think this book is so gorgeous and romantic, and I love the characters that Harvey created in here. Georgiana and Nate feel so real to me, and they grab me from page one. I had to keep reading just to know what was going to happen next."

Rinn nodded. AJ stopped recording and saved the video. They were finding a rhythm in this. And while filming like this might have been the most awkward thing that Rinn had ever done, she always felt most like herself when she was talking about a book. That was her natural state, really. Books, she could do. Books, she loved.

Rinn nodded one last time. "And seriously, I'm not going to spoil anything for you, but you really have no idea how Harvey is going to end this. You also have no idea how life is going to come at these main characters. I love how surprising and engaging the writing is, and if you are one of the five people on planet Earth who has not read this book, I *strongly* recommend that you at least give it a shot. I think that it has the perfect blend of the most romantic moments combined with real-life drama and real-world lessons. I mean, do what you're gonna do, but to be honest, please check this book out. It's amaaaazing."

AJ stopped filming and saved that last video. "That was impressive."

"Oh." She tucked an errant curl behind her ear. "Thanks."

"Seriously, I'd never be able to film with someone else watching. I can't even record one of those drawing-live videos that I see everywhere, where artists do a warm-up sketch so people can see their process as they draw."

Hope and relief bubbled in Rinn's chest. She felt lighter, a little more carefree. "Oh, I was screaming internally. I usually don't film with an audience. Worst-case scenario my sisters come barging in and ruin the shot. But they stopped making fun of me once they saw the first sponsorship check that arrived in the mail." Rinn took the phone from AJ's outstretched hand. She focused on the screen, not looking at him as she spoke.

"Is it weird, turning something you love into a business?"

The tone in AJ's voice was so sincere that Rinn looked up. Stared directly into his inhumanly handsome face. "It is. And I guess it isn't. I don't have to worry about finding the money for college. And I've started saving up the funds for my sisters, too. It feels kind of poetic that my love of books gets to pay for so many educations. But it definitely adds pressure. To perform. To do well. To look a certain way on camera. To have a certain rate of engagement for every post."

"You don't have to look any way, do you?" AJ was still so sincere.

Rinn checked her phone. She didn't know how to talk about the fact that she often wondered if the reason she succeeded as a Latinx girl with a book account on the internet was because she was half-white and because she was ethnically ambiguous-looking. That she must have benefited from some strange proximity to whiteness and that she was benefiting still by the way her account had grown. That she didn't know if she deserved all the followers that she had amassed.

She didn't have satisfactory answers to any of these questions. But she wore her hair curly so that her inheritance from her father—his black coiled texture—would not be erased. It would be seen every day by all the people who followed her. And she highlighted creators of color as best as she could. She did regular spotlights on Own Voices novels. She tried to talk about the stories that maybe other people had missed.

It didn't feel like enough, though.

"I do have to look a certain way. I mean, it's the internet, so it's not like how I look has to be perfect. But it matters. It's like I have to follow the rules I set up before I realized I was setting up rules. I'm not sure if that makes sense."

AJ's face scrunched up thoughtfully. It was a delightful expression. "No, it doesn't. But I believe you. I do gotta ask—why do you work here? I mean, your account is massive."

"Massive for books is still not massive given what people can get paid for social media," said Rinn on a laugh. It was true that, given her following, she probably didn't need to work a regular summer job anymore. But Rinn had two baby sisters. She was saving her internet money for all of their educations. She was putting it into special educational accounts for each of them. None of them were going to go into debt to go to school. Not if Rinn could help it. She was putting this book money to good use—debt-free college for her and for Gloria and Renate.

But that meant Rinn had to have another source of regular spending money. And even though she had initially chafed against the no-tech restrictions of Wild Nights, Rinn had come to appreciate the time away from her online persona. She'd take the bus to the blue line on the L and then walked the rest of the way to work. She felt independent. Like she could just be a regular girl working a regular job rather than this thing that had spiraled out of her hands and belonged more to her followers than her anymore.

But Wild Nights belonged to Rinn. It had belonged to her as a customer and now it belonged to her as an employee. She couldn't imagine a world without it. It was the one space where everything could be all right.

She had to do what she could to save it. Rinn clicked through and posted the videos. She'd been able to geotag them, thanks to re-adding the store to Google Maps.

Rinn and AJ both started walking back toward the checkout counter. It was a natural and easy silence that Rinn didn't take for granted. She'd learned through years of filming vlogs that she could quite literally talk to a wall. Or a camera. But companionable silence was a rare and precious thing.

Just before Rinn swung behind the register, AJ bumped his shoulder into hers. He stretched out the book in his hand again. "You forgot this, by the way."

It was that next Sayers murder-mystery novel. Rinn took it and decided maybe, now was as good of a time as any to actually flirt with AJ. Maybe, with the magic of this moment, it would work. "Thank you, I—"

Rinn opened her mouth, when a heavy *thud* sounded in front of her. Rinn jumped back as two full grocery bags of books landed on the counter. Her pen got knocked off the register, her glasses slipped down her nose, and AJ made himself scarce. He hated dealing with the resale customers.

Rinn didn't blame him.

"Are you open?" An aggressive-looking man stared at her. He had a sharp, angular face and a direct sort of disposition.

"Uh. Yes?" Of course they were open. How else could the man be standing in the damned store, *ruining her life?*

The man folded his arms across his chest. He was athletic and sun-weathered. He had one of those faces that could have been between forty-five and sixty-five—the kind of tanned white skin that had been left out in the sun to dry out, like leather. Rinn couldn't help but think of a romantic lead in a historical novel who had aged. Straight, rugged nose. Deep-set eyes, heavy eyebrows. Piercing stare. A rough voice saying horrible, sarcastic things. "Are you not sure if you're open?"

This was why Rinn was attracted to the sensitive, artistic type. They didn't go around shouting to get their way, bullying young women who had little power to do anything but apologize. "I'm sure we're open, sir. I'm just not sure what you're trying to ask me, since you couldn't be talking to me if we weren't open."

"Don't get smart," he snapped.

Rinn was never *trying* to get smart. It was just sometimes the things that flew out of her mouth seemed to be registered that way by adults. "I'm sorry, sir. That was not my intention at all. I mean—are you trying to ask me something specific?"

The acquiescence relaxed him back into his earlier commanding tone. "I want to sell these books. Obviously."

Rinn looked back at the bags. It was a lot of nature books and philosophy tomes. It was going to be worth twenty-five dollars, at the most. She raised her arm, pointing toward the back of the store. "Oh, then yes. The sales counter is open. It's in the back."

"There's no one there." He raised his eyebrow like he'd gained a point.

Rinn was left to wonder why there was nothing remotely sexy about a man who acted like an actual romantic hero in real life. Lord Byron must have been the absolute worst. "Well, I'm sure if you wait a minute—"

"I already did that." He crossed his arms again, like his time was more valuable than her time.

Rinn hated arguing about her personal worth via a dollar-per-hour rate. She'd gotten into enough of those fights on the store floor that this time she ducked down and dug under the register and grabbed the BACK IN A MINUTE! sign. When she popped back up, the man had one of those frozen, annoyed expressions on his face. Then she placed the sign on the register, and his features relaxed again as he read it.

"All right, let's go." Rinn headed toward the sales desk, practically sprinting so that the customer wouldn't demand she lift his grocery bags filled with books. He could carry his own freaking stack of dead male philosophers and bird-watching books.

Rinn made a big show of setting up the register for sales. Checking in with her badge and opening and closing the register so that he knew she had hurried over in order to check through his books quickly. The sales desk was the official one place in the store with internet access—other than Jo's laptop—so that they could look up the going rate for any books that came through the door. There were apps for that now, but the phone ban made using one of those impossible.

The man huffed and puffed and set the bags onto the sales counter.

Rinn gave him her brightest smile, cutting off whatever horrendous sarcasm he had been rehearsing as he'd lugged his books back across the entirety of the store. "If you give me a minute, I can tally these and give you a total. I'll just need your ID."

"Sure." The man got out his ID, and Rinn handed him a clipboard with a paper to sign his name and write his other information.

Rinn double-checked the ID against the number that he had written down. Then she smiled again. "Feel free to look around the store while you wait."

The man shook his head incredulously. "Kid, I'm trying to get rid of books. Not buy more of them."

And you just ruined me telling the love of my life that I was in love with him, so I think we're even, bud. "I'll just be a minute."

A new pair of hands slapped the sales desk, and Rinn looked up, expecting to paste on her most patient, but also most threatening smile. It was the *Please do not make me go get my manager* smile, because Rinn knew that Jo would always be on her side. Jo, blessedly, never thought the customer was right when they were behaving aggressively with young female staff. Instead, Rinn looked up to see Imogen's girlfriend, Lena. She was clicking her shining, stiletto-shaped, baby-pink nails against the counter.

Oh no.

"Hey there, sunshine. Any chance you've seen my girlfriend?" Lena was smiling like she'd lost track of her keys or her phone or something. Like Imogen was an everyday kind of thing that she misplaced and there was no harm in it.

Rinn sputtered. She had never been very good at being put on the spot. It was honestly possible that Imogen hated Rinn, but Rinn felt protective of her the way she would have any of Wild Nights' employees. They didn't have to like each other, but they did need to look out for each other. "I. Uh. I think. Well. Imogen is here. She is definitely here. She's probably here."

It was just that Rinn was a horrible liar and probably couldn't cover for a person if the saving of the world depended on it.

Lena gave Rinn a look of skeptical confusion. "Yes, I know that. She told me she was working today. She jetted from my house so fast yesterday that I wanted to drop by and give her this. She left it at my house." Lena held up something. It was a black leather jacket, as though Imogen didn't already own the world's supply of those.

"I'll go see if she's available." Rinn made a move to leave the register.

But of course, the bird-watching man saw her, like he was some kind of hawk. "Excuse me, miss, you haven't finished tallying my books yet."

"I need a quick second to go look into something for this woman here, sir."

"She doesn't look like a customer." The man eyed Lena, from her nails to her sleek bob to her denim jacket.

"That's rude," said Lena, completely nonplussed.

"Are you a customer?" Birdman folded his arms across his chest.

Lena shook her head. "No, but that's still rude."

The man waved his hands toward the books. "I rest my case."

Rinn groaned. *What, was this dude a lawyer as well as a grade A jerk and a freaking bird-watcher?*

Now Rinn knew that she couldn't stop Lena from going after Imogen.

It wasn't that Rinn minded Lena. On her own she was, perhaps, not somebody Rinn would have been friends with, but Lena was nice enough to make chitchat without being rude. She was the kind of girl who stuck up for herself and the things she cared about. Lena was one of those mouthy, popular girls you couldn't help but admire. And Rinn had never seen Lena bully another person or abuse her power over others.

But the two of them—Lena and Imogen—together was like reading a bad romance in a paranormal book. The kind of thing that works great in fiction, but in real life is just a plain mess. Sometimes Rinn wanted to save them from themselves. She usually resisted the urge. But after Imogen had shaved her head, Rinn thought they maybe didn't need to meet *right now*. Maybe, just maybe, Imogen needed some space. And not only from Lena, but probably from almost everyone.

"Can you wait until I'm done here? I can go grab her after that." It was a last-ditch effort, but Rinn had to at least try.

"Dude. What is with you? I can find my girlfriend on my own." Lena was losing her already short patience. It was only a matter of *when* her temper would switch, not if.

"It's just . . ." Rinn bit her lip. Then she released it, thinking of every clichéd heroine who bit her lip in consternation or confusion or concern. She was clearly thinking too hard about paranormal romance. Rinn was not a clichéd heroine if she could help it, despite the earlier heartbeat-in-her-throat thing.

She would be honest with Lena, and in turn, Lena would respond with a calmness and responsibility. Right. "She came into work in, well, A Mood. And while I'm sure she's fine now, I think, she maybe might not be. And she seemed to be radiating *Need alone time and lots of space, please do not mess with me today.* And I thought, maybe, I should go get her, or warn her, or something.

Or maybe you could come back later. When she's had time to calm down. Either of those would work super well, I think."

Lena held up her hands. "I promise not to fight with her in the middle of the bookstore."

Rinn raised her eyebrows, really not buying it this time.

Lena sighed. "That was *one time*."

"It's not *you*, Lena. I think she'd fight with anyone right now." Of that, Rinn was certain.

Lena crossed her arms over her chest. "I'm not leaving this spot until you tell me where she is."

Birdman glared at Rinn. Lena glared at Rinn. And Rinn couldn't really glare back at both of them at the same time.

Rinn had to backtrack. She didn't want to send Lena to Imogen. But she also didn't want the two of them to get into another knockdown, drag-out, yelling match on the store floor. Plus, Rinn also didn't feel like being yelled at *again* from a man trying to sell—as she had just tabulated—$15.47 in bird-watching and philosophy books. He was already going to be mad enough that his books were worth next to nothing. Rinn had to make an assessment and make it fast. "I think she's out back."

"Thank you," said Lena, tilting her head. "Now, was that so difficult?"

But Lena didn't wait for Rinn to answer her, instead moving out toward the back door. And Rinn was sure that whatever waited for Lena outside, difficult was only the beginning of it.

8

Mad Girl's Love Song

Imogen didn't know how to have this conversation with Jo. It was obvious from the way Jo was talking that she was basically admitting to the fact that the bookstore was closing.

It didn't matter why. It didn't matter how. Imogen could read the truth in all of Jo's looks. That Jo had kept secrets, better than Imogen had ever suspected. In some ways, this made Jo more like a regular adult than Imogen had thought possible.

Jo kept the truth from them to keep them safe.

Lied to them.

Just because Jo was in charge and she thought that made her more adept at dealing with these kinds of things. All the things that grown-ups remained silent about welled up in Imogen's chest. Reminded her that they never ever spoke about the nothing that was swallowing her up—the nothing that was pervading the edges of her family and taking a grip in her home.

I found myself within the middle of a dark woods where the straight way vas lost.

Imogen didn't mean to think in poetry. But her mother had been obsessed, and obsession was a catching thing. *Have you read the Suheir Hammad yet, habibti? What about the Mary Oliver? Did you get to the Dante this week?*

All that Shakespeare hadn't been part of some random literary obsession. Mama had read through the Arabic language, then through the Persian. Wallada bint al-Mustakfi. Al-Mutanabbi. Hafiz. Nizami. Abu Nawas. She'd read her way through both canons and beyond. And then she'd started in on the English. Aphra Behn's plays in verse. She'd cleared her way through the Romantics—Byron and Shelley and Keats, yes, but also Mary Robinson and Joanna Baillie. Imogen's sister had been named Wallada. Imogen had missed a normal name by six volumes.

Miss by an inch, miss by an entire culture.

Imogen had resisted the poetry for a while. But her mother was infectious with the stuff. And the internet was now littered with poets—some good, some not so good. But all worth reading and trying, in Imogen's opinion. And while Imogen had no talent for the stuff on her own, she devoured so much of it.

"Are you listening to me, Imogen?"

Imogen's vision cleared, the scene in front of her came back into focus. She could see the taut concern all over Jo's face. "Sure."

"Then what did I just ask?" It was the kind of phrase adults used all the time. But Jo didn't have any of the censure of Imogen's teachers. Jo's entire face was slanted with concern.

Imogen wondered about that. About how adults' faces looked so tightly held on, but also, nearly falling apart, falling down. As though the facade they put on to seem normal could break at any time.

Imogen was tired of the facade. She answered honestly this

time. Because she couldn't—or maybe she just wouldn't—make up a response to what Jo had been asking of her. "I don't know."

Jo wiped her hand across her mouth, rubbing for a moment before deciding to speak again. "Look. I don't know how you found out. But you can't tell anyone. I'm trying to figure out how to fix this mess."

"Jo, everybody knows."

Jo held her hand across her mouth. "Of course they do. Of course they all know that the bookstore is closing."

And right as Jo was saying that was when Lena decided to walk out the back door of the store and into the alleyway. If she'd been a scooter, or a motor vehicle of any kind, she'd have come to a screeching halt. As it was, she froze, through the door but still holding it open, like she couldn't decide whether she would be more disgusted with herself for staying or for going.

She looked at Imogen—taking in her fresh haircut in all its glory—and then rearranged her face into a placid, controlled expression.

"Hey, Lena," Imogen tried. Maybe if she acted like nothing had happened, then Lena would act like she hadn't heard anything and everything would be totally fine.

Lena was still holding the door open. "Did you at least save a lock of your hair for me, or did you throw it all away in the garbage like you always do when you're done with something?"

So much for that theory. But Imogen wasn't going to hesitate. "The garbage."

Lena barked a laugh. "How could I have doubted you?"

Imogen had nothing to say to that.

Lena stubbed her toe against the ground, then looked over at Jo. "Wild Nights is closing, huh?"

Jo put her head in her hands. She looked up at Imogen. "Oh God, I did not mean—"

"No," said Imogen, swallowing hard. "It's cool. Lena, you're not going to tell anyone, are you?"

It didn't matter that they'd fought last night. The way it felt like they fought every night. Lena wasn't a gossip.

Lena let go of the door, decided to stay in the alleyway for better or for worse. "No."

The door clattered shut in the background. Imogen tried not to look at it, tried not to look away from Lena.

Jo stood. She waved her hand in the air across her face—must have been another mosquito. "Lena, why don't you come back later? Or at least, go inside and, like, swear on a stack of whatever book you find to be holy not to tell anyone. And then you can talk to Imogen later."

Lena waved her hand in the air, and Imogen saw that she was holding one of Imogen's old, worn leather jackets. "I promised I wouldn't tell anyone. I don't break promises."

Imogen winced. Lena noticed.

Jo hung her head in her hands. "This is a disaster."

Lena clearly didn't have a verbal argument for that, but she crossed her arms and began positively fuming. And Imogen was tired of watching Lena fume.

It wasn't Lena's fault.

It wasn't either of their fault, really, that they were like oil and water together. How they had ended up dating was anyone's guess. Attraction had been a messy thing, in Imogen's experience. She was drawn to the beautiful and the uncompromising. She loved Lena's spine of steel. But steel was supposed to sway with the wind. Lena bent for no one, not even Imogen.

"No," said Imogen. "It's cool. She can stay. I need to talk to her."

Lena looked like a satisfied cat after a territory war over a particularly desirable box.

Jo looked at Imogen. "You sure?"

Not really. "Yup. I'll be back in soon. This won't take a minute."

As Jo left, Lena turned to Imogen. "What do you mean, *this won't take a minute*?"

"Lena, we can't keep doing this." Imogen's voice didn't break.

"Doing what?"

"Fighting." Imogen kept away any show of nerves. Kept her voice steady.

"We're not only fighting." Lena reached out, trying to grab Imogen around the waist.

Imogen flinched away. She had to stay strong here. Touch would loosen her resolution.

Lena's eyes hardened. She pointed at Imogen's shaved head. "Fine. Are you going to blame this shit on me, too?"

Imogen closed her eyes, shook her head. It was a show of weakness, but at least Lena had already agreed. "It's not your fault. Maybe it's not even my fault. I don't know. It's shitty. Everything is shitty."

Imogen opened her eyes. She looked into Lena's. She needed Lena to believe her, she needed Lena to understand.

Lena reached out, but then dropped her hands, thinking better of it. "Let me help."

"You can't."

"I could if you'd let me."

"You really couldn't. I don't want to play games anymore. We're no good. You know we aren't."

"We're all right," Lena hedged.

But Imogen had made up her mind. She wasn't dragging anyone else into this that didn't have to be a part of it. And she and Lena had always been wrong for each other. They wanted each other, sure. But it wasn't a beautiful kind of wanting. It was a raw and feral thing, and Imogen didn't know much, but she knew that kind of wanting wasn't love. It was something else altogether. And the two of them had twisted it until they both had become barbed, latching. It would destroy one or both of them in the end.

Oh what fools these mortals be, indeed.

"We're not all right. We're mostly everything that *isn't* all right."

Lena looked like she wanted to hiss or spit or maybe both. "So that's it. You gonna ask if we can stay friends?"

"We were never friends."

"Jesus, you can be cruel."

"I'm not." Imogen reached out for Lena's wrist, but this time it was Lena's turn to pull away.

"I think the problem is that you're waiting for someone else to save you."

Imogen shook her head. She wasn't waiting for anyone to save her. She was trying to save the bookstore. She was trying to save this space for everyone in it. Imogen was probably the *last person on earth* who needed saving. "You know I'm right. This is it, for us. This is as good as we ever get, and it's not even decent. Can't we call it? We're two people who aren't good or bad. But— God, Lena—we're bad for each other. You have to know that."

Lena shook her head. "You can't just sit around here, acting like you've got all the answers when you clearly don't want to talk to anybody. When you'd rather shave all the hair off your head than talk about a fucking feeling. That was a nice speech to give. But you should see a counselor. Not unload your bullshit onto Jo."

Lena was wrong. Imogen hadn't been unloading on Jo. She'd been looking for the truth. And she'd known that something was going on with Eli and with Daniella and with that strange shipment. She'd only had one card to play, and it had been a request for the truth.

Not that Lena would understand that.

"Just go." Imogen didn't flinch as she said it.

Lena nodded once, threw the leather jacket on the ground, then fled inside. With that, Lena was gone. And Imogen was alone again, like she wanted.

Imogen didn't pick up the jacket. She left it there to bake in the sun.

There was only one thing to be done, really. It was time to go to the break room and investigate what the hell had been going on with that delivery.

9

Dulce et Decorum Est

11:09 A.M.
Daniella

Daniella hefted a box onto the pile they had made in the back corner of the office. It was right by Jo's desk, but that seemed overt enough to remain, for now, covert.

At least until Jo started asking questions. After that, none of them would be able to stop the inevitable. But Daniella was hoping to stall for time as long as possible.

"Oh, look," said Eli. "Jo has a pack of those old glow stars."

"Eli, are you going through Jo's shelves rather than stacking boxes?" How Eli could take Daniella from a zero to an eleven out of ten on the irritability scale was never not stunning to her.

Eli shrugged. "You're on the last one, and I saw these on the shelf. Do you remember these?"

"Yeah, but my mom wouldn't let me have them. She said they were wasteful. Or was it pagan? I dunno—I couldn't have them." Daniella grunted and lifted the last box. "But I always wanted them. To put them up in my bedroom and to make a map of the stars. One of those little-kid dreams you have."

Unlike most people she knew, Daniella loved that astronomy involved math. She had wanted to make an exact replica of the night sky. But, of course, Mom hadn't seen it that way. It was money they didn't have on an idea she didn't understand.

"Funny to think of you having little-kid dreams."

"Yes," said Daniella, rolling her eyes so she didn't have to hold his gaze. "Hilarious."

When she finally looked at him, Eli was smiling like he'd just discovered a new stash of comic books. Daniella did her best to hold on to her disgruntled expression. They stood there, the two of them staring at each other for a moment.

"Hey, Daniella, are you going to take your lunch break soon?" AJ Park walked into the break room, looking perfectly disheveled, and it honestly did nothing for Daniella. She wished it did sometimes. Then Daniella could fall in love like a doe-eyed, fairy-tale princess—just like Rinn. But Daniella was too far gone down her own particular path of cynicism for that.

The problem was, Daniella was so caught off guard that she nearly dropped the box in her hands. She knew she looked guilty. She had just honestly forgotten that anyone else was in the store, other than her and Eli. And Jo—of course, Jo. Daniella's focus had been so singular—that was all.

AJ tilted his head. "What's going on?"

Daniella set down the last box. "Nothing."

Yes, that was very believable. All that was missing was breaking eye contact and whistling.

"Super nothing," said Eli with a grin, like he couldn't quite help himself.

Daniella had been wrong. Eli sounding as guilty as he ever could was what had been missing. Now the picture was complete. The two of them looked incredibly guilty now. No whistling required.

"Uh, you guys. Come on. Even I know something is up." AJ raked his hand through his hair, trying to get the strands that always fell forward out of his eyes.

Daniella looked at Eli, and they locked eyes for a moment. He didn't nod or move his head in the slightest. But she knew what he was thinking.

Let him in on it.

Daniella wished she could read minds with anyone other than the angelic-looking criminal in their midst, but that was life for you. Angelic criminals were Daniella's purview, the way handsome, soulful, kind artists never would be. "Eli's a total screwup and spent merchandise money on a bunch of fake but collectible Air Jordans."

"You really had to put that in the worst light, didn't you?" Eli didn't even sound surprised, like he could read her right back.

Daniella shrugged. Her words had been harsher than she had meant for them to be. But Daniella had felt betrayed by her own thoughts in that moment. "You ask for my help, you suffer the consequences."

"Apparently," said Eli.

"None of this explains anything." AJ was scratching that gorgeously disheveled head of his.

And Daniella still felt nothing. God really could be cruel, as her mother so often liked to say. Though, usually, she was saying that in reference to having Daniella as a daughter. "Eli here was taken advantage of late on the internet last night. And now we have a whole lot of fake merchandise to unload so that he doesn't go to jail."

AJ blinked. "I think somebody needs to start from the beginning."

So Daniella did. She told him about the email that Eli found. About his crackpot plan to flip the Jordans and make back the money. About how the Jordans had turned out to be fake and how Daniella had found Eli's discrepancy easily by going through the inventory. And then, Daniella decided to tell him her great plan.

"We're going to off-load these back onto the market. Easy flip, at least get the money back that Eli lost, and nobody will have to be the wiser. It'll look like an account glitch. I mean, we might lose shipping, but that's not the worst thing to explain away. We've probably got to sell them on a different market-place, so the original seller doesn't flag the post for fraud and so nobody else that saw the listing gets suspicious."

"That's your grand plan?" AJ was unconvinced. His whole face scrunched up so that his eyebrows were furrowed and his lips were pursed.

"Yeah. It's brilliant." Daniella folded her arms across her chest.

"And pretty immoral," said AJ, flattening his mouth back out into a skeptical line.

"Dude, she's getting us out of this mess and with a time crunch to boot. Daniella's a genius." This was Eli.

"But. You're just passing the problem along to somebody else. That's not right. You know that's not right." That was AJ.

Daniella snorted. "What's right and what is expedient are two different things."

"How do you know we're not just saddling somebody else

with the same problem—if not worse?" AJ sounded like he was giving a lecture on morality or ethics or something to a giant philosophy hall. It was nauseating.

"We probably are," Daniella fired back in the same tone. "But that's not *my* problem. The nine thousand dollars missing from our inventory and a store that is about to close is."

"No, it's his problem." AJ pointed at Eli.

"I resent that," said Eli.

"So do I," said AJ.

"Shut up, both of you. If the bookstore closes, we'll be out of our home base. We could all go out and get regular jobs at a diner or a fast-food place or an ice cream shop or one of those crappy retail jobs on Michigan Avenue. This place is home whether or not we like it. I can't sit by and wait for everything to close. I have to do something. I don't agree with Eli's methodology, but I do agree with what he was trying to do. He was trying to save this place."

Eli raised his eyebrows at Daniella's use of the word *methodology*, and she just scowled back at him.

"Look, maybe those jobs aren't half bad," said AJ.

"That is so not my point." Daniella crossed her arms again.

"I just. I don't want to belong to the kind of place that's preserved at the expense of someone else. I don't want to save my home by throwing someone else under the bus." AJ was so somber that it nearly undid Daniella.

But she found her footing quick enough. Daniella hadn't lived through her father's death and her mother's grief only to be unable to keep her eye on the prize. "Then what do you suggest we do? Have Eli go to jail? Let the bookstore close?"

"Are those really the only options?" AJ raked his hand through his hair again.

"Yeah. That's it. Save the nine thousand dollars in inventory. Attempt to save the bookstore. Off-load all of these faulty Jordans onto the market. Hopefully we can flip them onto some other unsuspecting schmuck and at least make back our money. If we get really lucky, we can make some money off this. That's literally all we have got."

AJ shook his head. "You're too mercenary for me, Danny."

Daniella clenched her teeth. "Fine. I'm the mercenary bitch. But at least when the chips are down, I know what call I'm making. Do you? Do you know what side you're on? Or are you just gonna hide in the mystery section and wait it out?"

AJ said nothing. He shook his head, turned, and walked out the door.

"If it's any consolation, you've got me convinced," said Eli as soon as they were alone again.

Daniella chucked a handful of plastic stars at him in response.

10

O Captain! My Captain!

11:12 A.M.
Imogen

Before Imogen could reach the break room, she was waylaid by Madame Bettache, who was flagging down Imogen from over in the classics/literature section.

Madame Bettache was a French Tunisian woman who had moved to Chicago shortly after her husband's death. She had deep brown skin and perfectly coiffed hair. She had a collection of scarves—Hermès, Imogen had later found out—that were given to the widow by her late husband as presents after each of his many business trips. Imogen had never seen the same scarf twice, and Madame Bettache came into the store weekly.

Imogen knew all of this because Madame Bettache had told her.

She reminded Imogen distinctly of one of her aunties. And so Imogen had started to call her *Madame Auntie*. Without Madame Bettache's knowledge, of course.

About a year and a half ago, Madame Auntie had come in saying she wanted a copy of *An Unnecessary Woman* for her book club. She had confessed to Imogen that she really only joined the book club for the social aspect.

That was when Imogen had known that Madame was a gossip.

But her original book club only met monthly, and Madame had gone from coming in once a month to once every two weeks to once a week. She had been picking up book clubs the way her husband had picked up scarves. For a while, Imogen had thought it was all for the chatter and the sense of importance that belonging to a book club must give to Madame.

That was, until Imogen had spied a battered, dog-eared, tabbed copy of *White Teeth* that Imogen had sold her the week before in Madame's expensive handbag.

Madame Auntie had found her love of literature. And even though she hadn't found it until she was sixty-five, she'd been making up plenty for any lost time.

"Hello, Madame Bettache," said Imogen when she reached the literary fiction section.

"Habibti," said Madame, pinching Imogen's cheeks like a proper auntie. Her scarf today was navy and yellow with nautical touches throughout. "This week, we read *The Song of Achilles*. Did you get my copy?"

Madame was constantly ordering copies into the store, and Imogen was constantly scrambling to find them. Half the time Imogen had to call the suppliers herself just to get the special order in. Otherwise, Madame wouldn't get books. The scramble reminded Imogen of the way the books had been shelved recently. Like a strange scatter plot.

"Hamdullah, habibti." Madame Auntie gave a catlike smile. "But you look sad. Are you sad? Have you been eating enough? Where is all your hair?"

That startled a laugh out of Imogen. "I'm eating plenty. Here, let me get your book."

Imogen found the one copy of *The Song of Achilles* that had, magically, been included in the last shipment without Imogen having to yell at a supplier for the copy. She'd hidden it behind a stash of cookbooks on a display table especially for Madame. It was the only way to ensure Madame would have her book. Imogen didn't understand how all the special orders were going missing in the past nine months.

After Imogen handed over *The Song of Achilles* and had her cheek pinched one last time, Madame Auntie simply said, "I keep looking." And she ducked off to keep browsing for more books.

Sometimes Imogen wondered if there really was a book club anymore. Or just this woman, furiously reading the classics in her third language. It was tough to say.

A sinking sense of dread returned to Imogen. If she wasn't able to figure out what was wrong with the store. If she wasn't able to piece together everything that was broken, what would happen to people like Madame Bettache? Where would they go?

Not that Madame was a charity case. She clearly had money to burn. A home to live in. She was well provided for. But she seemed to come alive in the store, surrounded by stories. It was a feeling Imogen understood well. She often felt lonely around people. It was in this old store that she felt like she was a part of anything, really.

Imogen stood for a moment, as reality sank in. The store was closing. She'd broken up with her girlfriend of nine months. She should feel something. She was hoping to feel something. A regret, maybe. A pang of longing. Something, anything, to *feel* again.

But—*nothing.*

She felt neither pain nor pleasure, neither relief nor regret. She simply was—numb and motionless. Waiting for the world to happen again.

She'd thought herself cured this morning. What a joke.

Imogen ran her hand over her head. She was grasping at that feeling of relief. That sense that she had cleansed the old and was now someone new. Someone who had shed the weight of what had been before. And for a moment she felt it. She felt that she was not trapped in who she had been, in who her mind had tried to shape her into being. Felt the delicate prickle of her freshly shorn hair against the palm of her hand.

But now that sensation was gone, replaced with the awareness that she had no idea who this new Imogen was. She had no idea who she wanted to be. And even if she did, she had no idea how she would get there.

Imogen leaned against a bookshelf, must have been the manga section, ready to sag against its weight. Ready to give in again. But she had to pull herself off this bookshelf. She *had* to investigate.

Imogen made it all the way to the door of the break room when it clattered open, slamming against the back wall. Brooding Art Boy came out of it, looking like he could have taken down all the bookshelves in the store, like that opening scene in *The Mummy.*

Wham, wham, whoosh, boom. A row of shelves and books toppling over like dominoes.

Imogen could see the rage flickering in his eyes. Understood it better than she understood herself. For a moment, he said nothing. And for an even longer moment, Imogen said nothing. She'd never heard Brooding Art Boy string more than four words together. Much less thought he was capable of slamming a door against a wall or destroying an entire bookstore.

But it seemed imperative, really, that she talk to him. Imogen gestured to the bookshelf beside her and said, "Wanna sit?"

"More of a lean, isn't it?" But he took a place right beside her, letting the shelf bear his weight as well.

And that sagging nothing in Imogen's chest lifted for a moment with the knowledge that Imogen was not alone. That someone else felt this crushing weight of existence as much as she did. That someone else needed to lean against a wall and take a break from the world for a little while.

She could help. She *needed* to help.

In truth the sun does not rise.

"What is with today?" he asked. The question was almost to Imogen, but also, almost to the air or to the books.

"Today?" asked Imogen. "It feels like this every day, doesn't it?"

He turned toward her, as though he were seeing her for the first time. "Maybe. But I've never had it feel like this."

"I have," said Imogen.

"For how long?"

"You know, I don't know." Imogen pressed her tongue up against the back of her teeth as she thought for a moment. "Right now it feels like forever. But when I think about it, I know that there was a time before, you know?"

"A time before?" Art Boy's focus was intense. Like he didn't look at many people, but when he did, it was with his whole being.

"Yeah," said Imogen. "What about you?"

He thought about that for a moment. His eyes went up; he bit his lip. Then he relaxed his whole expression and began to speak. "Sure, it was this morning. Before I found out what Daniella and Eli were up to."

"Oh God. What is it?" She felt the need to kiss her fingers, to touch her forehead, to touch the sky. Cool Girl and Eli always reminded Imogen of an engine—one spark would get the whole motor running. Alone they were trouble. Together, they were combustible chaos.

He raked his hands through his too-long hair, getting it out of his eyes. "It's just, did you know the bookstore was going to close?"

Imogen turned and stared at him. *Combustible. Chaos.* "When did you find this out?"

"Fifteen minutes ago." He shrugged. It could have been the nonchalant shrug of an art boy who didn't care. But it wasn't that. That the shrug didn't mean *It doesn't matter.* No, it said, *It matters more than I know how to say, more than I have words for.*

Imogen wondered if he actually was a real art boy, or if she'd just slotted him into a category because of his disheveled hair and his worn-in jeans and his quiet demeanor. In that moment, he could have been anyone. But he wasn't anyone. And he wasn't Art Boy, either. He was AJ, plain and simple.

"How?" Imogen didn't know why she asked it. But she needed something to say. Some time to process her thoughts. Some way to delay the truth from sinking into her own mind.

"Ask Daniella about it. She and Eli have a whole scheme to fix it."

"What kind of scheme?"

AJ shrugged again—that shrug that spoke volumes and refused to be silent—and said, "Ask them yourself. I don't think it's my secret to tell, even if I don't think it'll stay a secret much longer. It's too big for that."

Imogen felt a rage firing up inside of her again. Perhaps it wasn't much, but at least it was *something.* Because it hadn't just been Jo who had been keeping secrets. It had been Cool Girl. And Eli, too. But Eli seemed like the kind of boy who didn't just keep secrets. He looked like he dealt in them. Cool Girl having that kind of power and knowledge—over the place that Imogen felt safe—gave Imogen a sudden burst of feeling and energy.

Imogen pushed up off the wall of books, ready to do battle with Cool Girl and her minion. Ready to, verbally at least, slay them both. But then she stopped as she opened the door, remembering what a good listener Art Boy—no, AJ—had been for the moment. "Hey. Thanks."

AJ nodded, like he knew and he understood. "Sure. Anytime."

AJ, Imogen was learning, was the kind of person who didn't use all that many words to communicate, but he was honest with all the tools he did use. His nods and his shrugs and his raking his hands through his hair were true and real. He wasn't a performer. Imogen understood with vivid, sudden clarity why Little Miss Perfect had a crush on him. Not because Imogen herself wanted him. But it was impossible not to understand that the person who spent her day performing for the camera would be drawn to the one who couldn't fake his way through social niceties.

Imogen was *done* with social niceties.

She flung open the break room door and stormed in. There were piles and piles of boxes, neatly stacked, all along the back end of the room by Jo's desk. Not *in the way of* Jo's desk. But conspicuously away from the door. And close enough to Jo's desk that they were hiding in plain sight. A notebook sat on Jo's desk. That *had* to have been the ledger. Had to have been further proof that something was amiss.

"What in all of hell is going on?" Imogen sounded like her father, constructing idioms out of his second language. But she was too pissed off to care. Because she genuinely needed to know what in all of hell *was* going on.

"Who told you anything was going on?" Cool Girl crossed her arms over her chest in a deeply defensive posture.

There was something about that. The way Cool Girl deflected. The way she projected. The way she made an honest question into a volley at the other person that set Imogen's teeth on edge. Made her so angry, like it wasn't only her mind or her body that was angry. It was deep in her bones. Practically a riot in her soul.

They were two people who never had anything in common other than this bookstore. And the bookstore was closing, which left them with plain nothing.

It was that crossing of the arms that told Imogen this more than anything else. Told her that they were two girls who were never going to get along and were made to fight with each other, almost on a visceral, cellular level. As though the smallest pieces that made up Imogen were diametrically opposed to the tiniest pieces that made up Cool Girl.

"Nobody *needed* to say anything. There's a rat here. Dead for a ducat and everything." *Oh God*, the Shakespeare had come directly out of her mouth now, but there was no stopping herself. Imogen was finally *feeling* something, and even if what she was feeling was rage and betrayal, she would use it while she had it. Before she was deflated again, into that awful nothingness that spread outward from her chest and consumed her entirely, in body and soul. Imogen tried to muster a spark of gratitude for the feeling, but she couldn't. She was rage and rage alone.

Eli, for his part, looked between the two girls like he would do anything to *not* be involved. Except she could tell, from the way that he was edging closer to Daniella, that he was very, very involved and must have had no way out. He was central to this play, and no matter how many secrets he dealt in to get out of it, he would still remain the focus of this drama. He touched Daniella's elbow, reaching for it almost absentmindedly, instinctively.

He'd picked his side, then.

"Out with it." *Out, damned spot! Out, I say!*

And then Cool Girl made a decision. Imogen watched it as it coated her face. She dropped her arms. And her smile went wide and malicious. "Didn't you hear? Wild Nights is closing. We are trying to do our best to flip some merchandise and actually help. Rather than shaving our heads and parading our depression all across the storeroom floor."

This was not the first time that Daniella had wielded the truth like a weapon at Imogen. Wasn't even the third time. Over the past year of working with Daniella, Imogen had gotten used to the barbs. The way Daniella lashed out at anyone and anything that she had momentary power over. It was a cheap trick, and Imogen spent most of her time ignoring this about Cool Girl.

But this time was different. This time Cool Girl had scored a direct hit.

Imogen ran her hand over her fresh buzz cut to bolster her resolve. She'd had enough. "What did you two do?"

"None of your business," said Cool Girl.

But Eli chimed in. "She deserves to know."

Cool Girl shook her head.

But Eli kept going. "I thought I was buying some kicks to flip for a profit. It turns out, they're fake."

"So?" Imogen didn't understand.

"So I used the store's petty cash. So the merch is worthless unless Danny here can find someone else to off-load it onto." Eli shrugged.

"No." Imogen shook her head. "You can't do that. You *didn't* do that."

"He did, and we will," said Daniella.

She was so sure of herself. So utterly unflappable that Imogen did the first thing that came to mind in order to just *rattle* the girl—

"You can go to hell, Cool Girl." It was the only time Imogen had used the nickname to the girl's face. Imogen watched as the shock registered across Daniella's expressions.

Good. The girl *deserved* to be shook and rattled and jolted, after what she'd done.

"What did you call me?" Daniella uncrossed her arms. Stared the kind of stare that should have turned the floor to molten lava.

"Cool Girl. The Coolest Girl in the Fucking World." Imogen wasn't backing down. Despite the intimidation tactics. Despite the fear that was now fighting with the rage. Imogen was on a roll and would not be stopped. "Too cool to think about anyone else on the planet. Too cool to honestly *feel* something. Too cool to show yourself to the world. You sit behind your crossed arms and your snippy little catchphrases, and you throw everything you feel back onto everyone else so that nothing ever sticks to you. Must be nice to be above it all, Cool Girl. Must be nice to never have to *feel* anything."

Imogen knew that last part wasn't true, but she didn't care. She could give as good as she'd gotten. She was heaving as she breathed. Her chest rose and fell like she had just run a mile, which, honestly, had to have been at least two years ago when she was forced to for that President's Challenge in PE. Thank God she wasn't a freshman anymore.

And Daniella—somehow calling her Cool Girl out loud had made Imogen stop calling her Cool Girl in her mind—just stared back at Imogen. Imogen watched, saw the way that shock and awe warred with rage and frustration on her features.

What the hell did Daniella have to be frustrated with?

Daniella pointed. "Get out of here, Azar."

"With pleasure," said Imogen, with a bow. "And when I do, I'm telling Jo what the hell is going on here."

That set Daniella in motion. She grabbed at Imogen's upper arm. "You wouldn't dare."

"Watch me." And with that, Imogen wrenched her arm out of Daniella's grasp, grabbed for the notebook off the desk, and swiftly exited onto the bookstore floor.

11

Things Unknown But Longed For Still

11:21 A.M.
Rinn

Rinn knew she was technically still on register duty. She was supposed to stay there and not move. She was *supposed* to deal with any questions from customers by sending them around to whoever was floating on the store floor. She was supposed to stay put.

Rinn had not stayed put.

She was wandering around the first floor, trying to make the most of the bright summer light as it flooded through the windows. She had gotten an excellent repeating, looped video of the roller girl, just swaying lightly from where she dangled from the ceiling.

Rinn looked back over all the content that she'd made in the past hour—largely just rows and rows of books. Some of it she'd have to edit at home. But most of it would be perfect to post with just a few tweaks that she could manage on her phone.

Rinn scanned the first floor of the store with her gaze. She could see most of it from her vantage point. Over in the literary fiction section was that French lady with the big, dark hair who was obsessed with Zora Neale Hurston and Rabih Alameddine. Rinn could capture a photograph without getting the woman's face in the frame, though, so she snapped it quickly.

Rinn tried not to take identifying pictures of people without asking them first. The backs of their heads were, in her mind, fair game. But faces and eyes and even a tattoo—she wouldn't take a photo including those without permission.

In the children's section was a mother in her twenties that Rinn regularly noticed reading and flipping through books on running a small business while her son read picture books. But Rinn was even more cautious about taking photographs of children, so she went up to the woman, despite never having spoken to her before.

"Excuse me," asked Rinn, once she reached the seated woman and her child.

The woman startled, nearly jumping off the child-size stool that she sat on. She was holding not a business book this time but *The World Atlas of Whisky*. "Oh, I'm sorry. Do I need to put this back? I don't have to read it here. It's just, he's reading and I thought—"

But Rinn cut her off before the woman could finish. "No, no. Go ahead. I was just wondering if I could take your picture for some bookstore promo material. I didn't want to get you and your son in it without your permission. I mean, I should probably ask *everyone*, but I'm so used to being on camera that sometimes I forget. I won't put his face in it. He's just tucked into that book and so were you—tucked into your book, I mean—and it was just a really beautiful moment."

The kind of moment that Rinn wanted to preserve. The kind

of moment she wanted the rest of the world to see was possible here at Wild Nights Bookstore and Emporium.

Rinn held out her hand, the one that wasn't holding her phone. "Rinn Olivera."

The woman took it, shaking hands with her. "Rashida Johnson."

Rinn let go of the handshake. "Can I take the photo?"

"You don't give up easy, do you?" said Rashida.

"I try not to," said Rinn.

"Right. Go for it. As long as my little man here's face isn't in it."

"Excellent." Rinn smiled. "Just act natural."

Rashida raised an eyebrow, like she was skeptical that she could do that. But Rinn backed away slowly, and Rashida slowly got absorbed again into the content of her book.

Rinn used the grid feature on her phone and lined up the shot perfectly. The backdrop of the children's section just made the whole shot look like it could have been a portal to the realm of the fey.

"Thank you," called out Rinn. She gave a wave to Rashida as she left.

Rashida laughed and said, "Anytime."

Rinn had to show AJ these shots. After he'd helped her film video earlier, she thought he might appreciate these photos from all around the store.

Rinn gathered her curls into her hand, scrunching them slightly. She smoothed her fingers at the edges of her face, making sure there were no errant flyaways or baby hairs stuck to her forehead. She didn't mind a *few* baby hairs, mind you. But not an entire face-framing halo of them, for goodness' sake. Then she tugged on her skirt for good measure, making sure there weren't any weird wrinkles in the front. She smoothed it down the sides.

Rinn hated wrinkles in her skirts. She took a deep breath and stepped around a bookshelf.

Imogen was pacing in the self-help section. Imogen didn't look up. She must not have heard Rinn approach.

Before Rinn could stop the collision, Imogen paced directly into her. If either of them had been going any faster it would have been a shoulder check, but luckily, Imogen hadn't been going any faster and Rinn had at least stopped her forward momentum before they'd crashed into each other.

Rinn winced, not from the pain but because she was waiting for Imogen to yell or to vent her frustration.

But Imogen hardly registered that she'd been knocked into at all. "Oh, sorry, Rinn. I didn't see you."

Which was a normal response for most people, but an odd one for Imogen.

"Are you okay?" asked Rinn.

"Yeah." But Imogen didn't even make eye contact. She stared off into the distance—like she was trying to read the spines of the books two sections over. "Okay."

Rinn reached out. Because she was a masochist, possibly, and was maybe looking for Imogen to yell at her. And she touched her on her shoulder. "Are you okay?"

"Sure," she said in the same tone as before—distracted, unregistering. "Sounds great."

"What sounds great?" asked Rinn.

"Great. Super. Superb." And then Imogen walked off—still heading in the same direction she had been walking when Rinn had run into her, but not really noticing where she was going much herself.

Rinn turned and saw that Jo was coming down the aisle, and Rinn needed to scoot back to the register if she was going to avoid getting yelled at. There were so few things Jo would get upset about, but not being at the assigned location during shift was, understandably and definitively, one of them.

That and using Jo's laptop. Or, theoretically, taking a pen from her baggie full of vapes. But everyone used Jo's vapes, so that didn't seem like a *real* rule. Even Rinn had tried it—though she'd coughed up a storm and hated it. She'd also had to brush her teeth in the break room bathroom afterward, just to get the taste out of her mouth.

But she hadn't been too stuck-up to *try*.

To be fair, everyone knew Jo's password for her laptop was *thebatman*. It was just that all the employees had decided that using the laptop was one step too far. Where the bag of vapes were fair game, the laptop was off-limits. It was one of those rules that everyone who worked at Wild Nights had figured out without ever saying it out loud.

Rinn was nearly there, nearly back to the register.

"Rinn," said Jo, startling Rinn. "What are you doing? Why are you not at your station?"

Rinn found a smile. Of all the people to notice her, why did it have to be *Jo* noticing her when she wasn't at her post?

God could be cruel. "I'm going on break. I was going to go find someone to relieve me because it's almost lunch." Rinn sounded guilty to herself. She heard the overly bright, overly enthusiastic tones in her voice. She wished she could keep her cool just once in her life. She tucked her hand that was holding her phone behind her back, stuffing the phone into the waistband of her skirt. It was hanging on by a PopSocket, but that was better than having her phone confiscated.

Again.

"Not today." Jo pinched the bridge of her nose. Then Jo's

phone pinged, and Jo looked down at the alert. Her whole face scrunched up, staring at her screen, but she kept on talking to Rinn. "I need you to go back to the register. I'll send someone to give you relief. I just really need things to go smoothly today. You know what a big day this is. Brock Harvey is unfortunately making an appearance at the store, and I really need a win right now."

There Rinn took offense. "Whoa, Jo. It's *amazing* that Brock Harvey, author of *When We Were Us*—aka my favorite book in all of existence, and my favorite author—is coming to *our* bookstore. Jo, you know that's amazing."

Jo looked up from her phone and gave Rinn a look that she might have once taken as withering but now understood to be pitying. "Sure, kid. It's great."

"No, Jo. It's the best." Rinn tried to positive-attitude her way through this, but it wasn't easy.

Because Jo deadpanned back. "Spectacular. Spec-fucking-tacular. Just written by an author who sent in the most inappropriate author photo I have ever seen—no, please don't ask me about it—and I had to go scouring the internet to find a solid image to use on our store poster. Now get your butt back to the register, do you hear me?"

Rinn had, but new questions were taking hold in her mind. "Jo, can I ask you something?"

"Only if it means that you'll go back to the register after I answer you."

Rinn was about to ask if Jo knew that the bookstore was going under. If she was aware that something was wrong with Imogen. But off the harried look on Jo's face, Rinn came up short. She changed her question at the last moment. "Do you think that I have a chance with AJ at all?"

Jo shook her head, like she wasn't sure how they got to this part of the conversation. "I'm sorry, I asked you to go to the register and you're asking me if I think AJ likes you?"

Jo moved from pinching her nose to each of her individual eyebrows. She was still looking at her phone, concern tightening her face. But it was a performative kind of worrying that Rinn could read well.

"I just. I like him."

Jo shook her head. "I know. We all know."

That had been unexpected. "You do?"

Jo switched to massaging her forehead. "I mean, maybe not AJ. But yes, Rinn, we all know."

Rinn stared at Jo. She might need to throw up now. Or just bury herself underneath the remains of Wild Nights after it went out of business and never come out ever again.

Jo reached over, touched Rinn on the shoulder. "Can you please go back to the register now? I really, really, really need you to stand at the register. And not move. Until someone takes your spot. That's literally all I need from you. And you're still really struggling, and I need a verbal confirmation that you can do this for me."

But Jo's previous revelation hit Rinn like a ton of bricks, all over again. "Wait, everyone *but* AJ knows?"

"I don't even know why I bother. Like, why do I try?" Jo shook her head.

Clarity ran through Rinn. Her whole body was alert, ready. And she had only one thought in mind. "Should I tell him?"

Jo nodded along. "Yeah, of course you should. Of course that is where this day is going."

"Jo. I've got to tell him. That I'm in love with him. Don't I?"

Jo sighed. "Sure. Fantastic. Now. Can you please—get back to the register?"

"So I shouldn't tell him? That's what you're saying? Like what do you think my odds of success here are?"

"Rinn Olivera." Jo just shouted it at this point. She must have been trying to startle Rinn back to the register.

But Rinn was too focused now. Her head was too clear. She knew she needed to tell AJ how she felt. Rinn would not be intimidated into jumping straight to the register. She had to save the bookstore. She had to tell AJ how she felt.

And then Imogen barreled straight into Jo. As she did, Imogen dropped the notebook that was in her hands and fell over.

Rinn went over to Imogen, to see if she needed any help getting up. "Are you *sure* you're all right? You keep, like, running into people."

"I'm *fine*," said Imogen through gritted teeth.

Rinn did her best to not take this personally. As Jo helped herself up, she picked up the notebook that had fallen in the collision. She looked at the cover and flipped it open. Imogen's face went all scrunched up and concerned, watching Jo flip through the notebook.

"Wait," said Imogen. "Don't read that."

"Why not?" Jo looked up, stared at Imogen's expression, then closed the notebook. "What in the hell is going on?"

12

Into the Mouth of Hell

11:46 A.M.
Daniella

"What's going on with what?" Daniella had made it to the floor just in time to watch Jo pick up the notebook filled with the inventory numbers. The notebook itself wasn't incriminating in the least.

The expression on Imogen's face, however, told Daniella that her odds of getting out of this unscathed were slim to none. She was going to try anyway, though.

She had pushed Imogen too far. Daniella could always tell when she'd hurt beyond repair. She had no sense for it, in the moment. But afterward, Daniella could tell. She'd flown too high and too close to the sun with her barbs. She had to have finally hit a tender spot on Imogen.

But Daniella wasn't going to back down now.

Even if Imogen had clearly geared herself up to talk to Jo and tell her the truth.

God—had Imogen already told Jo?

Daniella had made it this far in life with sheer determination and brazenness. She'd not stop now. "Is everyone okay? That sounded like a nasty spill. I heard it all the way in the break room."

Jo wasn't buying that for a second. She reached out and touched Daniella's arm, trying to ground them both to this plane of reality. "Daniella. What is going on?"

Daniella took a deep breath. She wasn't going to crack. She wasn't going to throw Eli under the bus. She wasn't going to succumb to Imogen's threats or Imogen's awful opinion of her. She was going to swagger her way through this one, just like she always did. If Imogen had thought she'd been a *cool girl* earlier, that was nothing compared to what Daniella would be now. She'd find the ice in her veins. The coolest girl in the fucking world? *Just you watch.* "Look. It's all fine. I'm fixing it."

"You're fixing *what*?" Jo's tone and expression went serious. Her eyebrows narrowed together, and her mouth pressed into a flat line.

Daniella's heart rate rose until it was all she could hear. The rhythm of her own fear drowning out all sound and all sense.

Maybe Imogen *hadn't* told Jo yet.

Daniella cleared her throat. "There was a mix-up in the ordering. The other night, when I was closing."

"What kind of a mix-up?" Jo was unrelenting once you gave her something to focus on.

"A nine-thousand-dollar mix-up?" Daniella should have had more conviction in her voice. But she was lying to cover Eli's own lie, and she was having trouble finding any thread of truth that could give her story conviction. A lie was nothing without a piece of the truth in it.

"You ordered nine thousand dollars of inventory? We can barely clear a thousand in a week, Daniella. Do you know what kind of screwup this is?" There was no kindness in Jo's voice. No softening edge. No moment of understanding. Just a stone-cold panic. Just a vibrating anger that Daniella didn't know Jo had in her.

The mistake, Daniella knew, was a major one. She didn't need to be told that. She knew. She'd known since she found out. What she needed to do now, though, was stall for time. She needed for Eli to flee the premises and maybe drive out past the state line. "Look, I have a plan."

"No, you don't have a plan. You cannot possibly have a plan because you don't even understand the gravity of what you've done. You don't get what nine thousand dollars would do to a place like this. And if you don't explain what happened in ten seconds, you don't have a job anymore."

Daniella's throat went dry. She was not a snitch. *No one talks, and we all walk.* That motto had seen her—and her siblings—out of many, many a tight spot.

But she could tell that Jo was serious. That Jo wasn't messing around anymore. Jo was forgiving. But lying and covering up that lie with more lies was not within the boundaries of what Jo would ever forgive. To Jo, lies were the line. The point of no return.

Lies were how Daniella had survived this long in this world. She had lies for getting out of church on Sundays and lies for staying out late on Saturdays. Lies she told her family—that they were fine, that she was fine, that everything was *fine.* She had little lies—the kind she told to friends about how she felt about math or science—that added up to enormous lies, like the entire persona she had built in order to socially float her way through high school.

Perhaps these lies had made Daniella overly flexible with the truth, made her moral compass point somewhere other than true north. After all, what was a lie to a girl who pretended to be a poet on one corner of the internet all while she took videos of herself vaping on the other end just to be cool enough not to shake up the social hierarchy?

But lies had also given her a hard shell. And ability to withstand the worst of people. Somebody had to protect the bookstore. Somebody had to make the hard calls. Somebody had to be willing to do what it took in order to save all their asses. And Daniella—with her lies and her moral gymnastics—she had the heart of steel necessary to protect her and her own.

So maybe it was a good thing that she didn't have AJ's pesky moral compass to get in the way. Because the bookstore was *not* going under. Eli was *not* going to jail. Jo was *not* taking the fall. Daniella was going to figure all of this out. She had to.

Ice in your veins. A heart of steel. If you sink, you sink on your own terms.

Of course, that was when Eli came out of the break room, his usual charming smile totally wiped clean off his face. He was still holding the plastic stars that they had found on Jo's shelf in one hand.

He looked serious, and Eli never looked serious.

Daniella wanted to say something, say anything. But she was, for once, without words. Without sarcasm or a witty repartee. She was just a scared girl standing in front of an angry woman, trying to find her way out of a mess that was beyond her hands.

Jesus Christ and all the holy saints.

"It was me," said Eli. "It was my fault."

"Oh, wonderful, great. If only I knew what exactly you're at fault for." Jo put both of her hands on her face and pulled down, like she could peel off all her frustrations that way. "Love that nobody is giving me a straight answer about any of this. I've got

Imogen skulking through the store, throwing notebooks around. I've got Daniella answering questions with lies. And I've got Rinn staring gape-mouthed over there, with her phone—which I *took earlier today, mind you*—stuck in the back of her skirt like I wouldn't notice. I'm going to ask you all one last time. What *the hell* is going on?"

"I stole the money." Eli's voice didn't even crack or waver; Daniella had to give him that.

"You what?" Jo blinked. Just stared and blinked.

"It's gone. It's all gone." Eli wiped his hands against each other in an elaborate motion to show that everything that had been done could not be undone. "All the petty cash."

"Eli, it was nine thousand dollars. It can't all be gone." There was an incredulity in Jo's voice. Like she didn't want to believe it. Like if she believed what Eli was saying, she would have to take a whole host of actions that she had never prepared herself to take before.

And if Daniella knew one thing, she knew Jo would take whatever actions were necessary and good. Jo wouldn't like it. But she would fortify herself and she would do the right thing. Jo would turn Eli in if she had to. They were opposites in that way. Because Daniella would do anything to keep Eli *out of* jail.

The store stopped. The woman in the children's section. The stuffy old French lady. Myrna, who was sipping the last dregs of her coffee, sat right back down in the middle of getting up from her latest chair.

Everyone in the store stopped their act—whatever it was they had been doing—and watched. The employees were putting on a real show; nobody on the first floor, and few on the second floor, wanted to miss it. Even AJ, who avoided any kind of attention if he could, had found himself pulled by the gravity of the scene. He was on the edges of it, but he was still there. Imogen was still glaring, alternating between Daniella and Eli. Rinn's whole face was coated in horror.

None of them could avoid this now.

"Are you in some kind of trouble?" Jo was trying to understand, clearly. She had that focused look on her face as she stared at Eli. She had her hand on her hip. Her whole posture indicated—*I want to be on your side, Eli.*

So of course, Eli didn't take the peace offering. "No."

Jo slumped. She was still standing up, but there was a heaviness to the way she stood. Like she'd need to sit down in a minute. "Then this is all just a big joke to you? Is that it? Is this store a big joke to you? Am I a big joke to you?"

Eli shook his head—slow and sad and serious all at once. "No. I was trying to help."

Jo was having a hard time believing him—Daniella could tell from the furrow in Jo's eyebrows and the way her bottom lip was jutting out in a small, silent protest. And to be fair to Jo, it was a pretty unbelievable thing to have to hear, to have to swallow and comprehend and then come out the other side and find belief in.

"You were trying to help, so you *stole* nine thousand dollars." Jo said this slowly, just to make sure she was correctly repeating back what she had understood.

Even Daniella'd had some trouble with that one.

"It made sense at the time. I really thought I was helping. I really wanted to save the bookstore. I saw that it was going under, and I wanted to help. I get that I didn't help. But, I wanted to, you know. That's all I was trying to do from the very beginning—to help."

Jo turned away from Eli for the moment. His earnestness in this was a difficult thing for any of them to swallow. Jo looked at the crowd. Looked for other employees. "Who all knows about this? Daniella? AJ? What about you—Imogen? You're the one who was holding the goddamned books."

Daniella expected Imogen to throw someone else under the bus. To make sure they took the heat instead of her.

Imogen, however, shook her head. "You're the one who lied, Jo. You're the one who hid that we were going under. You didn't tell any of us that our jobs were basically defunct. You couldn't even give us the notice to find another job? What were you doing, hiding that from us just like any other grown-up? Maybe Eli screwed up. Maybe I saw more than I wanted to understand. But you knew what was happening and you didn't even give us a chance to help. It took Eli's late-night vigilantism to expose what was going on here."

Daniella watched Imogen in awe. She didn't know that Imogen was capable of that. That kind of intensity. Capable of anything beyond a surly expression and an eye roll. Capable of defending someone other than herself.

It was impressive.

Impressive, if you weren't Jo, that is.

"I'm sorry, Imogen. We're going under." Jo pinched her nose. "Are you happy now? I was trying to save up the money to buy part of a stake in the store so I could have some say in whether or not it sold, or at least make enough money on the sale to open somewhere else. I'd been gathering my resources as quickly as I could, but that's not happening now. I've got to pay back your goddamned money, Eli. Or turn you over to the cops."

"Jo—" Daniella tried to jump in. She had to tell her own plan. It wasn't great, and it wasn't particularly moral. But it would at least get back those nine thousand dollars. It would at least buy them back those two weeks and keep Eli out of jail.

Jo wasn't having any of it. She held up her hand, silencing Daniella in an instant. "Get into the office, Eli, while I figure out what to do with you. The rest of you get back to work, while you still can."

And that's when the landline at the register started to ring.

13

Nevermore

For a long beat, nobody moved.

Briiiing.

      Briiiiing.

The phone rattled a bit in its cradle.

        Briiiiing.

The sound of that ring, echoing throughout the enormous building—it was like the phone *knew* it was being intentionally ignored.

Only one person ever really called on that line.

          Briiiiiiiiiing.

Eli walked over to the receiver.

"Wait—" said Daniella.

But he didn't listen. He picked up the phone. "Wild Nights Bookstore and Emporium, this is Eli speaking, how may I help you?"

A muffled voice sounded through the receiver, but nobody could make out the words—though they were trying to desperately just judging by the fact that nobody was breathing for the moment. Or, at least, Rinn wasn't.

"No, sir. I will not put Jo on," said Eli.

The voice on the other end got louder, but no less easy to discern.

"Sir, if you'll give me a minute. Sir. You see, that was me. I ordered Air Jordans with the petty cash. They haven't been logged in the inventory yet. They're shoes, sir. Didn't seem right, logging them as inventory in a bookstore."

For a moment the voice didn't say anything at all. Then it came back rapid-fire, but softer.

Eli was having a conversation that could not only terminate his employment but get him into true legal trouble. Still, he kept his shoulders relaxed, his expression neutral. Rinn knew that Eli was posturing, but it impressed her nonetheless. Rinn couldn't posture if it would save the entire world. Honesty was her Achilles' heel.

"No, sir, they're fake," said Eli.

The voice responded equally quickly.

"Yes, sir. Okay." Eli nodded.

And then the voice said something decisive; Rinn didn't need words to understand that.

"Goodbye." Eli clicked the phone down onto the receiver. When he looked up, his whole face was dazed, like he'd seen God.

Rinn couldn't contain herself. "What did he say?"

"That was Archer Hunt Junior. He said to make sure that I

put the shoes in the inventory." Eli sounded almost dreamy as he spoke. "He said never to buy inventory without logging it into the system."

"What?" Daniella practically screeched this.

Eli cleared his throat. "He said to make sure to put the shoes in inventory. Then he was all 'otherwise, good job,' which is basically bonkers. And then he hung up."

"That can't be right." Daniella shook her head.

"And that's it?" Rinn had to know. She knew everyone else would be afraid to ask, but she needed to know.

"That's it," said Eli with a shrug.

Jo was put into motion by this. "All right, everyone, show's over. Get back to browsing. Get back to work. Eli—"

"Yes?" asked Eli, still with the expression that he'd possibly gotten away with a real murder.

"Stay out of trouble for the rest of the day." And then Jo walked off, clearly not wanting to deal with the rest of them.

Rinn, however, was unsatisfied. "Are you sure that's all he said?"

Eli finally had the sense to look insulted. "I'm not lying. He said, 'Good work, kid. Just don't forget to log the expense in the inventory.' And then he just hung up."

"It just doesn't make any sense," said Rinn.

"What?" asked Daniella. "Did you *want* Eli to go to jail?"

"No," said Rinn.

"So thank whoever you pray to that our problem is solved."

"It's *a* problem solved, Daniella. Not *the* problem," said Rinn. "We've still got nine thousand dollars missing that was probably going to be our payroll for the next few weeks. Without it the store is still definitely closing."

Daniella grunted. Even she had to admit that was still true, if inconveniently so.

But Imogen must have understood. "She's right. Didn't you say the bookstore is being sold?"

"Yes, that's what Eli read in the email." Daniella was well and truly put out by this point. Her entire posture looked like one giant eye roll waiting to happen.

It was impressive, honestly.

But that didn't stop Rinn. "That can't be right, either."

"Oh my God, Olivera. Stop trying to make up problems that you're the chosen savior for. The bookstore is closing. Count your blessings in the gratitude journal you clearly keep. Nobody is going to jail right now. Sometimes that's all you get in this life." And with that Daniella linked her arm around Eli and pulled him away from the cash register.

"But," said Rinn, looking to Imogen, the only audience that she had left, "he *can't* sell the bookstore."

"And yet, it looks like he's gonna. The man wins again." Imogen retreated back to the bookshelves—toward the art history section—without another word.

But Rinn's mind was calculating. The store actually *couldn't* be sold. That's why the store *hadn't* been sold all those years. It didn't matter that the land was valuable. It didn't matter how badly Archer Hunt Junior wanted to. The store literally *could not be sold*. Legally.

Unless, of course, Wild Nights Bookstore and Emporium was unsustainable as a bookstore. Rinn Olivera gasped out loud, though there was nobody left at the cash register to hear her.

MIDDAY

12:00 p.m.—4:59 p.m.

14

Madmen, Lovers, and Drunkards

12:01 P.M.
Rinn

A lull fell over Wild Nights Bookstore and Emporium. The customers had all gone quietly back to whatever they had been doing before the news had exploded across the store that Wild Nights was closing.

For a moment, Rinn stood dumbstruck. She couldn't believe it.

Could Archer Hunt Junior be intentionally sabotaging the store?

There was no other reason he wouldn't be mad at Eli. No other reason he'd said to simply log the Jordans as inventory. And he could profit so much more easily off the land than doing the work to run an independent bookstore.

No, it couldn't be. There had to be some other explanation. Some other more viable reasoning.

It was just that Rinn was having a hard time coming up with any better reasoning or any better explanation. In a few weeks there would be no grumpy Jo and no roller girl and no casually bumping into AJ. There would be no Wild Nights. And Archer Hunt Junior would somehow profit off the rising property values in the neighborhood. Rinn couldn't believe it. She didn't want to believe it. But instead of explaining away her reservations, Rinn's mind filled with questions.

What other explanation was there?

Why else would Archer Hunt Junior be totally cool with nine thousand dollars of petty cash going toward fake Air Jordans?

Had Hunt Junior worked out a way to sell the bookstore land?

How had he managed to make his case legal?

Rinn was thinking and walking, walking and thinking. She needed to pace to figure out the solution to problems like these. She needed to generate as many questions as she could. She understood *why* Hunt Junior was behaving the way he was. But she didn't understand *how*. She didn't even understand *what* he'd done.

She just knew he was motivated to get his money out from the value of the land and get it fast, while the market for gentrification in Wicker Park was still hot.

Of course, that's when somebody tapped her shoulder. "Excuse me."

Dear God. It was Birdman.

Rinn found her brightest customer service tone. "Hi!"

"Excuse me, miss, I sold books here this morning," he said.

"Yes." Rinn did her best to hold on to her smile. "I remember. What brings you back in?"

"Oh, I didn't leave," he said, in that manner that old men used where they sound like they're about to tack on *as a matter of fact* to the end of every sentence.

Rinn didn't want to hear it. "How may I help you?"

"Well, you see," he said.

And Rinn knew this was going to be a good one. A really great request, because it was all in his tone, all in his posture.

That sloping shoulder that seemed to say, *I have something very reasonable I'd like.* But the way he wouldn't make eye contact, that was very, *But if I'm being honest, it's a super-ridiculous thing that I know I'd like.*

"I got cash from the books I sold. But I've found some purchases I'd like to make." The man looked down, directing Rinn's gaze to the stack of books in his arm. "So what I'd really like is to use store credit, since it's worth more."

"I see." Rinn thought about it for a minute—he had requested the cash, not store credit. "But you've already got the cash."

The man nodded. "Yes, but I haven't spent it yet."

Rinn took a deep breath. "But you *have* the cash. It's in your wallet or your pocket."

The man nodded. "Correct."

"I'm sorry, sir, but if they've already cashed you out, the transaction is already logged. We can't reverse the cash transaction."

"Why not? Isn't it just like a return?" Birdman was so bewilderingly direct in his request.

"No, sir. It's not a return. It's redoing the original transaction." Rinn was trying to find her calmest tones.

"So just tell them to do that," he said.

"Do what?"

"Redo the original transaction."

"You want me to redo the original transaction? From scratch?" Rinn really hoped that this would work. Deflect. Live to fight another day. "You do know we'd have to find all the original books that you tried to sell just to log this all correctly?"

"Well, not from scratch, but yes, please." Birdman tacked on that *please* like he was a very polite person and he knew how the rules of society functioned and he was going to use all of them to get his way on this one.

And Rinn, she took a deep breath, and, rather than screaming, she redid the original transaction from scratch, because she was a real pushover like that. The books were still stacked right behind the register, luckily, so she didn't have to go looking for them.

Eventually, she gave Birdman his store credit—which, why he wanted store credit after finding out the store was closing, was really another matter that Rinn did *not* want to deep dive into. The cost of the books he was buying didn't take up all of the money he was making off the books. But far be it from Rinn to get into an argument about value propositions with this guy.

Besides, Rinn hadn't given up on figuring out this whole Archer Hunt Junior business. She didn't want to be right on this one. But she might be. She had to figure out what was going on to know for sure. The best person to talk to about any of this was the person who handled all the sales transactions for Wild Nights. And that was Daniella.

Rinn had to start there.

Only, Daniella was in more than a huff when Rinn arrived. She was standing with a chair in each hand. For a moment, Rinn thought that Daniella was going to ignore her.

But then Daniella blew some hair out of her face with a puff of frustration and said, "Can you help?"

Daniella didn't wait for an answer. She dropped a chair onto the floor with a clattering bang.

Rinn picked up the chair. It had landed perilously close to her feet. Maybe just now wasn't the ideal time to talk numbers with Daniella. Maybe she needed to help the girl out for a bit before asking for clarification on what was going on with Archer Hunt. "What are we doing?"

"Setting up the rows for the stupid Harvey event." Daniella grabbed her chair so that the back corners of the legs dragged along the floor, making a horrible scraping noise against the concrete section of flooring.

Rinn did try to be forgiving in many things. But she was tired of swallowing all of Daniella's petty opinions, especially when her favorite book was involved. "It's not stupid."

But Daniella kept on rolling, like a hunk of old Detroit steel and momentum. She wasn't going to stop until she smashed Rinn to pieces. "It is. The book is stupid. The event is stupid. The store is closing, and it is all *stupid*. It's just an author. Authors are just people. Stop glorifying them."

With that, Rinn had had enough. "Would it kill you to just honestly *like* a thing?"

"What?" Daniella stopped moving for a moment, stopped dragging her chair along its sad, screeching path.

Rinn caught up to Daniella and grabbed her by the arm to turn her around. "What is so wrong with people liking a thing that you have to crap all over it?"

Daniella swallowed, unused to this version of Rinn. Visibly thrown into unexpected waters by Rinn voicing an unfriendly opinion. "I don't have to crap all over it."

But Rinn wasn't about to take that as an excuse. She wasn't about to let any of this slide. There was too much at stake here. And Daniella, with her disdain and her secrets and her need to keep everything private, had already done enough damage to a thing that Rinn loved. "You do. You have to destroy everything that anyone cares about. You have to take something people love and make it a joke. You don't have to like the things that I like. You can hate them. But you treat everything with disdain, especially if it's something that other people really love. I'm so tired of that. This store is closing, but you don't even seem to care at all."

Daniella crossed her arms, buffering herself with bravado. "So. What's it to you?"

But Rinn had been watching Daniella. Rinn paid attention. She knew how to swipe for the jugular on this one. She knew how to defend herself against such reckless carelessness. "Are you really so out of touch that you disdain every feeling on planet Earth? Do you really not love anything at all?"

That seemed to land on her. Hit Daniella in a way that Rinn would have never expected. All of Daniella's posturing fell away. What was left was a wide-eyed girl, her face raw and a little shaken. "I have feelings."

"Show them for once." Rinn grabbed the chair out of Daniella's hand and started setting up the rows. "Or go find something else to do. You can find someone else's joy to destroy anywhere else in the store. Because I'm sick of looking at you."

Daniella stood there for a moment. And Rinn expected her to go, to flee, to run out on her. But instead Daniella went quiet, found the edges of the rows of seats and began setting up chairs there. It was a piece of Daniella that Rinn had never seen before. She almost felt sorry for her, seeing Daniella like that. Seeing the way she crumpled so easily.

But then Rinn thought about the way that Daniella had hidden such a huge secret from all of them. Had kept them from knowing that this place was going under. Had protected Eli after he'd screwed over the whole store in one night.

Would she even believe Rinn if Rinn told her about why Rinn suspected Archer Hunt Junior of sabotaging the store?

The only space Rinn felt like she had a place in this world would be gone. She could get another job, sure. But this was Wild Nights Bookstore and Emporium. The first place she'd found a copy of *When We Were Us*. Where Rinn had learned how to deal with difficult customers and that there was more than one way to catalog a collection. It also happened to be the only place she got to interact with AJ.

And when it was all said and done, the store was probably going to turn into something depressingly practical like a parking lot.

Was it all because Archer Hunt Junior wanted to sell his land and get out from under his father's will? Or was there another reason, a reason Rinn couldn't see? She couldn't take her assumptions and run with them. She had to find facts or proof before she went around accusing the owner of Wild Nights of trying to legally undercut and profit from his inheritance.

What a disaster.

Rinn put down one of the chairs in her hand. At least the seating arrangements were almost done for the Brock Harvey event. It was probably going to be the last bookstore event she ever worked.

Rinn had met so many authors in this space. Learned that authors were people she could meet and interact with. *Daniella and her stupid disdain and her need to always, always put people down.* Rinn continued to ignore Daniella as she set up chairs on the other side of the event space.

These events were one of the most magical parts of the job. That the people who made the stories she loved to read were actual real-live people—people Rinn had had the pleasure and the privilege to interact with. It was part of what had made books come alive. There was a person who wrote a book. There were people who read books. There were spaces where those two people could meet—sometimes online, but also, in these special, sacred spaces called bookstores. Because that's what it was, really, Wild Nights Bookstore and Emporium—a place where magic could happen.

Rinn picked up another chair from the stack and started

moving it toward the end of a back row. She almost had the line finished now.

A commotion broke out near the entrance to the store. But the sound of it—like voices and heavy footsteps and a wave of whispers—the sound moved so erratically across the space that, at first, Rinn couldn't tell where it was coming from. She looked around her, but she couldn't see anything from her vantage point. The noise shuffled and bounced through all the stacks of bookshelves. And then a man rounded a corner, followed by a woman holding her phone and looking down, and in her shock Rinn dropped the chair directly onto her foot.

Brock Harvey was in the bookstore.

Rinn flinched for a moment from the chair landing on her foot, but she didn't really feel the pain because—*Oh my God*—Brock Harvey was there in the flesh, and Rinn could barely remember how to breathe. He was wearing a checkered blazer with elbow patches; his hair was slicked back, and his shoes were these pristine white sneakers. He had on a V-neck T-shirt in the same clean white color, and his jeans were that perfect, pressed, dark indigo shade that important men wore when they wanted to indicate they were wealthy but casually so.

"And I don't know what you were thinking booking me here, Maya. You've really dropped the ball." Harvey said that at what Rinn considered a faux whisper. And then he started making his way through the setup of chairs right by the author stage.

Rinn ran up to him; she couldn't help it. She knew he had possibly just insulted Wild Nights, but she didn't think that he really meant it. He must have had a terrible early flight and a bad sleeping situation. Rinn had read about book tours online, and she knew how grueling they could be. Wake up at the crack of dawn, fly into a regional airport, then try to make it to an event, usually during rush-hour traffic. Finish the event, then sleep for a bit, and be back up at the crack of dawn for the next flight. Rinn would be grumpy, too.

But Harvey ignored Rinn as she approached. His body language made his avoidance seem almost *purposeful*. He went straight around to the other side of the chairs.

Straight for Daniella, who wasn't paying attention at all. She was absorbed with counting the chairs in the rows. With focusing anywhere but on Rinn.

Rinn could read that body language, too.

"Excuse me," Harvey said, reaching out and grabbing Daniella's elbow. "Could you help me?"

Daniella backed away, pulling her arm out from his grip, confusion palpable on her face. "Oh, you want Jo."

Harvey took a step closer; he didn't touch her again. But he wasn't giving her any space. He smiled a smile that looked like it should have been charming. But it wasn't. It made Rinn shiver.

"And who might *Jo* be?" Harvey asked.

"Jo's the manager. I'll get her." Daniella backed away again.

And then, before Daniella could turn, Rinn saw Brock wink. "You do that."

Daniella's expression narrowed, but she must have been more eager for the excuse to get out of there than to stick around and fight him about it.

Rinn stared at Harvey for a moment.

How was this the author of her favorite book? Maybe he was used to talking to adults. Maybe he had thought Daniella was older. But neither of those were satisfactory answers. None of those assuaged the instant distrust that was welling up in Rinn's stomach.

Rinn shivered again. "Mr. Harvey?"

That's when the harried-looking young woman—the one who had been trailing behind Brock—approached. She wasn't just in motion, she was full of nervous energy. She had on jeans and a pressed button-down shirt with a cardigan over the top. Her glasses were sliding down the bridge of her nose slightly, and her hair was what Rinn could only describe as floppy. She looked like she was about Jo's age, though she could have been younger. She elbowed Harvey.

At the prompting, Harvey turned his attention away from Daniella's retreating form and finally noticed Rinn. "What is it? Looking for something to be signed?"

"I mean, yes—that would be amazing—but I work here, and I was wanting to say how excited we all are to have you at the store." Rinn could hear the flatness in her voice. *Why wasn't this going according to plan? Why was he so different from the voice that narrated his books?*

Harvey sniffed and said, "Thank you," in a way that hardly implied gratitude.

And then, under his breath, but in a way that Rinn could still hear, "Jesus, they hire children here. *This place*, Maya."

Rinn took a step back. She smoothed her hands over her skirt. Was the polo she was wearing too juvenile? She'd been trying to dress up for the occasion. She'd steamed her skirt, and she'd made sure the polo had come fresh from the wash.

"Come on, Harvey. There are no small gigs. A sale is a sale, and every single one counts toward that final number. I'm sure more sales couldn't hurt season three." Maya's voice was overly chipper and enthusiastic.

Right. Season three. Of the TV show based off *When We Were Us*. The comment shouldn't have stung. It really shouldn't have. It was just that Rinn wished that she hadn't heard it, that was all.

Rinn smoothed out her skirt again, trying to conquer the feeling of resentment that was welling up in her chest. She could contain the feeling for now. She straightened her shoulders.

In all the hubbub of actually getting to meet Harvey, she hadn't even been thinking of the TV show. He'd been helping with the writing and the production of the episodes—most of his fans blamed the show for the fact that Harvey had stopped writing books. They'd all wanted a follow-up to *When We Were Us*; they hadn't gotten one. Rinn hadn't really minded the TV show before this moment—it got more people reading the book—but she had been a little bit disappointed that the show *had* taken away from any more books being written.

Rinn pasted on her bright smile and tried, tried, tried again. She put her hand out to Maya. "Hi! I'm Rinn Olivera, and I work here. I can take you to Jo if you like, or to the back room where you can sit and have some refreshments."

Maya took Rinn's hand and shook it. Then she looked at Rinn, a puzzled expression on her face. "Do I know you from somewhere?"

But Rinn didn't want to talk up her book channel. She wanted to be appreciated for herself as a fan and a worker at the bookstore alone. It didn't seem right, in this moment, to talk about the following she had built. She smiled, brighter and even more pasted on. She was excited for this. She had been excited for this all day. All week. "I've just got one of those faces."

Maya let go of her hand, gave a quick and friendly smile. "Yeah. Must be. It's nice to meet you, Rinn. I think a trip to the back room for some refreshments would be amazing."

Maya's friendliness, Rinn could see, was to overcompensate for Harvey's lack thereof. Harvey was eyeing the whole store as though the goth-punk-library vibe was a sad, odd thing. He looked out of place in the bookstore, which, Rinn had never *seen* an author looking out of place in a bookstore.

There was some undercurrent to Harvey that she couldn't place. Waves of irritation were rippling off him. But Rinn didn't know what she had done. She'd tried to introduce herself. She'd offered to take them back to a waiting area. She was doing everything in her power to make both Harvey and Maya feel comfortable. But in the end, she could tell that lingering disquiet was rolling off both of them. It was making Harvey surly and was making Maya overly bright.

"It's back here," Rinn offered, pointing toward the back office. "I can give you a tour if you like?"

But Harvey put her off again. "I've got it from here, kid. Why don't you give Maya that little tour of yours?"

Harvey was off and away before Rinn could even open her mouth to respond.

Maya gave an apologetic smile in response. "I'll take the tour. It sounds great."

"Sure," said Rinn. She no longer wondered why people said to never meet your heroes.

15

Handsome, Ruthless, and Stupid

12:22 P.M.
Daniella

Daniella was only stopped once on her way to the break room.

"Excuse me, miss," said a man in pressed khaki pants and a polo shirt buttoned all the way to the top button.

"Yes?" Daniella had asked with the last of her patience.

"Do you know where I could find some Italian food?"

Daniella had sighed and taken him to the cookbook section. But of course, that wasn't what the man had been looking for at all.

He'd been in search of *actual* Italian food. To eat. In a bookstore.

Daniella had almost lost her cool then. But she'd told him to put in *Lucia's* in his phone and run off before she'd given the man a lecture that bookstores do not serve pizza. Or pasta. Or ravioli.

Daniella slammed her way into the break room. The force of the door—the sound ricocheted through Daniella's chest. It was cathartic.

For a moment, Daniella understood why Imogen was constantly making noise. Screeching to a halt on her horrible moped.

Stomping her way around the store. Using her whole body to push open a door. It felt good, really, to make noise and be heard. It felt like she was calling on some primal form of existence. *I am here. You cannot ignore me. I exist.*

Of course, when she got into the break room, Daniella spotted Eli. He was sitting on one of the *Golden Girls* chairs. There was something so effortless and lazy about the way he sat—legs sprawled and relaxed, arms akimbo and hanging over the armrests while he managed to hold on to a mug of coffee—that Daniella found that the last of her patience had finally faded into nothing.

She was *not* going to say anything.

Daniella went over to the coffee maker to pour herself a cup of coffee. But, of course, there was only the tiniest of splashes left in the pot. A quarter of an inch or less. She sloshed it around, trying to will the derelict amount of coffee to turn into a viable cup.

Daniella grunted. She felt Eli's eyes on her, but she didn't look over at him, she couldn't look over at him. She was going to make coffee, and she was going to ignore Eli until kingdom come. Until she revealed herself as anachronisticblonde, which, for those of you watching at home, was going to be *never*. Daniella's mind kept spinning metaphors, ways in which she could clearly articulate in the most poetic and hateful of ways this simple truth: Daniella Korres was never speaking to Eli ever, ever again. Unto the end of the world.

She didn't care how dramatic that sounded. It was *true*.

Daniella opened up the top of the coffee maker and of course—*of course*—there was still a mess of coffee grinds in there. Eli hadn't thought to clean out the grinds or even to empty the pot. All he'd thought to do was pour out the majority—*but not all*—of the drinkable coffee left in the coffee maker and then sit with his stupid mug on the chair and act like he had done a good deed by not entirely finishing off the coffee. As though rational humans went around pouring themselves a quarter of a cup of coffee from the last of the drip-coffee sludge.

Typical Eli.

Daniella took the coffeepot into the bathroom, dumping the coffee grinds in the trash along the way. She pointedly did not look at the floor, knowing that it had to still have Imogen's hair all over it. Everyone was in fine form today, and Daniella would have to ignore all of them in order to avoid murdering someone. She focused on the bathroom sink, on rinsing out the last remaining dregs and sludge of the coffee. She turned the pot upside down, letting the final drips of water fall out before heading back into the main break room.

Of course, that's when she got to the pantry, pulled out a filter, and realized there was no coffee left in the jar.

Eli was still staring at her.

And Daniella couldn't help it. This time she looked over at him. Saw the way his eyes were taking her in. The way he missed nothing, not the tension in her eyebrows, not the clenching of her jaw, not the way her hands had curled themselves into tight fists. Daniella hadn't even noticed that, her fingers had so gradually moved together, as though by their own will. She stretched her fingers out so that they were wide, and the move made her hands feel electric.

Made *Daniella* feel electric. "What the hell are you doing?"

Eli had the gall to look absolutely flabbergasted. He pointed to himself and everything. "I'm sitting."

Irritation flared in Daniella's chest. How dare he give a smart-assed answer. Her ears were ringing, and her anger was at a low-level chant in her ears that nobody else seemed to notice. *How dare he how dare he how dare he.*

"Why are you sitting *there*?"

"Because I want to talk to Jo when she gets back?" Eli took the most casual sip of coffee in the entire world.

Daniella snapped. "Get out."

"Honestly, Danny, I would love to. But I've been having lots of hard conversations today, and I'd really like to not avoid this one with Jo. She deserves better than avoidance." And then Eli smiled like Daniella was in on the joke. Like she *could* be in on the joke.

"You do, do you?" Daniella couldn't believe this. She couldn't believe that Eli was sitting there calmly while all of their—no, his—plans came crashing down around his ears. She couldn't believe that he hadn't let her take the fall, either. That he'd *told* Archer Junior. That Archer Junior wasn't pressing charges.

The chant grew louder, more ferocious—*howdarehehowdarehehowdarehe*—until there was nothing left in her mind but those words. Nothing left but that rage. She couldn't believe she had *tried* to take the fall for him. Couldn't forgive herself for the attempt. "I don't give a flying fuck, Eli. Get out of here."

Daniella needed him out. Away from her. Away from the coffee that he had finished off. Away from the mess he had made. Why had Daniella even bothered to help him? *Why?* Why couldn't she look at Eli anymore after she had? Why couldn't she make a simple cup of coffee without Eli ruining it for everyone, but most particularly for herself?

Whywhywhy. Howdarehehowdarehehowdarehe.

Eli took a long drink from his mug. Then he put it down on a side table. For a moment, his whole face had screwed up like he was registering new information. Then he tilted his head. "Oh, I see. You want to pick a fight."

He said it as such a declarative thing—like he didn't even frame the idea as a question.

Daniella had to immediately push back. "No, I don't."

Then for good measure, Daniella grabbed one of the hideous floral cushions from the other *Golden Girls* love seat and threw it at him. "I want you to get out of here and leave me alone."

And, of course, the pillows bounced right off Eli's shoulders. Nothing stuck to him, not even couch cushions. The pillow hadn't even had the decency to land on a more vulnerable spot on Eli's body.

"Right. That checks out. You're not mad at me. You're not mad about the store closing. You're never mad about anything. You just want me to leave you alone and you are, of course, super calm and very fine."

Daniella lost it then. She toppled the nearest *Golden Girls* chair and then kicked it for good measure. Then she went over to the boxes and boxes and boxes of Jordans that she had spent all morning stacking, and she started throwing them into one another. A couple of the boxes burst open, the Jordans spilled out.

Eli was up in a shot. He grabbed her around the tops of her arms, gentle but firm. And then he said, "Danny. Danny, come back."

But Daniella couldn't find the way back. She was so angry. She wanted to light the room on fire. She wanted to upend Jo's desk. She wanted to tear down the world and hope nobody bothered to remake it again. "No."

"Come on, Danny." Eli's voice was so calm, so steady. "It's okay to be mad. Do you need to hit me with one of those cheap flowery chair pillows? Just let it out."

Eli looked Daniella in the eye as he said it. And somehow, Daniella had never noticed that Eli had brown eyes, not blue. She knew every freckle on his face, but she had somehow assumed the wrong color of his eyes. Given the rest of his coloring, they should have been sky blue, or maybe a sea green. But no, these were just a plain, clear brown. The realization grounded Daniella, again. She was coming back to her body after a flight through space and time and rage. The returning sensation started with a heaviness at her eyes with the threat of hot, angry tears. Then the sense that she had fingers and toes and they were hers and they didn't belong to the well of anger inside of her. Then she could feel her own breathing in her chest—in and out, but still not easy or smooth.

Eli didn't break eye contact. "It's okay, you know."

"No." Daniella shook her head. "I hate you."

"I know." He nodded, and suddenly Eli seemed like the kind of boy who knew the secrets of the universe.

"You don't know anything," said Daniella. It was a plea. A benediction. A desperate need to be spared this feeling. She blinked a tear away.

But Eli was ruthless. He let go of her shoulders and used one of his hands to wipe away the tear from her cheek. "I know more than you'll ever say. And I know why you won't admit it."

Daniella shook her head. He couldn't know anything. She never told him, and she never told anyone, really.

But Eli paid attention. And he must have been paying attention to Daniella. "I know you write poetry in that notebook when we're not looking. I know you take Calc BC even though you tell everyone you've got Algebra II to do over the summer. I know you have a weakness for astrology memes, and I know you'd rather dive into Lake Michigan than ever admit you had a feeling."

There was a callus along one of the ridges of Eli's thumb and Daniella could feel it as it moved back and forth across her cheek. She wanted to get out of her body again, go back into that place that was just white-hot anger. But she could feel that rough patch of skin across her cheek, and she could feel her breathing change to shorter, choppier breaths, and she was undeniably aware of the fact that one of her hands had reached out to play with a belt loop along Eli's jeans. She'd found her way back into her body, and she hated that it was Eli who helped keep her tethered there.

"You're trouble." Daniella's voice was lower than she'd meant. There was a tremor in there that she hardly recognized.

Half a smile pulled at Eli's mouth. "I know that, too."

And who was to say what might have happened next, had the door to the break room not swung open as Brock Harvey walked in.

"Oh, excuse me," Harvey said with one of those knowing almost-smiles that adults liked to make when they *knew things* even when it was none of their business. "I hope I'm not interrupting anything."

And it was like the poles on two magnets had been reversed. What had just pulled Daniella and Eli closer together now sent them propelling apart, across the room. There couldn't be enough space between them anymore. Daniella needed a canyon between her body and his. No, a galaxy. Then maybe she'd feel safe around Eli again.

"You're not interrupting," said Daniella before Eli could interject. She was still a little breathless, but she told herself that was because she'd leaped across the room. "Eli here was leaving, weren't you, Eli?"

For a moment, Daniella thought that Eli was going to protest, was going to claim that he needed to stay in the room because of Jo, because of something, anything. What a laugh—Eli trying to avoid trouble. Like he wasn't drawn to it. Like it wasn't his match in a perfect set of magnets. But instead he gave Daniella a steady look; he was looking for clues as to what state Daniella was in. Whatever he saw, he nodded.

"Yeah," said Eli. "I'm going to go and find Jo."

Daniella nodded as he walked off. Eli looked back over his shoulder once as he opened the door. But Daniella turned away from him. She took a deep breath and ignored the sound of the door closing behind him.

Good. Bye.

Except that's when she heard the low chuckle from across the room. "You seem capable for a pretty thing. Do you know if they've got anything else on offer other than bargain cheese and crackers in this joint?"

When Daniella turned around, she saw Brock Harvey smirking, like he knew a secret that Daniella never wanted to be told.

16

They Stuck Me Together with Glue

Nobody was at the register. That was Imogen's first thought. There was something about the sight of the store's source of income being totally abandoned that left Imogen in a place beyond sadness. A place where longing met up with inevitability and landed smack-dab into an awful metaphor.

Imogen turned away, running her shoulder into someone who was passing by.

"Oh, excuse me," said a girl who was about Imogen's age. She had brown skin and full lips and mischief in her eyes. She flashed the kind of smile that made Imogen want to lean in and ask about the nature of God.

Instead, Imogen leaned back, because she'd had enough of that kind of trouble for a long while. "No, that's on me. I didn't see you."

"Here for the Harvey signing?" The girl's voice was hopeful, for reasons that Imogen could not fathom, didn't want to fathom.

Imogen resisted the urge to say *God no* and go running in the other direction. She pointed to her name tag. "Nope, just work here."

"Lucky," said the girl with what was nearly a flirtatious smile.

It took all of Imogen's willpower not to bat her eyelashes right back. "Not for much longer."

Then Imogen shrugged, and turned around before the girl could say anything else. Imogen faced the register again. While she wasn't exactly a big fan of Jo right now, she wasn't going to leave the only source of money for the store completely vacant. There was enough mismanagement going on around here that Imogen didn't need to add to it. She was, if she could, going to temporarily destroy the horrible metaphor that was opening up a pitiful chasm of nothing in her chest.

Imogen should have foreseen that Little Miss Perfect would abandon her post for that absolute dirtbag of an author. Everything about that guy—from his elbow-patch jacket to his too-shiny hair—screamed, *I look up to Michael Bay.* Imogen was glad that she had ignored the girl waiting for a Harvey signing. That couldn't be the kind of girl for her. Imogen knew better than to say any of these thoughts out loud, though. She'd only get a dirty look from Daniella and a corrective comment from Little Miss Perfect.

Except, maybe Imogen wouldn't have gotten flak from Daniella, because that girl had made herself scarce. Maybe, for once, she and Imogen agreed on this one thing. That Brock Harvey ought to be avoided at all costs.

Imogen wasn't going to hold her breath on that one, though.

When Imogen got behind the counter, nobody was waiting in line. She checked the till, and all the cash was in there. She checked in with her badge and the register popped open. She closed it back again as she flipped open the paper holder.

Imogen never liked running out of paper while a customer was checking out. During a lull was the right time to change the paper over so she didn't have to worry about it at all. They—the customers—inevitably stared at her, wondering what was taking so long, and the moment was awkward, and Imogen would avoid that if she could.

Imogen never could remember where Jo kept the spare paper. She looked in the drawer under the register, but there wasn't any in there. She checked in the cabinet underneath the register, and there was nothing in there, either.

Imogen's kingdom for a roll of register paper.

Oh, maybe Jo kept it in the drawer on the far right. Imogen always forgot to check there. Half the time it was locked, so she always assumed important papers lived in the right-side drawer. It wasn't locked this time, though. It was filled with papers, which was a good sign. She lifted up the papers and that was when her heart stopped.

A gun.

There was a rational part of Imogen's mind that continued to work. Started speaking calmly and logically in her mind. Archer Hunt Junior probably put the gun by the register in the case of a robbery or a mass shooting or the end of the world. He was one of those paranoid kind of white men who must have felt that he needed a gun in all of his spaces, even the spaces he hardly ever went anymore. He had to be prepared. Imogen sensed that about him, from the way he banned the store from being posted on the internet to the way he checked in on Jo every day via the landline phone.

Archer Hunt Junior was definitely the kind of man to own a gun.

But there was also an instinctive part of Imogen's brain running at the same time. One that told her that this *was* the end of the world. That the gun beckoned to the darkness inside of her. Called to the void in her. Spoke directly to the nothing that she fought so hard against.

The nothing was winning. And then, in a flash, Imogen could feel—this piece of her that Imogen didn't realize she had—it awakened within her and reared up and found the last scrap of survival that was left inside of her and—

—Imogen screamed with every ounce of breath that she had in her. With the smallest slivers of survival that remained intact. She screamed like it was the end of the world because, for her, it could have been. She didn't stop screaming until people were all around her. Wouldn't stop screaming until someone took the weapon out of her hand and destroyed it. Nothing else would keep her from her banshee wail.

Jo was the first to break Imogen's screaming spell. "Imogen, honey, what is going on?"

"I found this by the register." Imogen set the gun into Jo's accidentally outstretched hand. Imogen swallowed, and her throat felt raw.

Jo's joking demeanor changed in an instant. She went rigid. She stared at the weapon in her palm for a moment, then she looked up at Imogen, her eyes wide and nearly wild. "Holy shit. How did you get this?"

"It was in the drawer with the extra rolls of receipt paper." Imogen shrugged. It was not a shrugging matter, but she found she couldn't do anything else in the moment. She didn't feel casual about any of this, but she felt like she had to do something casual to counteract the enormity of what she had gone through. It was an hour in an instant. A lifetime. She could sense the scream still there in her scratched-up throat, trying to claw its way out again, just in case.

Jo, for her part, let out a stream of profanities that ended in, "Goddamned Archer Hunt Junior."

Listening to Jo swear helped. Made Imogen feel like she wasn't alone. Like this wasn't always and forever on her. Like she maybe had help out there. They couldn't decide the big things, but others were there to swear on her behalf and take the gun away. The scream trapped in her throat slid back down, as though it was feeling safe enough to rest for the moment.

"I thought that this was under lock and fucking key. I had no idea the asshole stuck it in such an easy-to-find spot."

"You knew it was there?" Imogen couldn't believe it. Couldn't believe Jo would let a gun on the premises. Wouldn't warn them all that it was there.

"I knew that there was one. I knew that when Archer hired me, he told me that he had one. That there was a gun on-site. It was the one thing I didn't tell the employees, because you're nearly all underage and I know how tough that is, and I just didn't want any of you to even consider it. That it was there. And then I never found it, so I'd forgotten about it. He must have moved it recently. I would have known if it was with the receipt paper and moved it before this. I would never have left a weapon in that spot. Christ. What was that man thinking?"

"Is there any way to get rid of it?"

"Considering it's not mine, I don't know."

Imogen's hope fell.

Jo reached out, put her hand on Imogen's shoulder. "That doesn't mean I'll do nothing. Let me make some calls. See if I can't get rid of it."

Jo looked with disgust at the gun in her hand. She looked at Imogen, then back at the gun. She double-checked the safety, then put it in her jacket pocket as best as she could. She got out her phone and began typing at a rapid pace. She shook her head a couple of times but kept searching. She clicked with her thumb a couple of times, then held the phone up to her ear. "Yes, hello, is this the Naperville Police? Great. I'd like to schedule a time to drop off a gun for surrender. No, it hasn't been used in any crimes that I am aware of. No, it's not mine. Yes. Can I come by after I get off work today? Will someone be there late? I don't get off until nine. Okay. Yes. Okay. Sure. Thank you so much."

Jo clicked off her phone. "Good news, I can get rid of the gun. Especially since it's not mine and I want to stick it to that asshole. How dare he keep a gun, unlocked and loaded, on the premises where minors work. How *dare* he."

"Okay, Jo, you're starting to scare me." Imogen was registering the fury in Jo's eyes, the vibrating rage in her voice.

Jo took a deep breath. "Just . . . go help out on the floor. I have to find a place to stash this where no one else will be able to find it."

Imogen didn't need to be told twice. She grabbed a cart full of books and fled the sight of the counter.

Imogen was reshelving some cookbooks when she heard a voice from behind her.

"Do you read much prose, habibti?" Madame Auntie was standing in the stack. Her posture was ramrod straight as usual, but her head was at a tilt, making her entire body look like a question.

Imogen stared for a moment. "Sometimes? I didn't realize you were still here."

Madame Auntie waved her hands around, as though she

could merely wave away Imogen's question. And, honestly, she kind of did. "You read poetry, eh?"

"Yes." Imogen's words dragged out now. Had less of a direct question and more of a general wondering as to where any of this could possibly be going. "I mean, my mother gave me a lot of poetry to read as a kid. So I just got used to it. But I do read prose. You can't really make it through high school without prose."

Madame Auntie raised a single eyebrow. It felt like an accusation.

"At least, here, you can't," said Imogen, feeling the need to amend her statement.

"Believe me, child. You can go quite far in life without reading prose." Madame Auntie put her hand on her hip like she'd scored a point.

Imogen nodded. There was clearly no arguing with the woman. "All right. Is there something you'd like me to do?"

Madame Auntie shook her head. "I just thought you should know."

Imogen took a deep breath. Swallowed. Took another deep breath. Tried to find her steadiest voice. "Thank you."

And that should have been the end of it. But instead, Madame Auntie asked, "Your mother gave you poetry, yes? Where are your people from?"

Imogen knew the question well. It happened frequently enough. A part of her honestly couldn't believe it had taken Madame Auntie this long to ask her. "My people?"

"Your mother, your father." Madame Auntie tilted her head back and forth.

Imogen usually minded when she was asked that question. But it was different from someone who was similar to her. It was one thing when white people asked where she was from. But someone who felt nearly like an auntie, well, she could ask different questions. At least, Imogen thought so.

And so, without meaning to, without knowing why or what the consequences would be, she began to speak. True things, not sarcasm, not funny things. Real things. "My mom's family survived the occupation and the Six-Day War in '67. She was born in Chicago. My dad's family fled the civil war in Lebanon. He was born there, but he came here as a child. Before they were separating families. They've all been here for a while. But they remember things, you know? I think the poetry, it's her way of keeping the old ways. In her own expression, I mean."

Madame Auntie nodded. "I know. You remember things. And the things you don't remember, your parents and your family, they teach you to remember. They teach you to know what they carried. To carry it still."

Imogen stared at Madame Auntie for a moment. She wanted to call her Auntie, not just in her mind. She wanted to ask her. Questions about everything. About nothing. About the scarves and how many of them she had had and about her husband and how many trips he had gone on and why he'd traveled in the first place. About life before the internet and a time when the borders were open. About Chicago when it wasn't a beautiful city but a corrupt one, a posturing one. Or, a *more* corrupt one, at least. "Khala?"

Madame Auntie's mouth pulled into half of a smile. "Yes, habibti?"

"What do you remember?"

"This and that." Auntie's face dropped for a moment. Then she reached into her structured leather bag. The one that looked like it cost ten times what Imogen had paid for her scooter. She pulled out a black notebook. "You dropped this. Or your manager. I found it. I wanted to give it back to you."

Imogen didn't understand it. Why this woman, who had talked about her books and her book club and every one of the scarves her husband had bought and which trip he was on when he bought them, why she would suddenly clam up. But maybe those were easy things to talk about. Maybe real questions scared Madame Auntie just as much as they scared Imogen. As much as they scared everyone. Maybe telling a story was one thing but answering a question was another. "Thank you."

Madame Auntie cracked half a smile. "What's in this notebook, the one that you dropped?"

Imogen shrugged. "I got mad at Daniella, so I took what I thought was the evidence from last night. That Eli had stolen, I mean. When I found out the store was closing, I was so mad. I don't know if I've ever been that mad in my life. I was going to give it to Jo, but she figured it out anyway, about Eli and the money he had stolen and everything. I didn't even have a chance to open it. I was so scared, I think. I was mad, too, but also scared. I'm not sure if that makes any sense."

Madame Auntie laughed. "You would have had trouble with that, azzizati."

"What do you mean?" asked Imogen.

Auntie smiled with a wry twist of her lips. "I might have looked through the book. It is very good, if it is yours. No numbers. Just poetry and sketches. I had never seen poetry like that."

Imogen blinked. "What?"

"Just poetry and some drawings. I don't think you took the right books, if you were looking for money. Or maybe the right books didn't even exist. But I thought you were sad. Those poems, they're very sad. And mad. So much anger in them. I thought you might need someone to talk to. But, if they're not yours . . ." Auntie's shoulders lilted, almost like a shrug, but also almost like a little piece of understanding. Like she accepted what the universe would give and she would rather shrug than surrender.

Imogen's hands shook as she looked down at the notebook. It couldn't be. It just couldn't be. But somehow, deep inside of herself, she knew—or, at least, suspected—what she'd find when she opened the notebook. She delayed what seemed like the inevitable and said, "I *am* sad."

Madame Auntie nodded, like she'd known all along. "It's okay. I was sad for a long time, too."

"You were?"

Madame Auntie smiled. It was not a happy smile or even an ironic smile. It was a smile that laughed at the universe, rather than crying. "My husband died. And I know, I am not supposed to say these things now. My nieces all tell me, it's not right. But we had an old marriage. A long one. Traditional. He made so many of the decisions. I hadn't made a decision for myself—on my own—for forty years. I was . . . oh, what's that word. It's a beautiful English word. *Untethered.* I was untethered."

Imogen held her breath. *And how did you find your mooring again?* "Are you still untethered?"

Madame Auntie snorted. A proud expression of a proud woman. "No. My nieces made me go to therapy. *Go talk to someone,* they said. I hated it. Oh, I *hated* it. But they were right. It helped. I never told them this—that they were right. But they know, and they are smug about it."

Imogen laughed despite herself.

Madame Auntie shook her head. "And I found books. So many books. So much sadness and so much grief. But they taught me I was not alone. Told me my suffering was not unique. It was mine, of course. But everyone had their own. Every book was like it was written just for me and my sadness. And to not be alone, that was the important thing. The only thing."

Imogen nodded. She had nothing to say to that. No other question to offer. No polite ability to laugh away what Madame Auntie had said. And from the look on Madame Auntie's face, the woman knew it. So Imogen looked back down at the book in her hand. Maybe it wasn't what she thought it was. Maybe it was just a notebook full of scribbles and sketches. She flipped open to a random page.

And there it was:

In truth the sun does not rise, but Earth

Spins with all her might to bear creation

Imogen dropped the notebook like she'd been burned by it. Auntie leaned over like nothing had happened, handing her back the notebook, telling her to be more careful. Madame Auntie was feeling jumpy enough without books flying around the store. Imogen took the notebook back, not quite knowing why but also knowing she couldn't leave Madame Auntie there, holding the notebook in the middle of the air, hanging.

Because it turned out, Daniella Korres—the coolest girl in the fucking world—was anachronisticblonde.

And Imogen thought she might throw up.

17

One Wild and Precious Life

1:03 P.M.
Rinn

The worst part about giving this tour of the bookstore was that Rinn could tell that Maya could tell that Rinn had it planned out for weeks.

It was because Rinn *had* planned this tour for weeks.

"And over here we've got the store's old-school cash register," said Rinn as she died slowly inside.

"Wow," said Maya in a way that was meant to indicate that she was visibly impressed. Rinn could tell that Maya wasn't, and the fact that she was trying so hard was only making it all worse for Rinn.

Maya got up close to the register. "I haven't seen one of these since *I* worked retail when I was a teen a thousand years ago back in my hometown."

"Oh?" asked Rinn, swallowing every last inch of pride that she had left. "What's your hometown?"

"Houston," said Maya in that overly chipper way that she did when a situation was growing increasingly uncomfortable.

Rinn had learned this about Maya in the last half hour. Maya overcompensated for stress with overly performative cheerfulness. It was like seeing a version of herself reflected tenfold, and Rinn wished she could bury herself in a fort of books and never have to come out ever again.

"Wait, is that one of those credit card swipers?" Maya pointed to the imprint machine that was truly from 1996. To get it to work, Rinn would put the card in, then receipt paper, then she'd swipe the handle over the whole thing. It made a nice *katching-katchung* noise as she used it.

"It is indeed," said Rinn.

Maya picked up the device, wonder all across her face. "Can you even take imprints of cards anymore? I mean, why wouldn't you just use a Square account?"

Rinn opened her mouth to explain. That it added to the charm of Wild Nights Bookstore and Emporium. That yes, sometimes it was a drag that they had to write down credit card numbers since half of them didn't have an embossed edge anymore that would imprint against the machine. That sure, it meant sometimes Rinn spent her day arguing with credit card companies to make sure the charges went through, and they believed that Wild Nights wasn't some kind of fraudulent business. "It adds to the authenticity. I mean, I think our customers really enjoy it. The experience. Of an old machine. And we don't allow phones in the store. So it's like, part of the employees keeping to that as well. Because if we had our phone or a tablet at the register, we would . . . check it? I think. That's what Mr. Hunt always said. We'd be checking our phones and not working, and the customers would sense the inauthenticity of them not being able to use phones but us being able to use them."

But that reasoning sounded hollow even to Rinn. More of an

excuse not to update. More of a cover, a deflection. Not anything real or substantial. Nothing that couldn't be overcome with a sound business argument.

"But you've got electronic records somewhere, of sales, I mean?" Maya switched gears—out of her typical cheerfully-tap-dancing-through-uncomfortable-situations and into what was unfortunately genuine concern.

"I have no idea," said Rinn. *God, why didn't they have electronic records? Or a Square machine?* Those devices just hooked up to a phone and *swipe swipe*—you had a business.

Rinn's mask of polite friendliness fell as she thought about all the hours she wasted calling the credit card companies and taking imprints of credit cards and logging her transactions with a paper receipt. She felt a little bit like crying.

Why was Archer Hunt Junior doing this to them? Making them jump through so many hoops just to do the bare minimum of their job. Hoops that nobody else'd had to jump through for twenty years. Rinn had to talk to someone. Anyone. AJ? Imogen? Maybe Imogen since she dealt with inventory. "And that concludes our tour."

Maya gave her a strange look. "But. We just did a tour of the YA bookshelf and the cash register. Isn't there more to the store? Like that whole upstairs section?"

"Nope, that's it, that's all that you need to know," said Rinn, desperate for this torture to be over so that she could go and find Imogen.

"Isn't there like a famous bank vault filled with crime novels somewhere in here?" Maya turned around both ways, trying to see if she could spy the room over her shoulder.

Of course Maya would pick up on Rinn's favorite part of the entire store. "You're right. It's upstairs, on the left. Absolutely incredible. I swear I'm not just doing this because you're not Brock, but I have to go do something. Right now."

Rinn ran off before she could hear Maya's response.

Imogen was in the cookbook section of the store, reshelving books and talking to that woman with the collection of designer scarves.

Rinn called out to her. "Imogen. I need you for a second."

Imogen, holding a black book that she was possibly about to shelve, looked half-sick and half-relieved.

It wasn't Rinn's primary objective, but she had to ask again, "Are you okay?"

Imogen shook her head, like she was clearing water out of her ears. "Yeah. I'm all right."

"I've got to ask you a question," said Rinn. "It's about inventory."

Imogen's face scrunched up with concern. "You're the second person to ask me about that today."

"Who else asked?"

Imogen shrugged. "Daniella, actually. It was before I'd found out about Eli. I thought she was trying to cover her tracks, but maybe she was just trying to figure out that shipment that turned out to be all those fake shoes that he'd ordered."

"Did she say she knew anything, anything else, about the inventory?"

Imogen shook her head. "No, where is this going? We all know the store is closing. Why are you tracking down inventory?"

"I've just. I've got a suspicion here."

"Suspicion of what?" asked Imogen, eyebrows narrowed until a little V of a crease appeared between them.

But Rinn was already in motion. "I'll let you know when I find out."

Back in the corner of the self-help section, AJ was listening to music and double-checking that all the books were shelved properly. Rinn knew that's what he did when he couldn't handle any more customer service for the hour. Nobody wanted to talk in the self-help section. They wanted to keep their head down, picking out a book. Or their head down, reading a book.

"Have you seen Daniella?" asked Rinn, tapping him on the shoulder at the same time to get his attention.

AJ pulled out his earbuds, tilted his head. Rinn repeated the question.

"Last I saw, I think she was in the office," said AJ. "Why?"

Rinn waved him off with her hands. "I'll explain. I've just got to find Daniella first."

And so Rinn was off like a shot, trying to track down the threads of what was really going wrong at Wild Nights Bookstore and Emporium.

18

What Men or Gods Are These?

1:04 P.M.
Daniella

Daniella tried to take a step forward, away from Brock. She had enough experience to know when somebody couldn't be trusted. She had enough experience to trust all the instincts that were lighting up in her body, in her muscles. *Run*, they said. *Flee*, they begged. She continued to walk toward the door, trying to get out of the room, trying somehow to get there quickly but also, to not draw attention to how much she was rushing away.

The art of doing a thing so smoothly that nobody noticed it was happening was something that Daniella had perfected over the years. She had a light tread. An easy way of leaving the room so that she just disappeared. Those were, however, tactics that worked best in a crowd. A party. A full house. A room full of siblings.

Not an empty room with just Daniella and a man who was watching her every move.

Brock grabbed her by the wrist—his wide palm sparking a

jolt of fear through her body. "Don't hurry off. I've got you all to myself now."

"Stop." Daniella had never heard her voice so quiet. She felt her words grow small and dull. She had meant to shout it. But it was only that mere whisper that had come out of her mouth. That small piece of protest that didn't want to draw notice but had to speak up. "Let go of me."

His grip grew firmer. Then he leaned in, so that his nose settled in behind her hair and her neck. He took a deep breath in. "Now, you don't mean that, do you? I feel like we could be friends."

Daniella felt a shudder from her toes to a prickling sensation that shivered across her scalp. His hand was only in one spot, but she felt him everywhere. *Get off get off get off.* Did she say those words out loud or did she just think them? Why hadn't *stop* been enough? *Why hadn't no been enough?*

"Stop." This was slightly louder than the last time. Like a shot that had gone off in the quiet room. The piece of her that wanted to fade off into an invisible specter knew that it had lost. She'd have to start making noise, now.

"I don't think you need to get nasty." Brock's hold on her wrist grew insistent.

Daniella tasted real fear in her mouth, metallic and dry. A tannic, astringent taste. Like a cup of tea that had been left brewing for half the day in the kitchen. But, even then, Daniella wouldn't let the tea go to waste. She'd drink it. Fear was there to save her. And she still had plenty of fight left in her. She stomped hard—the heel of her combat boots coming directly into contact with the toes of his fancy loafers.

Brock let her go, just for a second, but a second was all that Daniella needed. She scrambled toward the door, before Brock had any more time to register what had happened, before he started shouting—Daniella had enough experience in this life to know that there would be shouting—and yanked open the door.

This is it. Almost there.

And that's when Rinn Olivera fell through the open door. She looked like she had been about to say something. About to ask for help for a task around the store. But Rinn didn't say anything at all. She squeaked, stumbled for a moment, and then found her footing at the last second. She took in the chairs all over the place, she took in Brock Harvey hopping up and down on one foot. He transitioned from yelping to finding real curse words to screaming in the span of about fifteen seconds.

Then Rinn Olivera took a good long look at Daniella. She was assessing the bleached-blond hair and the wild look in Daniella's eyes, she had to have been. And then Rinn looked back over to the man even Daniella knew was her writing hero, the man finally finding his footing. It definitely did not look great for Daniella. Daniella didn't know what to do. She looked like she had attacked him. She had, in fact, attacked him. Just in self-defense.

Brock did know what to do, though. He recovered so quickly it was nearly inhuman.

"Just came in here and was assaulted by this hellcat. Don't think I won't tell this to your boss, miss." And then he gave Rinn that wink that he had tried to give Daniella the last time, when he had first walked into the store. "I know *you'll* understand, won't you?"

Daniella waited for it, the moment where the other shoe would drop. The moment where Rinn's anger would be directed at Daniella.

Daniella had enough experience that she knew, deep in her bones, that she always bore the brunt of other people's behavior, no matter who started what. No matter who was responsible for what. She was a girl, and it was next to always all her fault.

But Rinn surprised Daniella. She, somehow, was no longer charmed by the wink. Rinn flinched, almost like she had been spat on.

And Daniella was frozen, frozen, frozen.

How ironic that she had written a poem about how the earth would always keep spinning, when Daniella felt as though the entire world and time had stopped all at once. She lived here now. Among these boxes and files and wacky furniture and terrible men.

And then Brock Harvey adjusted his hair, slicking it back with his hand, and walked out of the room. He didn't seem to have registered that he'd lost Rinn Olivera. He didn't seem like he'd lost anything at all. It was a saunter, his exit. The walk of a man who believed he owned any place, any space that he moved through.

Like he owned her.

Rinn came closer slowly. She reached out her hand, intentionally not touching or grabbing Daniella. Just reaching out, ready to accept. "Are you okay?"

But *okay* was so far from it that Daniella could only swat Rinn's hand away.

Daniella put a hand to her chest, right over the bone there. There was a horrible pain growing there. She tapped on the hard bone in the middle of her chest. *Her sternum, right? Was that what it was called?* If she could just press on it, maybe she could let out a breath. Maybe she could take in a breath. She kept pressing, tried gripping with her fingertips, but none of it helped. None of it did anything. Daniella still couldn't breathe.

"Daniella?" Rinn took a step closer. "Danny?"

Daniella didn't look up. She instead found a rhythm with her body. Forward to her toes, backward to her heels. Forward, toward the knocked-over chairs. Backward, toward the boxes of evidence of all of Eli's bad decisions. "Get out of here, Rinn."

"I wanted to check on you." Rinn's voice was somehow both quiet and resonant. Not loud, but not a thing that Daniella could ignore.

Rocking forward and back wasn't helping. The tapping, tapping, tapping on her chest wasn't helping. If Daniella could just get a deep breath in, everything would be okay. She would be okay. Nothing had happened and she was lucky and if she could just draw in a breath, that would help. Daniella knew it would help. "I'm fine."

"You're shaking back and forth and doing this weird tapping thing on your chest. I'd say that is decidedly not fine. Like if you were an old dude, I'd be worried you were having a heart attack or something."

"Oh, would you?" Daniella stood, rage flaring. She stopped rocking; she stopped tapping. She made herself as large and imposing as she ever knew how to make herself. "What about now?"

But Rinn was still looking at Daniella like she was convinced that Daniella could not possibly be okay. And when Rinn had an idea, nothing could stop her, come hell or high water—that much had always been apparent about Rinn Olivera.

And then Rinn opened her mouth and proved all of Daniella's suspicions right. "You're not okay. There's no way you could be. I saw him. I mean, not all of it. But I saw you afterward, and I saw him. I know what happened."

"Oh, and you know everything about everything, don't you?" Daniella inched closer, she shoved her face directly into Rinn's.

"Take a deep breath. Deep breath in, deep breath out." Rinn said it in such a practiced, methodical way. Like she really had talked another person out of this before with a little bit of can-do and a sunny disposition.

It made Daniella want to scream into a void. It made her want to curl up into a ball inside of herself and become as small and invisible as possible. "Just let me ask you something, Rinn Olivera—do you, I mean, is there anything you aren't an expert on by reading a fucking book about it?"

Rinn took a step back. She was not expecting the person she helped to fight her, clearly. "I'm not just an expert from books."

But Daniella had more fight in her still. She had hours, days, months, years of fight in her. It didn't matter that she couldn't breathe. It didn't matter that she wished she was small and invisible. She was clearly being seen, and she would do anything, anything to get out from the microscopic gaze of Rinn Fucking Olivera. "Articles, too? How delightful. Is there any time in your measurably perfect life that you have learned by actually experiencing it? Or are you the world's greatest living expert on second-hand knowledge?"

Rinn swallowed hard. She opened her mouth. Then she closed it. But then, she seemed to come to another decision and said, "You're a bitch."

That's when Daniella's hand went flying.

There was a *crack* and then dread—furious and intense.

There's no way that hadn't stung, because Daniella's palm stung. A numbness overcame Daniella. Shame, hate, fear, anger all washed through her. A knowledge that she had become her mother. It consumed her until she wanted to crumple, to fall.

Daniella had never slapped another person in her entire life. Oh, she'd fought. Had just stomped on the toe of an overly handsy creep. But she hadn't ever actually slapped someone—just to get another person to shut their damned mouth.

Rinn stared at Daniella like she couldn't believe it.

Daniella couldn't believe it, either.

Then Rinn held her hand up to her face, wincing as skin came in contact with skin.

Daniella could see the red handprint forming, as if by magic, across Rinn's face.

Neither one of them moved. Neither one of them spoke. It was as if neither knew where to go from there. They were in some strange and unknown land. The rules were different. And what those rules were, well, that was either of their guesses.

19

Heart, We Will Forget Him

1:11 P.M.
Rinn

For a moment, Rinn flexed and tensed—ready to hit back, to step forward and fight. But then she saw the way Daniella had crumpled. It was her face, first. Then the weight in her entire body gave way. And then, Daniella had gotten back up, dusted off her knees, only to turn and flee, leaving Rinn alone in the office.

Rinn had never felt more like she'd gotten it all so terribly wrong. That image of Daniella's crumpled face haunted her. Would possibly always haunt her.

Rinn realized she was still touching her face. She pulled her hand away, then touched back on her cheek. She winced. She was going to have a red mark there, Rinn was sure. Rinn wondered—almost as though she were outside of herself, looking on—if the red mark would be in the shape of a hand or not.

She hoped not.

Rinn took a deep breath. She exhaled. That's what all of those online meditation videos told her to do. The ones the school counselor had told her to watch. Something about finding mindfulness with breathing. Finding your body and rooting yourself into the present by paying attention to the rhythm of oxygen in and oxygen out of your body. Rinn still felt all the tension rolling around in her stomach, but the deep breath did help. Did allow her to relax her shoulders, get her stance to loosen, get her mind to pull away from fight-or-flight mode. Rinn took a deep breath and decided—against her impulse to avoid—to go after Daniella.

But Daniella was not anywhere on the first floor. Not anywhere in the larger back storage room, either. Rinn took the stairs two at a time, hoping to find her somewhere upstairs. She heard a noise above her. Books slapping against the floor. Books slapping against each other. Rinn dared to hope it was Daniella. Though what Rinn planned on doing after finding her was anyone's guess. Yell some more? Apologize? Rinn didn't have the answer. But she was in pursuit, and she was not about to give up. Rinn never gave up if she could help it, and she always believed that she could help it. Everything, Rinn assumed, was in her power if she tried hard enough and got just a little bit lucky.

The school counselor had called that *a control mechanism*, but Rinn couldn't quite see what was so wrong with control mechanisms.

Rinn followed the sound, or so she thought. It was difficult to pinpoint. It kept ricocheting off walls and bouncing so that at first she thought it was in the dollar-book section, then the old romance novels. There old romance trade paperbacks melted into the classics and then into the adventure books in mass market fiction. Depending on the book they could go for anywhere between $4.99 and ninety-nine cents.

But still, no Daniella.

And still, no source of the sound. She went past the hanging roller girl by the back set of stairs and went around the memoirs from the mid-twentieth century that were stacked up on an old player piano. She passed the dollar-record collection and stopped right by the bank vault door. That's where the sound was coming from—bargain mystery and crime in the old repurposed vault. Made sense why the noise had been reverberating around the floor and impossible to pinpoint.

Luck, it turns out, was not on Rinn's side. Daniella was not to be found in the old bank vault.

Eli.

He was sitting all the way in the back of the vault, his legs crisscrossed. He was sorting through used books to put in the section. Hence all the slapping sounds. He was taking all of his own frustrations out against the inanimate objects. Rinn touched her cheek reflexively at the sound.

Better to slap a book, really. It was a thought Rinn wouldn't have had before an hour ago. She was big into treating books as preciously as possible. She wanted to respect the written word. But there was still the stinging sensation that prickled through her cheek.

Rinn stared at Eli for a moment, unsure what to do. She could back out of the vault and pretend like she hadn't found him.

But then again, maybe Eli could help. Daniella at least trusted him, and Daniella must have needed someone she trusted right now. At least, that's how Rinn assumed Daniella felt. But Daniella had been harder to pin down than anyone Rinn had ever met before. Rinn turned, about to vacate the vault again, when her shoe squeaked against the floor and gave her presence away.

Eli looked up. "Oh, hey, what's going on?"

"Aren't you supposed to be in the office?" Rinn's voice came out sharper than she had intended.

"Yeah, but Danny kicked me out, so I'm up here hiding until she's out of there. Is the coast clear? Can I go down now?" Eli asked the question so wide-eyed.

Rinn shook her head. If only he'd been there. If he'd been in the room, maybe Harvey wouldn't have attacked. Maybe there would have been a way to have saved Daniella from him. But Eli had left the room, and Harvey had walked in, and Maya had left him alone, and Rinn hadn't thought to go with him, and nothing could be avoided now. It wasn't any of their faults. It was Harvey's. The consequences were all that were left to be dealt with now.

Rinn came to a decision. "I need you to go check on Daniella."

"Why?"

Rinn hesitated. This wasn't Rinn's story to tell. Rinn didn't even know exactly what had happened. She'd seen only the aftermath of it all. The wild, wide-eyed hurt on Daniella's face. The rage building in Brock Harvey's. That he has so smoothly smothered it to appear genteel and proper. Rinn might have been naive, but she wasn't stupid. There weren't many reasons a girl risked her employment to stomp on a guy when she was left alone in a room with him, but none of them reflected well on the dude.

Rinn also wasn't sure what that meant for her freshly slapped face, and she didn't want to think too hard about that, either. "Look, I can't really say. But I can say that she needs a friend and not to be alone right now. Don't ask her too many questions. Just go be a friend to her."

Eli stared for a moment. "I'm not sure that we're friends."

Rinn felt her rage boiling up inside of her. "What else would you be?"

Eli looked at her for a moment. "Not friends."

Rinn stared back, unwilling to yield in this. "She needs a friend, Eli. Can you do that? Can you go and sit with her and make sure she's not alone and not be a jerk about it? Or are you going to sit here and argue over the semantics of friendship before dealing with the fact that Daniella has an actual problem?"

Rinn didn't realize that she cared quite so much about a girl who was so rude to her, but that was life. Fall in love with boys from afar and treat mortal enemies like friends. Just a regular day for Rinn here.

But Eli was a difficult creature to keep on topic. "Is that a handprint on your face?"

Rinn backed up. Shook her head. "No. I don't think so. Not really."

Eli raised an eyebrow. "Which is it?"

Rinn blinked. Why couldn't she behave normally when she needed to tell a white lie? It wasn't even a huge lie. She needed to be able to cover herself for like ten seconds and her body was in absolute revolt. "I don't think so."

"Why wouldn't you know if it was a handprint?"

"Do you see any mirrors up here?" Rinn attempted to deflect.

But, of course, that's when Eli pointed to the mirrored surface hanging in the middle of the bank vault full of books.

Of course Old Mr. Hunt had put a freaking mirror in here.

Rinn looked into the mirror. It was a flash of an image, then she looked away. She didn't really want to register what she'd seen. "A handprint."

And Eli, who seemed most of the time like the most impulsive boy on the planet, just stood there like he had all the time in the world. "Any explanation for how a red mark the size of a hand got on your face?"

Rinn crossed her arms, fighting the shame flushing through her. "Yes. There sure is."

"Are you going to share with the class, Ms. Olivera?" Nobody could mock the tone of an authority figure like Eli.

"No." Rinn did her best to steady her breath. "Are you going to go find Daniella?"

"How did you get that handprint on your face, Rinn Olivera?"

It was a leading question, and Rinn, heaven help her, fell right into the trap. "It wasn't her fault."

Eli stared for a minute. He looked, well, mad. It was odd. He wasn't a particularly large boy. But he seemed larger suddenly. Puffed out. Barely in control and not in an impish or fun-loving sort of way. "What the hell did you say to her?"

"I'm not sure. I think Harvey came onto her. And I wanted to know if she was okay. And she lost it, Eli. She lost it at me."

"She lost it at you for no other reason? Are you sure you didn't *say* something? Daniella doesn't fly off the handle for no reason." That tensed threat wound its way through Eli's voice.

It was the first time that Rinn had heard Eli use Daniella's full name. "Why am I supposed to know how to handle this? Because I'm a girl? I'm *trying*, and somehow that doesn't count for anything, but I ask you to try for once and you say you're not even her friend. What the hell is that supposed to mean, Eli? Why can't you go talk to her? Why do I have to know how to do everything around here? You have access to the internet, too. You can figure out how to help a girl after a dude has been creepy to her. I am *tired* of being the one keeping it together." Rinn was out of breath by the time she got to the end of that speech.

Eli stared for a minute. Then he nodded, turned on his toes, and ran out of the vault and down the stairs. As soon as Eli left, Rinn sagged against the bookshelf.

She was tired. She was scared. A girl she knew had been harassed. Her favorite author in the world had done the harassing. She was pretty sure that the store's owner was the reason why the bookstore was failing—and that while he had the motivation to sink the whole enterprise on purpose, she had no idea how or even what he had done. Eli had expected her to know how to handle the aftermath of Brock Freaking Harvey perfectly. Daniella had made fun of Rinn for trying to handle everything perfectly. Rinn's breathing got shorter and shorter, shallower and shallower, until there was little air left for her to take in.

Rinn knew she needed to calm down. Knew she needed to take a deep breath and prevent herself from hyperventilating. Knew that this was a panic attack. She hadn't had one in ages. But she knew the name of what was happening to her. Knew that all of her safeguards and control mechanisms were failing her now.

It was just that knowing she was having a panic attack didn't stop it from happening.

As she opened her mouth to take in a deep breath, she broke into sobs.

In the middle of the old, echoing bank vault, Rinn began to cry.

20

Awaiting the Arrival of the Uncertain

1:19 P.M.
Daniella

Daniella was, she was pretty much certain, just about the only person who knew how to get to the roof of Wild Nights Bookstore and Emporium.

The view wasn't all that great. It overlooked an unremarkable square of downtown Chicago and was blocked by some of the old, original skyscrapers from the late 1800s that surrounded them in Wicker Park. It was one of those facts picked up from walking around the city. Usually by a family member who liked acting like a tour guide to visiting relatives—standing at the center of a group of people they had corralled into listening to them—talking about some young architect nobody had heard of outside of the city, who had both built a particular building *and* who had maybe met Frank Lloyd Wright or Louis Sullivan or whatever. Daniella had overheard enough to pick up which buildings were famous nationally and which ones were famous locally. But it didn't matter that everyone on the street had an opinion about half the buildings in the greater Chicagoland area. This one, this rooftop, felt like it belonged to Daniella because nobody else ever came up here.

Just her and the mosquitoes.

The warm breeze blew across Daniella's face, and she took a deep inhale.

Daniella preferred winter in Chicago. She knew that was insane to most people. But she liked the way the snow dampened everything. Made the world go quiet. Muffled the hustle and bustle of the streets below. There was a sense of camaraderie in the winter, of communal survival. There were puffy coats and crunchy snow beneath her boots. There were two layers of scarves and her favorite pompom hat. The air smelled cleaner, too.

No mosquitoes in winter, either.

The breeze on the roof was freezing in the winter, but nobody else would dare go up there when it was fifteen degrees out. She'd grab a hot mug of anything from the break room just to keep her fingers warm so she could sit up on the roof for an extra ten minutes in the winter. Sometimes it would snow and she'd watch as the little flurries melted into the steaming mug.

Today, however, was one of those smoldering, stinking days of summer that Chicago was infamous for. The kind of heat that would really stagnate were it not for the breeze slowly lifting off the lake. She slapped at a mosquito buzzing around her arm. And of course, on today of all days, Daniella heard the jiggle of the door handle. Somebody was coming up onto *her* roof.

This would never happen in the winter. *Never.*

The door swung open, and Eli poked his head around.

"Wow, I knew you came up here sometimes, but this is really the world's worst view of the city."

"Shut up." But Daniella didn't have the heart to put any force behind the command.

And Eli knew it. "Bet you thought you were the only one who knew how to get up here."

"I *was* the only one who knew how to get up here." Daniella crossed her arms over her chest just to emphasize her displeasure.

"Nah," said Eli, the door clicking behind him as it closed. "I figured it out ages ago. But I knew you liked to come up here alone, so I tried not to bother you. And now I don't even regret it because, really, this is the crappiest view. I can see straight into someone's overstuffed office and the back alley of a building that probably has a very nice facade, if I could see it. You can always tell the buildings that have nice facades because they're really shitty on the back side. Like all the money went to the front and the front alone."

"Eli," said Daniella.

"Yeah?" He looked so earnest as he said it. Like she really was about to say something nice and supportive.

Daniella shook her head. "Stop talking."

"Alright," said Eli, and he perched down beside her. "You gonna say anything?"

"Nope," said Daniella.

"Fair enough." Eli moved out from his crouch so he was reclined back on his hands.

And so they sat there for who knows how long, their fingers inches apart, their bodies both leaned back. The sun was hot and sweltering—except for that lazy, steady breeze that kept coming back from Lake Michigan, reminding them that that lake effect they'd been told about one day in earth science class hadn't been totally bogus.

Not that Daniella thought science was totally bogus. It was, in its purest form, observations based in math, which Daniella loved. But there was something about learning a thing and feeling its effects on her face that made the idea of that science feel real to her. The lake effect was true because she was sitting on a roof and the air hadn't stagnated. The climate was changing because the winters in Chicago were whiplashing between relatively mild to polar vortex. Daniella shivered. But it wasn't from thinking of winter or polar vortexes or snowstorms. It wasn't even from the breeze, because that was a comforting thing, keeping the sweat from accumulating under her armpits and beneath her bra. Keeping the mosquitoes off her face.

But the shiver went through her whole body again. She had to let it out somehow.

And, finally, Daniella said it, because she needed to tell someone, even if she was mostly just telling herself. All she needed was for that shiver to stop. Needed it to never take hold of her again. "Brock Harvey attacked me in the break room like a creepy psychopath."

"Jesus," said Eli.

Daniella laughed. It wasn't funny, she knew. But somehow, his anger gave her license to laugh, to giggle. To release all of that pent-up energy in a strange bubble of joy rather than the cracking release of rage that Daniella had let out on Rinn. "It's fine."

Eli reached out now, took Daniella's hand. It was a gentle hold, meant to make her pay attention. He released it as soon as he had her eye contact. "You know it's not fine, right?"

Daniella nodded. "I know. I know it's not fine. But it wasn't the first time, and as much as I hope, I don't think it's the last time. So I'm fine, and it's fine. It's not okay, and it's never okay, and maybe, somehow, I'm not okay. But I'll have to be, and also it's fine."

"And you say my logic doesn't make sense." Eli shook his head.

Daniella shrugged. "You know what I mean, though, right?"

"I do," said Eli.

Daniella looked over the edge of the roof. She could make out the horizon, in a sliver between two other brown-gray buildings. She didn't look, but she reached out for Eli's hand, threaded her fingers through his. "I'm glad you came up here."

For a moment, everything stopped. It went muffled and quiet, like it was winter. In that moment, the roof was no longer Daniella's. It was both of theirs. It was this—two hands intertwined on a rooftop over a city.

"Me too," was all that Eli said. But he said it like he understood. That he was welcome there when nobody else was.

Daniella looked over at him—he was still staring at the sliver of horizon like she had been. What Daniella really wanted to ask was *How did you know about the poetry?* but she couldn't ask that, not yet. It was too real of a question. "How'd you know about the astrology meme thing?"

"Pops up in my feed all the time. It took me a while to figure out who it was. I kept assuming it was all these other people. But it was you. It had always been you." It was Eli's turn to shrug. "Isn't it funny how we make all these assumptions, but in the end we've always known the answer? It's just not obvious. I mean, you love math. It would make sense that you like stars. Like telling a story about stars."

"Yeah," said Daniella. "It's never obvious. The best things are always a secret."

"The best things?" Eli leaned back, his hand still entwined with Daniella's.

Daniella leaned back with him. "Definitely."

He looked over. "Tell me a secret, then."

Daniella laughed. It felt good to laugh. Felt good to forget everything that was making her head spin—hangovers and creepy dudes and poor girls she'd slapped—and just laugh as she looked into Eli's solid brown eyes and counted his freckles. "I think I'm in love with you."

Except Daniella hadn't meant to say that at all. She'd meant to say she writes poetry, which was a safe secret, an easy secret. Not for anyone else, but Eli already knew that one, so it might not have been as scary.

Instead, she'd gone and told a secret that she'd been keeping from herself for years.

Eli's hand tensed in her own. "Look, you're going through a lot right now."

Daniella's tensed right back, so that what had been a soft, gentle touch was now two hands, gripping for control. "Don't tell me how I feel."

"I'm not," said Eli.

Daniella pulled her hand away. Wrenched it, more like. "You are. You know you are. You don't get to decide how I feel. It might not be convenient, but it is true. I love you."

"You can't." Eli shook his head. His eyes were wide.

She looked at Eli. He was tense. Daniella knew that kind of tension well. He was afraid. She felt it nearly every time somebody told her that they liked her, that they thought they loved her. How funny to see the expression now, rather than to feel it. To be its recipient rather than its instigator. To know that she cared and that the person didn't care back.

To know that she had been right about love all along. That it was a threat to her when somebody felt it. And it was a threat to others when she was under its sway.

"I can, and I will." Daniella knew a rejection when she saw one, when she felt one. The knowledge didn't make the sting go away. Didn't make her heart stop hammering or make her breath come back any slower. She got up. She took strides as long as she possibly could and wrenched open the door.

Eli was shouting at her from behind. Maybe telling her to stop. Maybe asking her to wait, for him to explain. But Daniella didn't need explanations. She had seen enough. She didn't need to be let down kindly or gently. She needed to get off this roof. She didn't want one of her favorite places ruined by the sensations running through her. She didn't always want to think of the fear and panic on his face when she thought about the roof at Wild Nights Bookstore and Emporium.

Because that's the other thing Daniella realized as she was leaping down the stairs, two at a time. That might have been the last time she ever sat on the roof of the store. She'd have no further memories there. And her last image of the space—her very last one—would be that horrible wounded expression that was on Eli's face as she turned and fled the sight of him.

Daniella reached into her pockets for a pen. She was going to write down, to draw, to scribble, to at least take these horrible feelings and make them useful or productive. But Daniella patted herself all over. She didn't have a pen. She reached into her bag. She found her notebook and let out the most enormous sigh of relief.

But then she opened it.

This wasn't her notebook. This was the old ledger with all the bookstore's finances in it. And if she didn't have her notebook— her sacred, precious poetry notebook—that could mean only one thing.

Daniella's secret book of poetry was floating around the bookstore for the entire world to find.

21

Left No Light to Guide the World

1:47 P.M.
Imogen

There was a strange hiccuping sound coming from the second floor.

Imogen looked at Jo, who looked back at Imogen.

"Okay, but do you hear that?" Imogen had to know. It was the oddest sound. Almost human. Almost like a crying infant, but also almost like a whimpering dog. Imogen didn't even know what could be making that kind of sound.

Jo nodded. "Definitely. I definitely hear that sound."

"But what is it?" Imogen was mystified. She'd gone into the office, looking for everyone. Half the staff was missing, and something was clearly up. She'd found Jo instead.

"No idea, but I've got to go check on what it is before the few customers we do have hear it and get scared off." Jo started to walk out of the office.

"I'm coming with you," said Imogen.

"What? Are we glued at the hip now?" Jo's sarcasm reached

some pretty peak levels for someone who was trying to show she cared so deeply.

Imogen didn't mean to go straight to a childish, petulant place. But her knee-jerk reaction could not be helped. "Sure, next thing you know I'll follow you into the bathroom."

Jo sighed. "Fine. I'll give you a lecture about boundaries and sarcasm later. First, to the mystery noise."

It took them a minute. The sound warbled around the second floor, with no distinct source. A thudding added to the warbling, creating even more distortion to the sound. The rhythm and the whine echoed and bounced until it sounded like it was coming from everywhere and nowhere all at once.

Jo waved Imogen over. "It's got to be coming from the bank vault. The vault is the only room in this entire building that does that."

Imogen didn't have an argument there. She couldn't place the sound at all, and she had no idea what could be making it.

Jo was clearly already picturing her own personal doomsday scenarios on what awaited her in the bank vault. "I swear to Christ if I find a stray cat I will lose it. I do not have the patience to deal with a feral animal today, not on top of everything else going on."

Jo stopped up short when she got to the door of the bank vault. Imogen nearly ran into her back. She stepped around Jo, trying to get a view of the scene.

It was *not* a feral cat.

Imogen looked to Jo for a moment. She wasn't sure why. Maybe it was instinct at this point. Look to the adult in the room to see if they actually knew how to handle the batshit insanity that was life.

But, of course, Jo didn't know what to do with a sobbing Rinn Olivera any more than Imogen did.

This was not the Little Miss Sunshine they were accustomed to working with, and Imogen could understand how this would freeze even the least adult of adults that Imogen had ever known. But Jo must have hit her limits when she caught sight of a girl sobbing maniacally in a room and throwing dollar-mystery novels across the floor.

Imogen had to duck under an airborne James Patterson. Jo took an Evanovich to the chest. But it was when the hardbound Sayers novels went flying that Imogen came to a decision. After what felt like a lifetime of standing still, of staying in place, of this strange, numbing immobility, Imogen didn't just want to take an action.

She needed to.

Imogen stepped forward, reached out, and gave the lightest touch she could at the upper part of Rinn's arm. "Hey, Rinn."

Rinn responded with a louder, wider-mouthed sob. She slammed what looked like a very nice copy of an original Nancy Drew onto the floor. Imogen did her best not to wince. Right now, a person was way more important than a book.

"That's okay." Imogen wasn't even sure why she'd said it. She didn't understand what Rinn had said, or attempted to say—not as words. But she understood the feeling. If there was one advantage to the way that Imogen had felt on and off for the past year, it was getting a sense of the feeling behind what people were saying. It was understanding what sadness was—sometimes more than a feeling—and that it was a thing she could almost taste, could almost touch at times, it was so real.

Rinn looked up, startled, but still crying. Her eyes were wide and haunted.

"We're going to go to the bathroom, okay, Rinn? I need you to nod at least once that you understand."

Rinn kept crying, but she also bobbed her head up and down. She got it. She really, really got it. She also apparently couldn't stop crying.

"Okay, and I'm also going to need you to drop that book. We don't need any more projectiles for right now. I promise if you still need to throw books after we go to the bathroom, you can." Imogen put a supporting hand underneath Rinn's elbow and helped Rinn off the floor. Rinn didn't resist or try to protest. She dropped the last book in her hand. That had only been *The Woman in the Window*, so Imogen didn't even mind that one being left crumpled and collapsed on the floor.

Imogen half propped up Rinn the entire way to the bathroom, past a stunned Jo and all the way down the stairs, toward the break room. Rinn was still half-limp in Imogen's arms, but she still kept putting one foot in front of the other until she got to the back.

Walking into the employee bathroom felt like returning to the scene of the crime, in some way. There was still a light dusting of her hair along the edges of the floor. Imogen hated that Daniella had been right about that. But the hair was the least of Imogen's worries right now.

Imogen turned on the cool water on the tap. She held back Rinn's perfect curly hair. "I'm going to need you to splash your face with that, okay?"

Rinn was still crying, but it was more of a whimper and less of a sob. She nodded again, then she leaned over and practically submerged her head under the tiny faucet, which, honestly, shouldn't have been possible given the size of the sink. Rinn took a startled breath as soon as the cold water hit her face. Her breath shuddered, and then she dunked her head again and began using her hands to splash her entire face. Rinn let out some breaths—Imogen couldn't tell if they were shock from the cold or from the change in states. To go from crying to not crying was in and of itself startling.

Imogen had forgotten. It had been so long since she'd cried. She'd been so sad, but she hadn't cried in ages. Hadn't let it out. Had simply held on to the sadness until it was all consuming.

For a while, the only noise in the room was the running of the tap and the water splashing across Rinn Olivera's face. She pulled herself up from her final submerge under the tap and—with a face dripping with water and melting mascara and a few wet pieces of hair—Rinn sputtered out, "Brock Harvey is a fucking creep."

Imogen nearly dropped Rinn's hair. "What did he do to you?"

"I saw him." Rinn shook her head. Her eyes were still closed. Like she was telling herself something she couldn't quite believe. Like she was remembering the story and she had to get it right, but she also didn't trust herself. Like she'd been taught to never believe herself when she had to say horrible, true things out loud. "I heard him come on to Daniella. She tried to get him to stop, and he didn't listen."

"Shit."

Rinn ducked her head back over the sink. She grabbed the edges, like Imogen had this morning. Perhaps guarding against reality. Perhaps trying to make sense of her own memories. Imogen wouldn't ever know for sure. But she could see the flinch of pain followed by the peace of shutting her eyes against the world for just a moment longer. "She stepped on him—stomped on his feet or his knee or whatever—and then I walked in. I heard her saying *stop* and *no* before I opened the door. I couldn't get the handle open fast enough."

"Jesus."

"And then I tried to find her. And I made it all worse. I was trying to help, and I made it worse. God, I don't even know if she's okay. All I wanted to know was that she was okay." Rinn slowly pulled up from her stoop over the sink. Her face was still dripping, still a mess.

Imogen grabbed some paper towels out of the dispenser and handed them to Rinn. "Let's get you back together in one piece before worrying about her, okay. We can worry about her in a minute."

Rinn took a shuddering deep breath, but she didn't start crying again. "You're good at this."

Imogen took the heel of her hand and made circles against the top of Rinn's back. It was a soothing gesture she'd learned from her mother. That her mother had done when she'd been unable to sleep. "I've read a fair number of self-help articles on the internet. They have all sorts of tips. But most of them can be summarized by the flight-safety-info tip—put on your mask before assisting others."

"Is that what you're doing?" Rinn asked, her eyes direct and so questioning that Imogen could only give her the truth.

"No. Definitely not." Imogen let out a small, hard laugh. "Why is your face red on one side? Or more red. It's just one cheek and your nose."

"Daniella hit me." There was something so sudden about the way Rinn was relaying information. Like she was finding the truth and processing it as she said it aloud. "She slapped me, and I deserved it. I couldn't help her."

Imogen shook her head. "The only people who deserve to be smacked in the face are Nazis, TBH."

Rinn sniffled. "Why are you being so nice to me?"

"*Am* I being nice to you?" Imogen had to look everywhere but at Rinn.

Rinn's voice was the steadiest that it had been in the last half hour. "You know you are."

Imogen began wiping down the water off the sink. She still didn't look at Rinn, and that gave her the buffer to say the truth. "I don't know. I guess I always thought you had this perfect life with your perfect social media presence and your perfect hair and your perfect attitude and your perfect happiness and your perfect ability to make friends. You never seemed human. And it turns out you're just as capable of being cracked as the rest of us. I don't think I've ever seen somebody throw a tantrum by launching books across a bank vault, but I guess there's a first time for everything."

Rinn laughed a little—a sad, self-aware sound that stabbed Imogen right in the heart—and then tilted her head to the side. "Of course I do. Everyone has the ability to be cracked. Most people have a hell of a lot going on under the surface. If there's one thing I've learned from building a social media following, it's that. People reach out all the time, telling me what's going on in their lives, why they're struggling with reading. Everyone's answer is different. But everybody's got something going on under the surface."

Rinn reached out for Imogen's hand. It was the beginning of something small and precious and tentative. An offering of peace. A moment of truce. Or perhaps, friendship. "I think we need to go and find Daniella. And I think we need to talk about Archer Hunt Junior."

It was a strange request, but Imogen took her hand, and together they both went in search of the coolest girl in the world.

22

The Melancholy Mourner There

2:19 P.M.
Daniella

Daniella was *not* going to cry. She was done crying. Sure, she felt nauseous. And sure, she felt the pricking sting starting from behind her eyes. But she was not going to cry. Not a single tear, thank you very much. That was just sweat around her eyes because it was so hot out right now.

She leaned against the brick wall, and then slumped down it.

She was fine. She was okay. Everything would be all right.

Daniella reached around her knees, trying to steady herself against herself.

She stretched her fingers out, digging them into the concrete, like that was digging them into the sand at the shore. Like she was at the edge of the lake and she needed to ground herself to keep from drowning.

A cool metal feeling interrupted the sensation of grating, gritty concrete. Daniella looked down.

A half-empty vape pen.

Daniella took the vape in hand. She looked at it for a minute.

It wasn't the shade of the menthol, minty-green flavor. It was a metallic, slate gray. That could only mean one thing. Inside was a partially used weed pod. One of the mythical few weed pods that Jo had bought and kept hidden in her bag o' vapes. Daniella's hands shook as she clicked it back to life. She didn't feel them shaking, though. She watched them shake, fiddling with the plastic sliding lid. Like she was watching herself fail rather than feeling herself go through any motions.

Then the door crashed open and Daniella nearly jumped out of her own skin. The vape pen fell to the ground, having flown out of her hands. It was Rinn and Imogen. They were holding hands the way friends do—palm over palm, their hands neatly enfolded in each other. It was a careless kind of affection, and it gave Daniella a pang to see it, though she couldn't have said why.

Imogen was the first to lower herself onto the ground. She ducked to a crouch and then she plopped next to Daniella's legs. She looked at Daniella for a moment, then she caught sight of the flash of the metal of the vape pen. She reached for it, flipping it through her fingers the way drummers do with their pens. Maybe Imogen knew a lot of drummers, too. Maybe she was a drummer. Daniella had no clue. There was so much that Daniella didn't know about Imogen. She hadn't realized that before. But in one little finger twirl, Daniella saw how much she didn't know. Saw everything that Daniella had been too busy to pay attention to.

Everything was always right in front of Daniella, and she never seemed to see it until it was too late. If she was being honest with herself, she could have. But Daniella was done being honest with anyone, starting with herself and ending with the rest of the world.

Rinn was more tentative. She stood on the other side of

Daniella's feet for a minute. She didn't really look at Daniella. She didn't look *not* at Daniella, either. It was this strange, distant gaze. Rinn saw Daniella, but she wasn't looking at her. Rinn saw Daniella, but she wasn't quite avoiding her, either. Limbo, trapped in emotional purgatory.

I've done that to her. I've made her afraid of me.

Daniella wished she could apologize. For what she said when she'd been so afraid. For what she'd done. She wished she could go back, undo most of her day.

Most of her year, if she was being honest with herself.

But Daniella didn't have a time machine. She just had poetry and a bad attitude. Daniella looked up, willing Rinn to look at her. And like magic, it worked. They stood there, eyes locked for a moment.

"I'm sorry," said Daniella. It seemed a paltry thing, that apology. "I'm sorry for hitting you. I'm sorry I took everything out on you. I'm sorry."

Rinn seemed to make up her mind. She nodded, almost to herself, and then turned and sat beside Daniella. "I'm sorry, too. I shouldn't have called you a bitch when I could tell you were feeling vulnerable."

Daniella didn't say anything else for a minute. None of them did. They all sat there in a strange, comforting silence. Imogen with her twirling vape. Rinn with her tapping foot. Daniella with her shaking hands. Melting together into a concert of wordless symphony.

Daniella couldn't have said how long they all sat there like that. But she knew she had to be the one to break the spell. She knew it the way she knew when the rhythm was off in a poem. By instinct, by feeling. By hard-won knowledge that made her feel witchy and portentous even if she knew she wasn't. "I hate being alone, you know. I always have. I think it's because I grew up in that house with my mom. Full of siblings but she made it feel so empty that it felt haunted. And not even haunted by my dad. He died in a hospital. But it felt haunted by her, somehow. By all her candles and all her prayers and all her hours on the icons when she wasn't in church. I love the saints; I did as a kid. But she just made it this space filled with her memories and everything she hated losing. And so I hated to be alone in that place. And I hated being stuck there with nothing to do."

Imogen stopped twirling her pen. Rinn stopped tapping her foot. They were both watching her, rapt. Daniella had that ability, she knew. To tell a story. To capture people's attention. It sometimes felt like her one and only skill in this life. That it was a sickness to need an audience. But with these two, it didn't feel like that. It felt like something else altogether. Like connection, maybe. Like a lifeline, too.

"And so I started going out. First it was to parties. Then on dates. If you can call them dates. Hanging out. Anything to get me out of the house. And then I found this place, here. A job. I had so many places to get out. A party one night. A boy another. And then work. Always had work. Always had school, too. It was something to do, you know? To keep from being stuck at home. I couldn't stand it at home anymore. What my mom needed to cope was so different from what I needed. My brothers and sisters, they all escaped, too."

Imogen spoke up first. She spoke so casually. Too casually for Daniella's comfort. "I found this, by the way. In the break room."

Imogen tossed a notebook at Daniella.

Daniella's heart practically stopped for a minute. There it was. Her book of poetry. "Did you read them?"

"I didn't have to," said Imogen. "I've read them all already.

Online. Every last one of your poems. You know they're beautiful, don't you? You write what I think we're all too scared to say out loud. You draw these scratchy, horrifying things. Your work is so brave. So fearless. And then in real life you're this. You're just as scared as the rest of us. I feel like I just found out my hero is actually a Russian bot."

Daniella nodded. Anger was something she understood. "Sometimes, I feel like my rage is infinite."

"You really are a poet, aren't you?" Imogen still sounded mad, but also, a little like her fury had deflated. Like the bite behind her anger was gone.

"Against all reason, yes." Daniella shrugged. It seemed the safest gesture.

Rinn, who had been watching the two, just nodded. "A regular Mr. Darcy."

Daniella looked up, squinted. "What?"

"You liked poetry against your will, against your reason, and even against your character?" Rinn looked slightly less certain of herself now.

Both Daniella and Imogen shook their heads. They didn't get it.

Rinn looked away again, embarrassed. "Never mind."

Daniella, however, reached out, took Rinn's hand for a moment, just to get her attention. "No, don't be ashamed. Just because I don't get it. I mean, I feel like secretly writing poetry is how I ended up like this in the first place. You at least talk about the things that you love. You at least can share them with people."

Rinn flushed all the way from her neck to her hairline. "Thanks."

Daniella tapped the cover of her notebook. She looked over to Imogen. "Where'd you find it?"

"Break room. I thought it was the financial ledger." Imogen

was watching Daniella the way a wary cat watches a stranger in their home. *Friend or foe?*

In for a penny, thought Daniella, *in for a fucking pound*. "I make these. I think Imogen knows that now. But here they are."

Daniella cracked open her notebook and she started to show them her poetry, her drawings. She showed them her process. The space she had made for herself—so that even when she was stuck in a place she didn't want to be, she still had a kingdom of her own to build and to conquer.

There were the early sketches next to later poems. The first couplets, the first sonnets that Daniella had ever tried. The attempts at odes. The starts of something a little bigger, a little more epic. Then the later stuff—the development of her style. The scratchy lines of her drawings became more prominent. Her poetry became surer. She was rolling out couplets with ease by the end of the notebook. But the work, it was all there, in this notebook. Every crossed-out line. Every poem she posted. Every one she didn't. This was Daniella's holy space. This was the one place where she'd let herself be free.

Rinn reached out and took the notebook in hand first. She flipped through the pages, reading. She smiled at a few places. She had this quiet, steady focus when she read. She stopped midway through, then she passed them to Imogen, who took the notebook reverently in her hands. Imogen held the book like it was sacred and precious, and Daniella wanted to turn her eyes away and not watch. But she was riveted by the sight that someone took such care with her work. That the words and the drawings that she put on the page meant that, even to one other single human. It was a revelation. A benediction.

Rinn picked up the discarded vape pen. She clicked it once. "I hated these things, you know."

Daniella stared at her, trying to figure out what Rinn Olivera was doing, knowing how to even work a vape pen.

There must have been a look of total horror and confusion on Daniella's face—the same look that was mirrored on Imogen's face, too—because Rinn looked at her and said, "What, you think I don't watch any videos but my own?"

But Rinn had said it with a smile, so Daniella knew it wasn't a mean-spirited kind of teasing. And that's when Daniella's eyes must have totally bugged out of her sockets. Because Rinn Olivera, the most perfect of all the social media influencers—she was into *books*, for God's sake—took a hit of the vape pen.

Rinn coughed for a solid minute. "Yeah, I still hate that thing."

She passed it to Daniella. But Daniella was too stunned to take it.

"Why'd you do it, then?" Imogen accepted the pen next, took a hit, and blew out smoke. She offered it wordlessly to Daniella.

This olive branch, she could at least understand. Daniella took the peace offering and smoked it once. She tried to hand it back to Rinn.

But Rinn shook her head. "We're bonding, right? I had to try something."

Imogen and Daniella laughed.

Rinn waved their laughter off with a flutter of her hand. She got up and dusted off her pleated skirt so that it held no wrinkles or debris from the asphalt. "All right, ladies. There are two things on the agenda. The first is I think we should go and tell Jo what an *asshole* Brock Harvey is."

"Ugh," said Daniella. Rinn was right, of course, but that didn't mean Daniella had to like it.

"Definitely," said Imogen, with a nod. She'd put the disposable vape back down on the ground where they'd found it. Like the last two hits were to be passed along to the next person who stumbled across the alleyway and needed them.

"And the next item on the agenda?" Daniella did her best to make a Very Serious Face, but she cracked in the end and puffed out a laugh instead.

Rinn simply straightened her shoulders in response. Daniella felt her resentment for Little Miss Sunshine shift. Bloom outward from her chest into another feeling altogether. Something almost like respect and startlingly close to admiration.

"The next item on the agenda," said Rinn, "is that I think that Archer Hunt Junior has been tanking this store. For at least a year. If not more. But I have no idea how. You two have got to know what he's been doing. All I know is why."

"What?" asked Imogen.

"No, not what. *Why*," said Rinn.

"Oh my God. That would explain the inventory orders going down," said Daniella. "I noticed the inventory orders were down when I checked on Eli's Air Jordan purchase this morning. Sales are down, but sales are only down because inventory is down, and we're not even honoring any of our special orders."

"Systematic mismanagement," said Imogen. "That's what it is. Nothing is shelved right, and there are guns out in the open of the store, and the customers are being deliberately pissed off. No wonder we're getting fewer and fewer sellers at the sales counter. The special orders not being honored—God, that makes so much sense. I kept wondering why nothing I was notating in the inventory was ever there the next week. But why?"

"Because he can't sell the place unless it's no longer viable as a bookstore." Rinn gestured wide, her arm trying to convey the whole space of the store.

"How do you know that?" asked Imogen.

"It's what Jo said. On the tour. When she hired me," said Rinn.

"You remember your employee tour with Jo?" Daniella stared.

Rinn smoothed out her skirt again. "Yes, I do."

Daniella held up her hands in a gesture that was as close to *mea culpa* as she would ever get. "Fair enough. I've just never paid attention to what anyone said on a tour."

But Rinn, being perfectly insufferable, said, "Oh, you probably have, you just don't realize it. We pay attention to tons of things we don't realize at the time. But they become the voices in our head anyway."

"Sometimes I wonder if she's human," said Imogen, a little bit of awe in her voice.

"She is," said Daniella conspiratorially. "That's the worst part."

But Rinn just stretched out her hand to help Daniella up. Ignoring rudeness the way she always did, with such aplomb. "Are you going to help me break the news to Jo or not?"

Daniella didn't think. She took Rinn's outstretched hand, and together they were going to save their little corner of the universe.

23

Scratch a Lover and Find a Foe

2:57 P.M.
Rinn

In retrospect, maybe kicking the door—which was already ajar—all the way open so that it slammed and reverberated against the wall might have been going a bit far.

Rinn had startled both Jo and Brock Harvey—who were sitting across from each other at Jo's desk. They both looked directly to the door, and they were both staring at Rinn. Daniella stood next to her, frozen in position. Imogen was on the other side of Rinn, offering her presence as support. And Jo looked concerned that any of them should be there.

Brock looked so smug, and it took all of Rinn's incredible amounts of self-control that she had honed in over the years of literally working with other humans across the internet to not continue kicking into the room until she got to Brock's horrible, smirking face and his perfectly gelled and receding hairline.

How had she ever admired this living cesspool of a human?

Perhaps Rinn had less self-control than she realized because Imogen had grabbed hold of the upper part of her arm. She was shaking her head—not a *No, don't do it*, precisely, but more of a *Wait just one minute.*

Rinn would wait a minute, but then she might be done waiting for all eternity. Because whatever it was that they were about to dole out, Brock Harvey had it coming. As much as Imogen had slowed and halted her forward motion, that didn't stop Rinn from pointing her finger directly at Brock Harvey and saying, nearly on a shout, "Get him out of this store."

The about-face, in terms of Rinn's sheer adoration of the man not a couple of hours before, left Jo gobsmacked. She stared at Rinn. Then she turned her head and stared at Harvey.

Harvey was, of course, prepared for this. "Just because I won't give you an autograph before all the other fans who will be in line tonight, that doesn't mean you have to get in a snit with me, little girl." Then he turned and rolled his eyes—oh so performatively for Jo—and said, "Fangirls," as though it were under his breath.

But he knew it had been audible. They all knew. They had all heard.

That was when Imogen had stopped holding Rinn back and took her own step forward. She got right up in Brock Harvey's face, which startled even Brock Harvey. Imogen pointed directly at his chest without touching him. The threat of her was plain and obvious. And then Imogen spoke in clear, commanding tones that Rinn didn't know anybody their age could use. Didn't know anybody her age who had it in them. "This isn't about a fucking autograph."

Well, that had gotten everyone's attention.

That is, if Rinn kicking down the door hadn't already gotten their attention, which it definitely had.

"Somebody tell me what is going on, and somebody tell me

right now." That was Jo. She was looking at Imogen, her body tensed. Then she was looking at Rinn, who felt as out of control as she ever had in her life. And then she took in the sight of Daniella, stuck in the doorway, unmoving and staring blankly. Jo looked over to Harvey.

Harvey opened his mouth, but Jo held up her hand. She wasn't having any of him at the moment. "Not you."

Rinn thought about explaining herself, but then she realized, it wasn't her story to tell. She looked at Imogen, who in turn looked at Daniella.

Daniella nodded. Took a deep breath. She took a step into the room, steadying herself on one of the old wicker chairs with the hideously printed cushions. Her words came out in a stream of truth. In a confession. No, a declaration. "That creep tried to come on to me while I was alone in the break room. He then grabbed me and tried to pin me down when I said no. Obviously, I had to defend myself, so I stepped on him to get out of his reach and then ran like hell. Rinn found me before I could run all the way out the room. She saw a lot of it."

"Whoa, your crazy employee attacked *me*. She stomped on my foot. Ask the little fangirl one. She walked in right as the crazy one attacked me. That's what I came in here trying to tell you."

Jo held up her hand again, turned, and gave Harvey a real mean stare. "I said shut it, Harvey. And I meant it."

Harvey went dead silent, like he hadn't expected that response from another authority figure.

"Jesus, is that why you came in here, trying to be nice to me? Did you really think I wouldn't believe my own employees? Over a guy who has that much gel in his hair and fucking elbow patches on his designer jacket? I mean, I get you don't think I'm that bright but, man, that stings." Jo looked up, looked to Rinn. "What did you see?"

"I heard voices in the break room. I heard Daniella saying no a lot, and then I heard some murmurs, a muffled shout, and then I fell into the room as Daniella opened the door and saw Harvey hopping on one foot and Daniella nearly in tears. I tried to help. I mean, I made it worse, but I tried to help."

Jo nodded. "Is that where you got the handprint on your face from?"

Daniella nodded. "Pretty much."

"See?" said Harvey, flailing wildly now. His gestures were large and buffoonish. He was a caricature of a man enraged. A comic. An old-timey print. "She's a crazy girl. A nutcase. She's violent, and she took her violence out on *me*. I could sue, you know. All I'm asking is that you fire her for my own safety and the safety of others around her. I mean, hell, they smell like a smoke shop. It's like Coachella in here, it reeks of weed, and it didn't before those girls came storming in here."

Rinn continued, calm as can be. She ignored the weed comment. Didn't even address it. "No, she was upset. She was still in a fight-or-flight response, and she still had so much adrenaline running through her. And I didn't sound like a friend, so she treated me—quite naturally—like a threat. I mean, it was wrong. But her actions are totally rational, given what she'd been through."

"Oh. Thank you. I mean. I'm still sorry I hit you." And then Daniella looked straight at Harvey for the first time since she'd come into the room. "I'm not at all sorry that I hit you, though. You deserved it."

Rinn looked over at Harvey, too. "I believed in you. In your work. In the things you said about love and growing up and family. And it turns out, you're just full of shit, aren't you? You're peddling whatever will sell to hide the fact that there's a horrible monster inside of you."

Harvey's eyes went wild, and for a moment, Rinn wasn't sure if he would pounce on one of them again. She could nearly envision his hand going flying, could see the spittle spewing out of his mouth. He looked primal and ferocious and everything that he had managed to keep down, just below the surface, was now visible to all of them.

But then Jo stuck out her hand, put it against Harvey's chest. "Sit down, Harvey. I'm not going to ask you again."

Harvey sat.

"I guess, from what you're saying, is that you deny all these claims?" Underneath her calm tones, Jo's voice vibrated with fury.

"Of course I deny it. You'd have to be an imbecile to think that I, of all people, would do that. I would never jeopardize my career."

Jo narrowed her eyes. And then she employed her beautiful, razor-sharp sarcasm with just one word. "Right."

Rinn had to clap her hand over her mouth to keep from laughing. Or snorting. Or both.

Brock Harvey turned a near purple shade of red.

Luckily for them all, the door to the break room swung open and in walked Maya. In her arms was a stack of Brock Harvey's books. She was somehow still able to look down at her phone and continue clicking through it. "Look—I know you don't want to sign any more copies than you have to, but most bookstores expect to have signed stock at the end of an event, and if you do it now you don't have to stay—"

The room was so silent that Maya stopped talking immediately. She looked up. "Uh. What is going on?"

"These *utter morons* are treating me like a criminal." This time spit really did go flying out of Brock Harvey's mouth. He seemed secure in his audience—like Maya would be on his side.

But Maya's whole face contorted into a series of embarrassed expressions that finally landed on a strange kind of determination that Rinn hadn't seen before. "God. What happened now?"

"What do you mean *what happened now*? They attacked me. And now their manager. Is. Not. Doing. Her. Job. And. Protecting. Me. Or my career. Because of her"—and here Brock decided he really was a caricature of an angry man because he used scare quotes in the air with his fingers when he said the word—"*employees.*"

But Maya wasn't buying it. The determination in her face really took hold. "First of all, that's not how you use those, Brock. I've been telling you. They are her actual employees. You can't scare-quote a thing that is actually true. Second of all, it was bad enough when you came on to me at BookCon, but how dare you go after these young women. They're teenagers, Brock. *Teenagers.*"

Jo, as calm as ever, looked over at Brock and said, "I'm having a really hard time believing that you didn't do these things, Mr. Harvey. My employees don't lie. They don't go around making things up. And Maya's experiences seem to back up what they're saying."

"No, they're thieves." He was shouting, and Rinn wanted to cover her ears, the noise was so shrill. "Don't think I don't know what's going on. We all heard what's happening here. We all know you're harboring an actual criminal."

Jo took a deep breath, like she had learned to center herself with one of those meditation apps. Rinn had always found those apps to be pretty helpful, truth be told.

"That employee is my responsibility to deal with. As is the fact that an author has come into my store and started assaulting the young female employees in my care. And considering that the first headshot that you sent into the store was you, shirtless, eating spaghetti that was getting into your chest hair, I'm having a real hard time believing you at all." Jo set her hands on her desk so that her hands were in a wide *V* across the space—she was in charge here, and she wouldn't let anyone take that from her.

"I did *not* assault anyone." Brock really was purple now.

Maya gave up, dropped all the books in her hands onto the floor, and put her hand in her face. "Jesus, Brock, not again. I can't with you. I really can't. I can't keep sweeping this kind of behavior under the rug."

This time, Harvey didn't have words. He lunged for Maya.

And without even thinking, without even hesitating, Jo grabbed Harvey and punched him right across the jaw. "Get. Out. Of. My. Store."

Harvey grabbed his jaw, howling. "I will be pressing charges. Don't think I won't."

Jo kept her chin ducked down, still ready for a fight, still on her feet as if she had to throw another punch. "You do that. But remember it's your word against mine. And I've got witnesses."

"So do I," said Harvey.

"No, you don't," said Maya quietly. "I quit."

"But she punched me in the jaw—I have evidence. And that little bitch stepped on me."

Jo shrugged. Her knuckles looked red, but she didn't flinch, and she didn't flex out her hand. She looked Harvey dead in the eye. "Chicago's a rough town, ace. Anybody could have done that to you. Doesn't mean it was me."

"You're a rotten crowd," he shouted one last time. "I'm worth the whole damn bunch put together. You're all a bunch of phonies."

And then—unable to even come up with an original parting shot—with a flap of his elbow-patches sports coat and still clutching his wounded jaw, Brock Harvey fled Wild Nights Bookstore and Emporium.

24

Folded in Each Other's Wings

Jo sat on the edge of her desk, holding her hand like it was a baby bird. There was a little bit of stunned awe in her voice as she spoke. "Never hit someone bare-knuckled before."

Imogen stared at Jo for a minute. Jo was staring at her hands. Imogen looked away, looking for anyone else in the room to register how absurd this was. Daniella raised her eyebrows but said nothing. Imogen looked to Rinn, who was wide-eyed with disbelief.

Then Rinn said what they had all been thinking. "But you *do* hit people with your knuckles wrapped?" The incredulity in her tone was pretty noticeable.

Or maybe it was irony. Imogen couldn't be sure. Rinn had this undercutting sense of humor. It wasn't like Daniella's sarcasm. There was no scorn in Rinn's humor. Just a level of self-awareness that made Imogen's lips twitch nearly into a smile.

Jo shrugged. "Sure. I box on Monday nights. I'm used to hitting and getting hit. Never realized the wraps were for my own protection as much as the other person's."

"Of course you wouldn't realize that. Of course you think that wrapping your knuckles was for the protection of other people." Daniella shook her head and did her best to stifle her laughter, but it was one of those impossible-to-control, sputtering things—under wraps for now, but capable of exploding at any minute.

"Hey, people get seriously hurt bare-knuckle boxing," said Jo in her most grown-up, most adult of tones.

Rinn, Imogen, and Daniella all busted out laughing then. Riotous laughter. It was at Jo's expense, that was true. But it was also at the day they were having. Imogen, at least, was laughing about creepy men and unsecured weapons, and the fact that Eli had tried to save the place they all loved by *stealing from it*. There was a power in laughing. It had been so difficult to find recently. But she felt it now. That she had taken back some sense of herself by laughing at everything that threatened to blow her over.

Imogen's face hurt, she was so unused to laughter, so unused to smiling. The pain of it on her face slowed down her laughter, but not her amusement. She recovered first. "You really aren't a proper adult, Jo."

Jo moved her hand like she was going to make a stern gesture but ended up wincing instead. She'd forgotten her knuckles were sore. Forgotten, for a moment, that she'd just punched out a famous author in the break room of their dying bookstore. "I don't think a proper adult could look after you hooligans. You're like those kids in all those movies that drive the nannies and the governesses crazy."

Rinn was the first to step in again. "Are you comparing us to the Von Trapp kids from *The Sound of Music*, Jo?"

They all started laughing again. This was one of the last moments they would spend with Jo, and they were going to spend them laughing, not crying.

Maya came back into the office, holding a small baggie of ice. "I begged the coffee shop next door to give me this. They said they weren't supposed to give out plastic at all, especially not to noncustomers."

Jo winced as she settled it onto her hand.

"Here. Let me help." Maya adjusted the bag of ice so that the pressure was more gentle as it landed on Jo's hand.

Jo still winced a little, but she also breathed out a sigh of relief as the ice covered her knuckles completely. "How'd you get them to give it to you?"

"At first I told them we needed it for an injury, and they wanted to charge." Maya focused very intently on the bag of ice. Not on Jo's hands. Not on Jo's face. Just that bag of ice.

Jo also focused on the bag of ice, but she also watched Maya's hands settle the bag. The focus of a woman determined not to look.

Imogen smirked watching the exchange. "So did you pay for it?"

Maya shook her head. "Nah, I told them Jo punched a creep and that changed their tune. Anybody who throws a left hook in order to protect a teen girl gets a bag of ice on the house. Annnd"—Maya pulled a card out of her pocket. It was one of those loyalty punch cards, and it had been fully punched out—"a free coffee."

"Wow. What a reward. A free bag of ice and a free coffee." Jo's voice was shaky, like she'd finally registered what she'd done. Like she didn't want to, but it was slowly dawning on her, all the same.

Imogen knew that feeling all too well. She rubbed the stubble of her hair at the back of her neck.

"As long as you didn't break any bones, you really do come out ahead," Maya said with a smile. She made eye contact, and she looked at Jo like maybe the sun was about to come out again.

Of course, that's when Eli came into the office, holding the landline that he'd dragged all the way through the store. AJ trailed in after him, clearly concerned about whoever was on the other end. None of them had heard it ringing, but Eli handed the receiver to Jo and they all knew without a word that it was Archer on the line.

Jo cleared her throat. "Mr. Hunt?"

And then Jo listened and said nothing for a solid minute. She just sat there, stone-faced, hearing whatever Archer had to say. And then she hung up without so much as a goodbye.

Nobody said anything for a long beat.

Finally, Jo said, "He called to congratulate me."

"On what?" asked Imogen.

"Punching Harvey in the face. Said not to worry, that he talked Harvey down from pressing charges. And said *good work* and then hung up the phone."

"He loves doing that," said Eli.

"Isn't it bad for business to punch a famous author?" AJ spoke up now. His whole face looked like he was trying to solve a problem, but he didn't even understand the question.

The events of the day really settled onto Jo and she slumped over onto the desk, defeated—no matter how many adorable women were smiling at her—banging her head lightly against the surface. Every beat punctuated a word. "I can't believe I got out of that one. I can't believe we got out of that."

"You didn't," said Rinn, piping in.

All heads swiveled to hear. Enough people said "What?" that Imogen wasn't sure who had spoken. Maybe she'd asked out loud, maybe she'd just asked in her head. Maybe everyone had asked.

"We didn't get out of that. Hunt just wanted a lawsuit. He wants the business to go under. He wants Wild Nights Bookstore to fail. Everything we've done today—Eli with his terrible inventory order and Jo punching Harvey—just adds to his case that this business is no longer viable. That he's allowed to sell this business free and clear."

"Oh my God," said Jo. "You're right. He can't sell the property as long as the business is still functioning well enough."

"He's been ordering way less inventory," said Imogen.

"And not putting in any of the customer orders," piped in Daniella.

"He's slowly been bleeding the place dry," said Rinn. "I think he's had this plan in motion for a while. Plus, he made sure that we could never tell anyone about it. No cell phones. No photos. No geotag even available. We're in a dead zone."

"Oh God." Jo must have felt it more keenly than the rest of them. "What am I going to do?"

But they were all thinking it, really. *What were they going to do?* Because the bookstore was still in trouble. Beyond trouble, really. There were still stacks of fake Air Jordans sitting behind Jo's desk. They were all going to be out of a job soon. It had felt good to best a bully and a creep. But all of their problems were still there, waiting.

"What do you need to do?" Maya started rubbing Jo's arm, the one that Jo had used to throw a punch at Harvey, and Jo whimpered in approval.

"I've got no idea," Jo said, her face into the desk. The sound was muffled, but the words themselves were clear. "I'm supposed to know, aren't I? I'm in charge. But I don't know what else I can do. I don't have any money myself. Everything I had saved was in that petty cash account. I wanted to buy a stake in the store. Prove I could do a better job of running it. But I was in over my head, and I had no idea Archer was undermining me the whole time. And it's not like anybody will give me a loan; my student loans are through the roof. I think I'm as maxed-out as I can be, especially given my income. Maybe I can refinance those. Do we have time to refinance those? Can I refinance those and add more debt to them? I mean, does it really matter anymore? All my dreams of saving this place have gone up in smoke. Actually, not smoke, no. They've gone up in Air Jordans and a fistfight." Jo didn't even laugh at her own bad joke. It was like she told it so she could express her misery in the worst kind of humor.

This was when Daniella stepped up, took charge. "Look, Jo, I have a plan."

"It's not a very good plan," interrupted Rinn.

"It's *a* plan." Daniella folded her arms across her chest. Daniella, Imogen was learning, was not one to ever cede ground. Daniella would charge forward, and she would protect herself against all odds.

But Rinn interrupted. "Let me guess. It involves unloading the merch back onto an unsuspecting person of the internet."

Daniella was about to fume. "It's a good enough plan. It at least keeps you from having to take out a shitty loan. It's not a *bad* plan."

Imogen realized in an instant that Daniella and Rinn were like wind and flame. They were only going to make each other worse. They needed a go-between, someone to ground them both. They were on the same side. They each saw the same problem. But with different perspectives. There had to be an intermediary—a go-between—or they would turn into a raging, city-wide fire.

Imogen made a decision. "Look, it is a plan. And while it is probably an amoral or even an immoral plan, it's definitely a plan. Good job, Daniella."

Daniella looked disgruntled but mollified.

Imogen was not quite finished, though. "But Rinn is probably right that unloading our problem onto the next person is not really a great or viable solution. We might be, like, endangering another Eli in another place. Like, the Eli of Nowhere, Minnesota."

Daniella snorted. "Whatever."

Rinn crossed her arms and glared. "It wouldn't be whatever to that person."

"But we'd live to see another day." Daniella was becoming increasingly less mollified.

Jo, meanwhile, had raised her head off her desk. She got out her phone and was clicking, clicking, clicking through it. "I'm going to find a loan. Like a temporary loan. A refinance. There's an app for that, right?"

"Probably," said Daniella.

"Definitely," said Rinn.

"Don't do that," said Maya.

"Oh God, this isn't even my phone." Jo was despondent. She whimpered again and put her head down on her desk. "I can't even open it."

Jo began digging through her desk drawers, looking for her actual phone, versus all the phones that she had confiscated.

It was Daniella's phone, there on the desk. Imogen recognized it because she had one of those flippy wallet cases. It was all black and busted, and there was duct tape on the places that were coming apart. It looked like it had been beat to hell and back, and there was no way any of the rest of them would do that to their phone case but Daniella.

Also, it had a small sketch done in Wite-Out on the back that looked exactly like her poetry sketches. Imogen wondered how she'd never noticed that before.

But Jo kept digging out phones.

Her phone. Imogen lived dangerously and didn't have a case on hers. She knew it was inevitably going to be destroyed one way or another. Or, at least, that's how she had felt. Looking at the worn, beat-up case that Daniella used, Imogen felt like maybe she ought to get one.

Rinn pulled out her own phone from the waistband of her skirt. It was white with a stack of illustrated books on the back. It looked like it had been drawn both by and for Disney princesses. If Imogen had seen that phone case this morning, she would have puked, it was honestly so nauseatingly adorable. It even had one of those handle things for taking better selfies. Now she just felt like the case suited Rinn, in that overtly femme kind of way.

Rinn was staring at the phones like they held all of the answers in the universe. "Guys."

"I don't think refinancing your student loans for Eli is the best use of money." This time, it was Imogen's turn to be the voice of reason.

"Do you think we should just roll over and accept that Archer Hunt Junior has been screwing us all this entire time?" Daniella was furious again.

"Guys." Rinn tried saying it louder this time.

"I can't think with you guys yelling all around me. Do I want an eighteen percent variable rate?" Jo was clicking, clicking, clicking through her own phone. She'd finally found it. *Tap, tap, tap.*

Daniella and Imogen both shouted no at the same time. They exchanged a look, and Imogen got the sneaking suspicion that Daniella was also much better at math than she let on publicly.

"*Guys.*" Rinn looked like she'd had it; she really did. Her hands were on her hips, and her stare was directly at the phones. Everyone stopped to look at her.

And as soon as she had everyone's attention, Rinn Olivera smirked. "Can I take a look at that property agreement?"

Jo raised an eyebrow. She'd at least recovered her sarcasm. "Why? Do you have a law degree we don't know about?"

Rinn shook her head. "No. But I think I have an idea."

25

Drowning an Ocean

Pissing off Archer Hunt, really, was an added bonus.

The more she looked through the property contract, the more Rinn realized that the plan itself was brilliant. Now, Rinn had to convey her brilliance to everyone else. They had to see. This was how they were going to save Wild Nights.

"Look," said Rinn. "Hunt Junior gamed the system, right? His dad handed over this enormous piece of land in the middle of Chicago. But there was a catch. Old Mr. Hunt made sure that Junior kept the store running. And so for a while, Hunt Junior did. But Junior must have reviewed the will, reviewed the clauses, because he realized he had this one out—Wild Nights Bookstore and Emporium had to remain open as a bookstore as long as it *wasn't* a financial burden. Only if running a store was a hardship could Junior sell. So he tanked the store so that he could profit off the land and the building."

"Yeah," said Daniella. "So?"

"So that's the *land and the building*." Rinn knew it was so simple, nobody had even thought about it. They'd been so unplugged, the easiest solution hadn't been available to them. But Rinn was making it available. They *had* to see it now. They had to.

Maya looked over to Jo. "Is she always this cryptic?"

"No," said Jo. "Usually it's getting her to stop that's the problem."

"Hey," said Rinn. "That's not funny."

But Imogen and Daniella were laughing. Rinn swatted at them, and they backed up, still giggling.

Rinn crossed her arms over her chest. "Look, I am having the most brilliant of brilliant ideas, and you are all sitting there laughing at me. Fine. Just think about it. This contract on Jo's computer is for the sale of the property, plant, and equipment. It doesn't say anything about the books."

Imogen looked skeptical at this. "I think the books *are* the equipment in a bookstore, Rinn."

But Rinn was not giving up on her idea. "No, they're not. The books are the intellectual property of the bookstore. And those special customer orders or preorders are like contractual obligations we have to fill."

Daniella's jaw dropped. "She's right, you know. Those preorders and requests are technically bookings, not sales. We can't log them as revenue until the customer collects them."

"Exactly!" Rinn was excited now. "Like, Archer Hunt Junior is selling the physical bookstore and the physical land. We're preserving the *metaphysical* bookstore—which is Wild Nights and its intellectual inventory. Guys, it's very legal and very cool."

Jo narrowed her eyes. "Books are not metaphysical, Rinn. You were throwing them around quite physically earlier today."

"But those books belong to the idea of Wild Nights. They

preserve the spirit of Old Mr. Hunt's will. If we can preserve the books, we can save the bookstore."

Daniella then managed to interrupt, cede to Rinn's point, and contradict it, all in one go. "Are you saying that the only way we win is to lose?"

Rinn was excited now. It didn't matter that she was being skeptical—if Daniella got where Rinn was going, if Rinn could get Daniella halfway there, then she could get the rest of them all the way there, Rinn was sure. "Yes and also no. It's that, by trying to set this place up to lose, Archer Hunt Junior also set us up to win because of the terms of his father's will. Because Hunt Junior watched from his weird-ass no-internet tower, doling out email cease and desists like *that's* his job, not running this place, he's probably not even thought about the books as an asset to the store. Just a piece of math that he has to manipulate in order to get what he wants."

Imogen was looking like she might be on board now. "He did refuse to place those customer orders."

"Exactly. He didn't honor those bookings. He gave up on the idea of Wild Nights in order to sell Wild Nights. He's not selling the store, not really. He's selling the building and the land. We can't save the building. But we can save the bookstore."

Everyone looked like maybe, just maybe, this was a plausible plan. It was, at least, a working plan that they could get behind that didn't involve scamming some other poor, unsuspecting person. And that was a hell of a lot better for Rinn, personally.

"It's a good idea," said Daniella. "I mean, it'll take time for any plan like that to work. And the problem is, we don't have any time. And where are we going to put all the books?"

That was a challenge if Rinn ever heard one, and Rinn loved a challenge. "Long term, yes, it will take time to rebuild a customer base. But short term, we need to get people into this store and buying stuff so we can afford a storage unit. We need to unload these Jordans. And I bet if we told my followers that these weird fake Jordans were for sale, they'd want a pair. And then—"

"Ohhh," said Maya. "That's where I know you. You're thebookbruja. OMG, I love your feed."

"Thank you so much," said Rinn, blushing. But she got back on target quickly enough. "Guys. This bookstore is this weird, magical place that nobody knows is here because nobody is allowed to talk about it, like, ever. And people love to talk about the places they love and share them. And if we just got the ball rolling, I bet this place would snowball. I bet everyone would want to grab a coffee from the coffee shop with the not-free-free ice and come hang out for hours and hours and hours, don't you see?"

Daniella shook her head. "You don't get a snowball effect in like two hours. You don't get it in even twelve hours. You can't *make* the store go viral. Do you really think people will buy fake Jordans just because it's for a bookstore? People aren't that stupid."

Rinn eyed Daniella back with the same expression. "I never said people were stupid. I said they'd want to buy the Jordans."

"Why?" asked Daniella. "They're fake. Nobody wants a fake thing when they can get the real thing. And people don't just help out a bookstore. This isn't a fairy tale, Rinn. This is real life. In real life, things don't go according to plan just because you've decided they will."

"Hey," said Imogen. "Let's hear her out."

Daniella folded her arms across her chest and said nothing. She stood stony and silent, waiting. But she wasn't arguing anymore.

"Thank you." Rinn nodded to Imogen, then went on, while

she still had her captive audience. "We can sell the Jordans as a bonus. Like we can sign them. Or we can ask for donations and then give them away as a wacky bonus that goes with donating to the bookstore. So the donations cover the merch. We'll at least pay for storage that way. And maybe even get some start-up capital for another space."

Jo looked up, half-forlorn, half-hopeful. "We don't have any way to take the donations. They'd have to be cash only. We can't charge them from the store and then not account where the merchandise was coming from."

Daniella, here, did the unexpected. "But Rinn's right. The shoes were never logged as inventory. And the store's finances are all on literal paper. Hunty Junior uses the world's oldest finance system. There's no way he could track a swipe attachment to a phone hooked back up to the original account that Eli took the money from. I mean, we could take cash, too. But I think digital is better. The digital payments won't look normal—but at least they won't look like theft? I can make sure it's all squared away for tax purposes."

Imogen looked at Daniella. "You know the tax code?"

"I've been helping out with the books for a couple of years. I've got the basics down. It's just math rules. I'm great with math rules." And then Daniella jutted her chin out to dare anyone to defy her on this point.

Rinn definitely wasn't about to. Neither was Imogen, by the waves of understanding washing across her face.

Jo, however, shook her head. "Even if we got all the logistics down, why on earth would anybody want to buy Jordans to save a bookstore that they haven't even heard of? What's in it for them?"

"I could put poems on them," offered Daniella, like that was the kind of thing she said every day. Like she was normally someone who bragged about being able to do accounting and write her poetry.

For a moment, Rinn didn't know what to do.

Maya broke the silence in the room. "You write poetry?"

Daniella jutted her chin out again. "Yeah. I do."

"Is it something people would have already heard of?" Maya asked.

It was her earnestness, Rinn decided, that tipped the scales. Rinn watched as it disarmed Daniella and all of her defenses.

"I've got a solid account." Daniella dropped her chin and went for that *I don't really care but actually I care a lot* shrug. "Nothing like Rinn's, but it's enough to pull some people in, I think."

"Her poetry is really beautiful," added Imogen. "It's legendary."

And then Rinn watched as Daniella flushed, just for a moment, before returning back to her original shade. "I could even do some doodles or sketches on them. People would pay extra for those. I mean, they might. I can't guarantee that they would. But it would at least add something so that you're buying more than fake shoes."

Rinn didn't want to make it weird by crying or anything. But having Daniella come to her side and then offer to put her work out there for the cause was really just so much. Rinn cleared her throat on a cough, to be sure she wouldn't sound emotional or choked-up, because she knew Daniella would hate it if she did. "Thank you. That would be amazing."

Jo stared at the girls for a moment. "That could maybe work. Two influencers plus lots of photos and content. And I like it a lot better than unloading our problems directly onto somebody else. I'd really rather not screw over somebody else down the line. I'd like to think I have a slightly higher moral compass than somebody selling detox tea. Maybe I don't. But I'd like to try to hold on to that idea of myself for as long as I can."

"And you wouldn't have to take out a loan that would destroy you," said Imogen, in what could almost be mistaken for a positive tone.

"I mean, I've already got student debt for the rest of my life, but I appreciate what you were trying for."

Imogen nodded, like she understood that Jo appreciated her effort at positivity.

Hell, Rinn had appreciated it. They all had.

But there was work to do. Rinn cracked her knuckles one by one. She rolled her neck, because this was about to get really serious, and she wasn't going to go into serious work with a stiff neck. She wasn't going to be slowed down by shoulder pain or anything. "Okay, first thing I need to do is tell all of my followers about this. And then I need to somehow update the Brock Harvey signing into a 'Save Wild Nights Bookstore' party. And then Daniella and Eli need to set up a station that looks good with all the Jordans on it. I can take video. I mean, I can't do my *normal* production value, but, like, I can at least get some good live-style shots and some good stuff for the immediate feed. And Imogen, I need you to help art direct all of my shots."

"Dude, no." So much for Imogen's positive vibes.

"Okay, I will art direct the shots, but I need you to take them. I've got some staged photos all around the bookstore that I have been planning for literal years now." Rinn was not about to give up, even if taking video really did freak Imogen out. "Oh, and we need to eventually recruit people. To box up the books. So let's put out some feelers for that. Though we shouldn't do that without a storage space."

Maya leaned in to whisper in one of those voices that the whole room could hear. "This is terrifying."

Jo gave her a pat on the arm. "It's best to let it happen."

Rinn ignored them both and their little adult bubble. She had shit to get done. "All right, and then after I post the photos, you all have to post the photos. And Daniella, you need to go out and buy one of those Square things we can attach to our phones. Can we do that quickly?"

"Worth a try," said Daniella, who was already tapping through her phone, hopefully looking up places to buy a credit card machine that attached to their phones.

"Good. All right, everyone know their jobs?" Rinn asked.

"Is she gonna say *break*?" asked Maya at that low whisper.

"Probably," said Jo, lifting the ice bag and testing to see if she could touch her hand without pain.

But Rinn wouldn't let someone tease her away from her favorite rally cry. Rinn didn't play any team sports. And she wasn't about to let some grown-up who used to work for the biggest creep in the world tell her how to end a meeting.

"Break," said Rinn.

EVENING

5:00 p.m.—9:00 p.m.

26

Master of My Fate, Captain of My Soul

5:00 P.M.
Imogen

There was something strange about watching Rinn filming herself.

It took away a little bit of the magic, made Rinn look a little bit ridiculous. After all, she was swinging a stick around on her phone, talking to the air. But also, it was endearing. To watch anyone put that much heart and soul and care into a thing.

For once, Imogen didn't feel tangential embarrassment at that. She normally would have, watching someone try so hard with so much determination and so little self-consciousness. But instead, Imogen was impressed with Rinn's dedication to a thing that she loved.

Of course, that's when Rinn flipped the camera around. "Say something, Imogen."

"Something," said Imogen, in an absolute panic.

And then Rinn laughed. Not *at* Imogen. But at what Imogen had said. Like it was funny. Like her horrible, awful, no-good dad joke was funny.

"Imogen is a riot," said Rinn with so much authority that Imogen nearly believed her on the spot.

Rinn clicked through her phone, posted the video, and then snapped the telescopic arm of her selfie stick back in place. "Okay. That was the easy part."

"*That* was the easy part?" Nothing about the way Rinn had held focus with the lens of her phone camera and continuously talked to it for four minutes had, in any way, seemed like the easy part.

Rinn nodded. And for such a sunshine-and-happiness kind of person, it was amazing how much gravitas she could lend to her statements. "Now we gotta go tell the Harvey fans waiting in line that he's not going to be at the bookstore due to unforeseen circumstances."

"The unforeseen circumstances being that he hits on teenage girls in bookstores and probably also his younger publicist and maybe any young woman who has the misfortune to cross his path while he's alone with them?"

"Yes, but hopefully we don't have to announce that to the entire bookstore because I think Jo's in enough trouble for punching Harvey as it is. I don't think we need to fan that fire, so to speak."

"I wish we could," said Imogen.

"Oh, we always can," said Rinn in that voice again that made Imogen *believe* her. "But it's a question of whether we should. If it's necessary, I think we should. But that's the problem with creeps. It's always on the victims to expose them and the victims to bear the brunt of what people believe. The vulnerable risk everything. The powerful can just point at everything that they have amassed, as though that's an argument against potential injustice and misbehavior."

"You know," said Imogen, "I'm starting to feel bad that I've never watched your book channel."

Rinn smiled. She really was made of sunshine when she smiled, but Imogen wasn't filled with envy at the sight anymore. Sunshine could be a calming and soothing presence. And there was no use resenting the sun for what it did best.

"The nice thing about social feeds is, you can always pick them up when you want. I know people say that social media is out to destroy us and we're all going in for the likes and the instant gratification." Rinn was walking briskly now. Approaching the line of people who were waiting in the retractable barriers that she'd set up. "And I get that, I really do. But it's also about connection and meeting people and reaching out. I think people want to blame technology because it amplifies what we already are. Humans are vain and selfish, and we're constantly jockeying for position on a scale that doesn't really matter and doesn't really exist. But we're also kind and we also share and connect and create communities across borders. Both are happening. It's all happening."

Imogen stared for a moment, then smiled at Rinn. "Yeah, I definitely need to watch your channel."

They were almost there, to the front of the line. But as Imogen's own anxiety was ramping up, Rinn kept firing off questions.

"What do you like to read?"

"Mostly poetry," said Imogen. "My mother taught me to love poetry, and now I'm stuck with it, I guess."

"But there's so many kinds of poetry! Shakespeare's poetry. So's Rupi Kaur. There's beat poetry and novels in verse. There's stories you can only tell with poems. There's also the early nineties stuff, like Suheir Hammad."

"You know Suheir Hammad?" Imogen had never met anyone who wasn't Palestinian who knew about her. She was like this great guarded secret. Of diaspora, of the American experience. Of colorism. Of the eliding ways that white supremacy affected immigrants.

Rinn smiled, completely nonplussed by the series of assumptions that Imogen kept throwing at her. "Sure do. Though I do have to give my librarian credit for that one. When I was diving into poetry so I could understand it better, she recommended her to me. She saw I was looking for Own Voices poetry. There's something in there, isn't it? It's like I've been haunted. She makes me feel like I've been haunted, but also, like I'm not alone for it."

"Yeah, like she's been talking to the jinn or something." Imogen hadn't meant to say it like that. Hadn't meant to lay it all out there like that. It was just that once she got started talking about poetry, all sorts of feelings came out.

Rinn stared for a moment. "Yes. It's exactly like that."

The relief of Rinn having agreed with her was beyond anything that Imogen could have imagined. It was like falling off a high wire, only to discover that there was a safety net to catch her. That there were rewards to vulnerability, along with the risks.

"You know it's okay, right?" asked Rinn. Only she said it more like a statement and less like a question.

"What's okay?" asked Imogen.

"To be depressed," said Rinn.

Imogen's response was knee-jerk, immediate. "I'm not depressed."

Rinn's whole face went thoughtful for a moment. "It's not a weakness. Depression isn't. I mean, I've got anxiety."

"You do?" asked Imogen.

"Sure," said Rinn. "I'm basically hard-wired for it. My brain just works that way, I think. I care a lot, and I want to make things that are really great. When I film or take photos. Like there's an edge there where I know my naturally anxious mind helps, because that's what's keeping me focused, keeping me paying attention to all the details I'm good at. The positive word for anxiety is conscientiousness."

"It is?" Imogen felt like maybe she was having this conversation underwater. Or in a space suit. The sounds were muffled. Her mind was trying to block it out. But still, she could only really hear Rinn's voice through it all.

"At least, that's what the therapist I saw said. The school counselor. I can only see her during the school year, but she helps." Then Rinn paused. Bit her lip for a moment. Released it once she had formulated her thought—Imogen could literally see the way Rinn thought across her face. "What I'm trying to say is, you can get help in all these different ways, like therapy and meds, for dealing with the ways in which your mind feels like it's against you. But, like, it's also still your mind, and it's also made you who you are. Like I'm built to be happy but maybe not built to be calm. Maybe that's just me, but for the longest time I was anxious because I had anxiety, you know?"

Imogen did know. She nodded.

"But some things just are. Not giving myself the space to have and deal with and learn from my anxiety was way worse than being a person with anxiety."

"Are you about to show me how to overcome my depression or something right now?" Imogen narrowed her eyes.

Rinn—*Oh my God*—she laughed. "No. I think you need a licensed professional for that."

Imogen didn't know what to say to that; she decided it was best to say nothing. They had reached the front of the line of the Brock Harvey crowd by this point.

"Excuse me," said Rinn. "Could I have your attention, please?"

But Rinn didn't shout. Didn't kick up a big fuss. She said it at a normal volume, and then she stood there, silently waiting for everyone to quiet down.

And then they did.

It was like watching a magic trick, that quiet assumption of power. It took patience, but the crowd slowly went silent, like a ripple that traveled from the front of the line all the way to the back. The last person to notice, the last person still talking, looked visibly embarrassed when he realized that everyone else had been silenced.

Imogen was in awe.

Rinn smiled. "Thank you all so much for being here. Unfortunately, Brock Harvey has had to cancel due to a scheduling conflict."

Everyone looked visibly disappointed. And, given that none of them knew what Harvey had done in the break room a few hours ago, Imogen couldn't quite blame them.

"But he *just* posted that he was going to be here today." This was from the guy in the back who had been the last one to stop talking.

Imogen looked out in the crowd. That girl that she'd spoken to earlier gave her a sly smile and rolled her eyes at the guy in the back. Imogen smiled back, an involuntary reflex.

And this was where Imogen was thoroughly impressed by Rinn. Because Rinn did not roll her eyes as she said, "Yes, there has been a change in plans. He will not be here. But I did want to let everyone know that there is signed stock copy if they would like. And we will also be having a huge bookstore celebration and poetry festival instead. You really should stick around. There's going to be a live reading, and our resident poet—Daniella—is going to be writing her poems across a whole series of fake Air

Jordans. It's basically bookstore community and poetry performance art at its finest, people. All of the proceeds are going to go directly into this amazing local bookstore."

A few people were nodding their heads along with Rinn. That Imogen understood. She was a rallier. A go-getter. A girl who just *wanted* to believe Rinn. Though a few of the disappointed audience members and skeptics still showed their displeasure.

The dude at the back was still not having it. "I don't understand why he's not here. He made it all the way out here to Chicago for the first time in like three years and he cancels an hour before? That doesn't make sense."

Rinn put her hands on her hips. "What's your name?"

The dude stuck his chin out. "Warren."

"Well, Warren. I'm going to tell you something. Everyone put down your phones. No recording. I don't want to get sued for libel or slander. Not that I've got anything worth suing."

Imogen double-checked to make sure her phone was on silent. She didn't want to miss this. Rinn's voice had gone all hushed and almost reverential.

No, not reverential. *Somber.*

Rinn waited until she had the entire audience's attention again. "Brock Harvey was one of my favorite-of-all-time authors. I run a book account, and *When We Were Us* is largely why I started my account, why I got so many people to start reading. Why I wanted to reach out and talk about books. I know, that's a lot. But I feel like I have to give you this context. Earlier today, Mr. Harvey hit on one of our underage employees. He's been asked to leave the store, and we're unfortunately going to have to cancel our event."

My God, was she good at this. Nobody dared even breathe while Rinn paused to take a breath.

"As you may or may not have heard, this bookstore is in trouble. So instead of celebrating a man who brought a lot of hurt into this space, we're going to celebrate our bookstore. We're struggling here, and we'd really love your support. We're also going to celebrate a young woman who is a poet, because that feels like justice today. We'd love if you stayed, ate some of the snacks and cakes we had ready for this visit, and instead listen to some rad poetry. We get if you'd like to leave, though. The choice, as always, is yours."

Rinn smiled. It wasn't her usual, ray-of-sunshine smile. It was a quieter thing. A smile that was a little bit sad and a little bit threatening. "Thank you so much for your time."

And then Rinn turned around, hooked her arm in Imogen's. And pulled her along. Imogen gave one last, confused smile at the girl, whose eyes had gone wide as she'd listened to Rinn speak.

Rinn kept walking. Imogen did her best to keep up. Nearby, Daniella was holding her notebook; her voice was fairly steady as she practiced her poem aloud. But her voice was a lie; Imogen could see her hand shaking as she turned the page.

"I warmed them up for you," said Rinn. "You're going to have quite the audience for your show."

Rinn winked, then let go of Imogen's arm. She went off, to go set up decorations for the party. Imogen watched as she wove in and out of customers, making sure they were staying. After a minute of watching Rinn work, Imogen looked over at Daniella. She could tell, of all the things that Rinn could have said, that mentioning the audience had *not* helped Daniella's nerves. Daniella's hands shook even more visibly as she read aloud this time.

Imogen sat down next to Daniella. "How's it going?"

Daniella looked up, her face stricken. "Oh, great. Super. Really fantastic. Looking forward to it."

"Oh, definitely. I can tell. You don't look like you're about to vomit or anything." Imogen nodded.

"Exactly. I feel stupendous. I regret nothing about this. I feel fine." Daniella nodded right back.

"Just as long as you're fine." Imogen nodded again. She figured Daniella would crack any moment now. When she didn't, Imogen just said, "Danny."

Daniella put her face in her hands. "I really can't do this. I can't."

"You mean you won't," said Imogen.

"No. I can't. I can't even post on my account that I'm going to be performing. I'm just. I'm going to choke. I can feel myself choking."

"So decide you won't choke."

"That's not how it works," said Daniella in a huff. Her words were a little muffled because her head was still down.

"I just watched a very small girl decide that an entire line of people would quiet down for her and they did." Imogen waited for Daniella's rebuttal to that.

Daniella's head snapped up. "I am *not* Rinn Olivera, and I am not going to *The Secret* my way through my life."

"No," said Imogen. "But I think believing in yourself a little bit couldn't hurt."

Daniella looked away for a minute. "I believe in myself."

Imogen raised an eyebrow because Daniella was never one to back off from a challenge. "Then act like it. Tell people who you are and where you'll be."

"It's not that easy," said Daniella.

"I don't think I said it was easy." Imogen had never thought that.

"You said to *just do it*," said Daniella.

Imogen shook her head. "Just because it's simple doesn't mean it's easy. I mean, I think I just realized that I've been depressed for the past, well, *while*. And, like, all the treatments for it are dead simple. They're not easy, though. They actually feel really complicated and difficult. It's just, they sound easy when someone tells them to me. Then I feel even worse. Anyway, don't do that. Don't feel even worse. Just do the thing. Don't avoid the thing."

"Wow," said Daniella. Then she pointed to herself and then back at Imogen. "Pot. Kettle. Et cetera."

Imogen stared at Daniella—stunned at her own self for a moment. "Wow, truly. You really do give the advice you need to hear, don't you? I mean, I can hear myself on this one, and the irony is unmistakable."

"That's okay," said Daniella. "I think it's advice I needed to hear, too."

Imogen nodded. "Just get up there and read your beautiful, ridiculous poetry. You love your own poetry, right?"

Daniella shrugged. "Sometimes."

That Imogen understood. "Then maybe try to channel that *sometimes*."

Daniella nodded once. She got out her phone. She flipped open the selfie mode. Looked at herself. Raked her hands through her frizzing blond hair, then gave up. She looked up at Imogen. "If I regret this, I'm blaming you."

Imogen understood. "Fair enough."

Daniella nodded. She hit record. "Hey, guys. So. It's me. Anachronistic Blonde. Coming out of my little hole of invisibility to tell everyone to get to Wild Nights Bookstore if you want to hear me read some poems."

"Don't forget the shoes," said Imogen in the background.

Daniella turned, and ran out of time on her footage. She posted it and flipped the camera onto Imogen. "Why don't you tell them about the shoes?"

Imogen cleared her throat. She could do this. If Daniella could read her poems, she could be on camera. "There's going to not only be poetry readings by your favorite poet over there, there's going to be signed fake Jordans with her art and poetry on it. Limited-edition collectors' items, people. You do not want to miss this. And all the proceeds will benefit the bookstore to keep it from going under. Damn the man. Save Wild Nights."

Daniella posted that, flipped the camera back to selfie mode, and said, "I don't know who the man is, but definitely come by and come save Wild Nights."

"You definitely know who the man is," said Imogen, even though she was off camera in that shot.

Imogen watched as Daniella posted the last video. "Well?"

"I do feel okay. Jittery but okay." Daniella shrugged.

Imogen stood up. "All right, then. Time for us to save Wild Nights."

27

My Noon, My Midnight, My Talk, My Song

5:41 P.M.
Rinn

AJ was lining up a new row of chairs. For a boy with such messy hair he was doing the job methodically. One right after another, dropping each chair into a line and then leaving a gap for an aisle. Then the next row, then on down the line, back the other way.

Crowds had been coming in since both Rinn and Daniella had put up their announcement. It had been a slow trickle at first, but there was a steadiness to it. Rashida Johnson came back. So did Charlene with the arm tattoos. Myrna had returned and found a seat at the front—one of the ones that Daniella and Rinn had already set up.

Jo'd had AJ set up more chairs just in case. Because most of the ones that Rinn and Daniella had already set up were nearly filled. Many, though not all, of the Brock Harvey fans had managed to stick around.

Rinn had figured she could do it. She could tell AJ how she felt. She could do anything if she rolled up her sleeves and got to work. That's how it had always been.

With AJ, all she had to do was time it right.

At least, that's what Rinn hoped would work.

AJ finished lining up the chairs. He dusted off his hands by wiping them together, then against his jeans. Rinn stepped forward—and of course—that was when Birdman stepped right in front of her.

Again.

Rinn wasn't even surprised at this point.

"Hello." Birdman gave a very formal nod.

"You're still here?" Rinn hadn't meant it to come out quite so sharp. But *dear God*, would this man ever leave the store? For someone who had been so hell-bent on getting his books sold *right away*, he hadn't left the place in hours.

"I am!" He was very excited about this point. Like he'd really won by making a day out of it all.

Rinn gritted her teeth. "How can I help you?"

Birdman sighed. "I'm so glad you asked. You see, I wanted to buy one of those poems that the other young lady is selling."

"They're for the bookstore," said Rinn. "Her name is Daniella Korres. She's a great poet."

"I believe that," said Birdman, a little more stiffly. "I just don't have any cash."

"Oh, you can use a card," said Rinn, finding her friendliest voice again.

"But," said Birdman. "I was hoping I could use my store credit."

It took everything in Rinn not to scream. "You can't use store credit for that, sir. This is a benefit for the bookstore. We need actual money for it."

"So when you give me credit it's not actual money?" He really did sound perplexed.

Rinn wasn't sure if she wanted to scream or punch this man

in the throat. She'd never been a particularly violent person, but she was really feeling it now. "Sir. That store credit is for store items only."

Birdman held up the Air Jordan, inked in Sharpie with a poem and a doodle. "But I'd really like to purchase this. And it's in the store."

Rinn, finally, accepted that there was no winning with this man. No logic he wouldn't undo. No reasoning other than his own that he would follow. He was never going to listen to her. She was never going to win him over. "Sir, just take what you want to the register and explain it to them there."

"But they said to talk to a manager."

Rinn took a deep breath. "Tell them Jo says it's okay."

"Great!" Birdman beamed. "Thank you so much, Jo!"

Rinn shook her head. "Anytime, sir."

Then she looked up, around the seating area, and of course, AJ was gone.

But Rinn Olivera was not going to give up now.

She went searching through the bookstore. Doing her best to avoid customers. She'd learned from years of turning on the charm that there was also a way to turn it off. To flip a switch and become the kind of magnet that repelled rather than attracted. She wasn't sure how to describe this. Other than, in some way, going invisible. She hadn't realized before she'd started filming for her channel that she was pulling focus, drawing attention. But she'd learned when harnessing that feeling, how to let go of it. How to totally deplete it out of her system and be somebody nobody paid much attention to at all.

It was working for her now.

Nobody stopped her as she moved along through the aisles.

Nobody approached her with more event- or store-related questions.

They didn't seem to notice her at all.

Rinn climbed the stairs, went under the headless roller girl. She wove in and out of the stacks of books, under the tunnel made out of books, until she found AJ in the dollar-music section. He was putting away a stack of records.

"That can wait until later, you know," said Rinn.

AJ noticed her and smiled. His smile lit up the whole second floor. "I know. I just wanted to get away from the crowds for a little bit. And I felt bad not doing some kind of work, even if it's not as important as what you're doing. I didn't want to hide and do nothing, you know?"

Rinn did know. She nodded. And for a moment—a second really—she stopped seeing the most beautiful boy in the world. She saw the quiet person who was worried about what to do when their skill set wasn't what anyone needed at the time.

The moment flashed and was gone. Rinn was still left a little dazed by how handsome AJ was. But Rinn realized that *that* was the person she wanted to know. The unsure boy just trying his best. She wanted more of those moments where she nearly forgot the effect that his looks had on her. "Hey, AJ?"

"Yeah?"

"You want to draw a poster that I can post onto my feed super quick? Can you work that fast?"

AJ looked startled. Really, honest-to-God startled. "You'd want me to?"

"Yeah," said Rinn. "As long as you're cool with me tagging you and your art account."

"Sure," said AJ with a slow grin. He reached out, touched the top of her arm.

It was such a simple touch, but it did these horrible things to Rinn's stomach. *Butterflies? Spasms?*

Did it even matter at this point?

"Thanks," he said. He grabbed a sheet of paper from a stack of flyers for a band that someone had left right by the records. He got out a Sharpie from his back pocket and started doodling. It was a quick sketch, but that was what Rinn had requested.

"You're the one that's got to draw a last-minute poster. I should definitely be the one thanking you." Rinn smiled back at him. She wanted to see that glimmer of him again beneath the glamour. She wanted to break her own spell. So she said the thing on the tip of her tongue. The words she never had the courage for before. She spoke without thinking. "Do you wanna grab dinner sometime?"

"Like a date?" said AJ, a puff of laughter escaping his lips.

But Rinn didn't think he was laughing at her. Almost like he had to ask as though it were almost a joke, just in case.

But Rinn was done with just in case. "Like a date. There's this place—the Chicago Diner—they've got the most insane cookie dough milkshakes on the planet."

AJ stopped scrawling for a minute.

Rinn stopped breathing.

"Sure," said AJ. He handed over the drawing.

Rinn looked down and snapped a photo of the flyer with her phone. She'd have it up and posted in no time. She smiled at him. "This is really great, thank you."

They stood like that, staring at each other, unsure of what to do next. AJ looked down first and Rinn assumed it was time to head back downstairs. But before she could move, AJ spoke.

"Before you go," said AJ, digging into the back pocket of his jeans.

Rinn waited, wondering.

He handed over a folded sheet of paper. "I made this for you."

Rinn took it. Her whole body was going on autopilot. She unfolded the paper, smoothed out the creases, and then looked at it. It was a drawing. It was two people, dancing almost cheek to cheek. A man and a woman. The woman had a cropped, curly bob. The man was blond and had a monocle. "Peter Wimsey and Harriet Vane. From the books."

AJ shrugged; Rinn smiled.

"Thank you," said Rinn. And then before she said anything to ruin it, Rinn turned and skipped down the stairs, hoping that the fund-raising was going as miraculously well as her love life at the moment.

They had an hour before their fates were decided.

28

Do Not Go Gentle

Daniella stared into the crowd with what could only be described as sheer fucking terror.

Even Rinn could not have anticipated this reaction, and that was saying something, because Rinn was the most positive person Daniella knew. Between their two followings, people had shown up. Also Rinn, with all her hustle and drive, had converted many of the Brock Harvey fans into Wild Nights fans. They were sitting in the chairs, waiting for the event to start. They were relatively good-natured considering the tone of the event had shifted dramatically.

So many people had showed up. What was it Rinn had said? *Book people rally.* She hadn't been kidding in the slightest.

The store was flooded with people.

Daniella was positive that she was going to vomit this time, and none of it was due to her hangover, which was now gone, or Imogen's hair, which had finally been cleaned up out of the bathroom. Forget her earlier bravery. Forget her outing herself as Anachronistic Blonde. Forget all of that confidence she had briefly built.

Daniella was going to throw up.

She was going to fail and she was going to fail by throwing up on the entire audience and there was nothing she could do about it. Her hand was already cramping from all the poems and doodles that she had drawn to ease her nerves before the performance. Her throat was constricting. And there were little spots popping in and out of her vision. She felt sweaty, everywhere, from her armpits to her hands to her hairline. *Oh God oh God oh God oh God* Daniella wished she knew who was the saint of poetry. Her mother was mostly obsessed with the martyrs. Daniella started reciting those in her head, using the rhythm of the familiar to lull her nerves, but it wasn't working. The martyrs had never failed her before.

That's when she felt a gentle hand at the back of her shoulder. "Hey."

It was Eli.

"I know you hate me right now," he said. "But could you take a deep breath? You look like you're about to hurl."

"I *am* about to hurl." But then the talking had forced Daniella to take a deep breath and man had that helped, even if she didn't want to listen to him at all.

"Look," he said. "I'm going to go warm them up. You got this. And trust me, they'll love you after they hear what I have to say."

Daniella glared at him. But the anger was better than the absolute terror, so she held on to it. Grabbed hold of the rage.

"Yup, that's it. Just be mad at me. You've got this." And then Eli grinned and alighted onto the makeshift stage.

"Hello, everyone." Both of Eli's dimples were visible as he grinned at the crowd. "So glad you could make it out to our little shindig, which is turning out to be a much bigger shindig than anybody planned. Standing room only left in the back. Hey, Danny, hand me your phone?"

Daniella, aware of every eye in the store staring at her, handed over her phone to Eli.

He opened it—*did the boy know everyone's passcodes?*—started a video, and began filming the crowd. "Everybody, wave."

Most of the people did, which annoyed Daniella to her core.

"Great, now that that's over with . . ." Eli tossed the phone back to Daniella.

Daniella, surprised, managed to catch it. She looked down. He'd posted the crowd onto her anachronisticblonde account. Daniella knew what he was doing. He was giving her social proof. He was building her up, just a little bit.

She hated that it worked.

"Hi, everyone, I'm Eli. And whether you realize it or not, I'm the reason you're all gathered here today. You see, late last night, I was going through the accounts here at Wild Nights Bookstore and Emporium and I made a discovery. This bookstore was going to close in two weeks unless we did something about it."

Someone in the audience gasped. The rest of the audience laughed at that response.

"I know," he said, putting his hand over his heart. "Tragic. And as somebody who is very bad at sitting still, I tried to do something about it. What I tried to do is flip Jordans."

This bit got a laugh out of the audience.

"I know," he said, winking. "Good for me, right? Anyway. I screwed up and bought some fake Jordans."

Eli pointed to the mountain of sneakers behind them.

"There they are, folks; get a long, hard look at one of my

most expensive mistakes, and trust me when I say, that's saying something. We've all spent the day trying to figure out what to do with them. Try to unload them onto another unsuspecting schmuck on the internet? I know, you're thinking, *That's immoral.* But the thought crossed my mind. I was ready to quickly get out of trouble. But in the end we decided to do something different. We decided to take my mistake and use it as a platform to give this poet behind me her own platform. In case you don't already follow her, she's got an account: *anachronisticblonde.* May I please present, and will you please give a warm welcome to, Daniella Korres."

The crowd applauded appropriately, and Eli waved Daniella onto the stage.

Oh God.

Daniella got out her phone. She stepped up to the mic. Then she closed her eyes, blocking out everything for a minute.

You love your own poetry, right?

Daniella looked out into the crowd. Imogen was there, smiling her ghost of a smile. Next to her was Rinn, nodding in that encouraging way that she had.

Daniella had no idea if she could do this. But she decided she would anyway. She had to try.

"'In truth the sun does not rise.'" Her voice was too quiet, she knew.

Daniella took another breath.

And then another. "'But Earth spins with all her might.'"

Just keep breathing, and maybe you won't vomit everywhere. "'To bear creation.'"

That was really the end of the sonnet. Daniella had finished the rest of the poem and had snapped a photo of it. But when she spoke it out loud, she knew she needed to say the ending couplet first. Knew she needed it to begin where the poem finished, for the symmetry of it.

She kept going, kept speaking. Maybe it wasn't any good. But maybe it was enough just to hear it out loud for herself. "'Each morning the day will break with new light.'"

Her voice grew stronger, grew more intense. "'While each night the sun flies far from the sky.'"

Daniella looked up, saw the crowd. Their faces were neutral, impassive. She closed her eyes briefly and then on an exhale recited the next line. "'When the morning comes with the sun's new cry, yet again she is born fresh and full bright.'"

The faces in the crowd blurred. She didn't register them anymore. Didn't know who they were. Didn't care. This wasn't about their reaction. She knew it mattered. But it wasn't about that. "'Just when you think the end is in whole sight—born from end is the beginning up high.'"

She had found her rhythm now. She'd found her pacing. The poem was like music, one beat following the next, each sound taking the form. "'In shrouds of clouds, the night attempts to wry the sun's light. The moon leaves the starless night, for fear of being the sun's epistle.'"

She knew some of the words were old-fashioned. "'Fear of the black, fear of what will unearth.'"

They were supposed to be old-fashioned. She was anachronistic on purpose. Looking for old forms. Looking for new ways. Her voice grew softer, but not from her own fears. Because the poem needed that sensation, and she had to give the poem its due. "'Fear of the pain, fear of trepidation.'"

And here was the grand finale. Proof that she hadn't just written a couplet about a hangover, though the hangover had prompted all the imagery. "'Tis folly that we see not a cycle: For in truth, the sun does not rise, but Earth spins with all her might to bear creation.'"

And it didn't matter, Daniella realized, if the crowd went wild or not. It didn't matter if there was thunderous applause or a polite clap. Because she'd done it. She'd performed her poetry, and she'd let her voice out of her notebook and into the world. There was nothing anybody could do to stop her ever again.

Daniella was infinite. She was invincible.

29

Hope Is the Thing with Feathers

The line to get Daniella to sign a fake Air Jordan wound around the store and practically out the door. Everyone had gone mental after that first poem. Daniella had talent, that was for sure. And then the context of that talent had sparked something spectacular. Nobody expected the peroxide blonde with Debbie Harry vibes to be the one who was into writing old-fashioned sonnets. And definitely hadn't expected them to be any good.

Rinn smiled, watching Daniella's stunned reaction. She was glowing—slightly confused as to how she'd ended up in this position—but glowing. It was like she didn't know that she could put a spotlight on herself for the things she cared about until this moment. Rinn loved getting to see people have that moment. Where they found themselves.

Rinn usually helped people do that by finding the right books for them. By encouraging them to read. But with Daniella it had been poetry. People were asking her to sign the Jordans and draw sketches on them afterward.

It was something to watch Daniella succeed like that.

Rinn went over to Imogen. "How's it looking?"

Imogen shook her head. "I mean, good. We've never cleared twenty-three hundred dollars in one night, let me tell you. Which is amazing, truly. But the problem is, it's either enough for a storage unit or enough for a storefront. Not both. Not enough for payroll, either, more than a few days. And we're definitely going to need to store the books while looking for a new space. Most of the people in line already bought their shoes because we made sure there was a pay first, sign after deal. So there probably isn't much more to come in."

"Is that all? Don't we have cash?" Rinn couldn't believe it. Couldn't believe they were going to fail after all of that.

Imogen shrugged. "A bit. We've got that store credit voucher from that guy who won't leave. But honestly, most people don't carry around cash. It's not a significant amount, not really."

They had failed.

Rinn found herself backing away from the crowds. Imogen said something, but Rinn didn't really hear her. She gave an answer. It was yes—no—maybe it was a no. It didn't matter. Rinn kept backing away. She couldn't process her thoughts. She couldn't sort through the idea of working so hard to come up short.

She made it outside to the back alley before she'd realized it. She didn't really think about how she'd gotten there. She knew she was finally alone. She thought she'd be safe from the failure that was swallowing her from the inside out. But the feeling intensified.

She was left alone with her own thoughts.

She wished she could cry again. Wished she could rage. But this feeling was more like the slow loss of feeling. She was aware of herself shutting down. Like she was outside herself, watching it happen.

Here stands Rinn Olivera, human failure.

Rinn slid down the alley wall, curled her knees to her chest, and held tightly on to herself.

She had failed.

Rinn had never failed at anything before in her life. She'd always managed to get it all the way across the line. Always managed to push through. But there was nothing left to push through. Here were the results in black and white. They didn't have the funds to keep the bookstore open. They didn't make the funds to see her vision through.

Failure. It was inevitable, and it was her own doing. Rinn felt that. It was the only feeling she really had left. She wasn't enough, and she hadn't done enough, and she would never be enough, maybe ever again.

The back door slammed open, and Imogen came out. Her face was all worried and scrunched up. "Are you okay?"

Rinn reached her arm out, and Imogen came and sat beside her. "Not really."

Daniella dashed through the door next. "I told them all I was having a hand cramp and to give me a five-minute break. Would you believe it, everyone was cool with it." Daniella paused, realizing that now was not the time. "What's going on? What happened?"

"The bookstore is going to close," said Rinn.

Daniella plopped down next to Rinn. "Of course the bookstore is going to close. Nothing was ever saved in a day, except in the movies."

"We failed," said Rinn. "I failed."

Imogen shook her head. "That depends on your definition of failure."

"There's only one definition," said Rinn. "We were meant to save the bookstore. We were the last hope. And we didn't get it across the line. We didn't even get close. Okay, we got close, but we either have to pick storing the books for a month or finding a storefront, and we barely have time to even do one of them. We can't even save the books. What was I thinking? We failed."

"Excuse me," said Imogen. "There I take umbrage."

"Ohhh, *umbrage*. Excellent word. I'll have to note that down in my notebook. It's got great syllabication, too," said Daniella.

"Thank you, Danny." Imogen cleared her throat. "I take *umbrage* at the fact, Little Miss Perfect, that you have a binary and totally bonkers definition of failure. And we all know binary definitions of anything are harmful and unhelpful."

"Have you been calling her that in your head the whole time we've worked together—*Little Miss Perfect*, I mean?" asked Daniella. "Because I usually think of her as Little Miss Sunshine."

"You're both very rude," said Rinn, at a loss for how the conversation was twisting and turning around her.

Daniella ignored this aside. "Wait, what was mine again?"

Imogen shrugged. "Cool Girl or Coolest Girl in the World."

Daniella tilted her head. "Hers is better."

"Guys!" said Rinn, feeling like she needed to take charge and focus the conversation.

Imogen's expression grew stern. "We didn't fail."

"We did. The bookstore is closing. We'll never see each other again. We'll never all work together again." And then, because Rinn really was feeling desperate, she tacked on, "Everything is horrible and nothing is good and nothing good will ever happen again. Bookstores are dying, and I can't change that. And I really thought we could be friends."

"Quit feeling sorry for yourself," said Daniella.

Rinn reeled back. "Excuse me."

"You heard me. Quit feeling sorry for yourself. We might not have saved Wild Nights the brick-and-mortar store, but we saved Wild Nights," said Daniella.

"Yeah," said Imogen. "And we saved Jo from taking out a terrible loan. Nobody is going to jail. Danny here announced she's a poet. And, like, you rallied all those people, Rinn. You got so many people off their butts and got them into the store for *poetry*."

Daniella nodded. "None of this should have worked. But it did. Maybe not all the way. Maybe not the way you saw it. But it worked because you believed it would."

Rinn didn't know what to say to that.

"We did that, Rinn. We all did it, and you got us there." Imogen looked over at Daniella. "Well, Danny helped."

Daniella slugged Imogen's arm, but in a playful kind of way.

Imogen paused for a moment. "There's this idea, I guess, in Islam—ummah, and if you translate it directly, it means 'community,' which is cheesy as hell. But really it's this idea that we share something together beyond any one tribe. Like back in the day everyone on the Arabian Peninsula was fighting and retaliating and fighting. But Islam was something they had in common. Something beyond their close-knit kinship ties. A thing bigger than any of them. And we did that today. I'm depressed, and Daniella is angry, and you're full of sunshine. Eli's basically a criminal, and AJ is an earnest art kid. And we all found this bookstore to be bigger than any one of those things. You helped us find that."

"I hadn't thought about it like that," Rinn said.

"Because you're so busy focusing on one binary definition of success that you've missed all the magic you made." Imogen crossed her arms. She was in a huff now.

Rinn reached out, touched Imogen's shoulder. "I'm sorry. You're right. Binaries are awful."

"Yeah, you better be. We all worked for you. You rallied us. Now you're saying we failed because we didn't save some awful, out-of-touch guy's bookstore. Well, good riddance." Imogen tilted her head away, like she was still upset with Rinn for suggesting that they had failed.

Rinn wanted her to understand. "It's just. It's my other home."

Daniella laughed—almost at Rinn, but a little bit the way she always did, laughing at what the universe would throw at her. "Same here. Same for all of us. But that doesn't mean it's lost forever. I mean, given what I thought was going to happen, just an hour ago, I'll take this win and every win like it. Look, I just accidentally confessed *my* feelings to Eli, and I didn't even want to admit them to myself."

"You would?" Rinn had never heard Daniella be so open. She'd never thought of wins on a sliding scale before. She'd only thought about results. "Wait, you did?"

"I would. And I did."

"Do you want to take them back now?" It was the only question Rinn could think of. The most important question at the top of her mind. She needed the answer like she needed air and front-facing cameras.

Daniella shrugged. "How can I? They're feelings. They might not stay true, but they were true. I think if I've gotten anything from performing my poetry, it's that I can't keep my feelings pocketed in little notebooks to keep them safe. I don't think anything really works like that."

Rinn was watching these two girls. They had been practically strangers to her this morning. Now they were like wise abuelas or tías or something telling her the secrets of the universe that they had learned from life. Maybe they weren't always right, but they definitely weren't wrong, either.

"Are we going to be okay?" asked Rinn. It was a question she needed to know the answer to.

"No idea," said Daniella. "But I'm willing to try if you are."

"Same," said Imogen.

Daniella put her hand in the middle of their little circle. "All right, hands in."

And all three piled their hands, one on top of the other.

Daniella smirked her mischievous smirk. "I say we go in there and celebrate that nobody is going to jail and nobody is going further into debt. Also, that I actually like you two fools and I never thought I'd hear myself saying that. And I say we throw a dance party on the roof when it's all over, because if Wild Nights Bookstore is closing, it's closing with a goddamned bang."

"Yeah," said Rinn.

"Agreed," said Imogen, with one of her own quiet half smiles.

"And then, I say we steal the roller girl on our way out." Daniella raised her eyebrows.

Rinn and Imogen said deal at the same time.

And then Daniella's smirk stretched out into a grin as she was about to say something when a figure popped out of the shadows.

"I'm sorry to be rude, young ladies. But I couldn't help but overhear that you're looking for a place to store all these lovely books." Madame Bettache stepped out of the shadows and into the light of the alley, like an avenging angel. She was stubbing out a cigarette under her foot, and she looked like a woman who knew about the world in a way that Rinn might never.

And in that moment, Rinn found her hope again.

30

But Still, Like Air

8:34 P.M.
Imogen

Imogen watched as Rinn and Daniella and Madame Auntie left the back alley. They were going back into the store and talking through how much space she had in her enormous brownstone that she now lived in alone and how much the bookstore could temporarily use. Madame Auntie said she could loan the space and they could pay her back for it.

Business, she said. It was all treating them like businesswomen.

Rinn was back to organizing and rallying. Imogen had watched as Rinn's mind began counting up boxes and shelves. She said she would enlist Rashida—who had stayed for the poetry event—and Charlene, who had come back especially for it. Daniella had immediately asked for fair pricing and whether there would be interest on the space as a loan.

Madame Auntie started quoting numbers, and she was talking about the ways in which she could delay the interest. She said she would write up a contract and that while it wasn't legally binding for them to sign it as minors, she would take their signatures on the document along with Jo's. Because she wanted to treat them like equals in this deal.

Imogen had stuck out her hand for a firm handshake. Madame Auntie had taken it solemnly and followed the other two inside.

Imogen had the outside to herself, now. She said she'd be inside to help them in a minute.

It smelled like the end of a hot day. Stinking and messy, horrible and baked. With the sun going down, the temperature ought to have been relieved of at least a couple degrees of its pungency. But it was still humid, and it was still summer, and it was still Chicago. There would still be mosquitoes, even after dark.

Imogen knew, deep in her bones, that she would miss this horrible little alleyway.

She'd miss the awful way it smelled and the way the breeze picked up at night, taunting her with the idea of cooling off but never actually doing the job properly. Maybe they really had saved Wild Nights. But Wild Nights was also closing, and she'd miss this original spot like a homeland that she knew she could never come back to.

A head poked out of the doorway. "Oh, it's you."

It was the girl from earlier. Her expression shifted from curious to delighted. Her hair was lit from behind—from the lights inside the store—giving her a slight glow, gold on the edges of her deep brown waves. "It's so cold in there. I don't know how an old building manages to stay air-conditioned in this city."

"Only at night, when we've all sweated our way through the day." Imogen waved because she was the most awkward human on the planet. "But hi. I was out here with a couple of friends."

"That's cool," said the girl. She was swinging the door back and forth in her hands. It was seesawing and making a tiny screeching noise.

"I'm Imogen, by the way."

"Olivia," said the girl with a smile. "But people call me Liv. Or Livy, if they'd like to die earlier."

The comment didn't hit Imogen the way she thought it might. She laughed, unlocking another small piece of her sadness. It was still there, but its hold wasn't as gripping as it usually was.

It was time.

"Olivia—Liv—I've got some stuff to finish up out here."

Liv's face fell slightly.

"But do you maybe want to come to a dance party on the roof after the signing?"

Liv's smile returned, full force. "There's gonna be a dance party on the roof?"

Imogen did her best to steady her breathing. "Yes, ma'am, there is."

"I'd love to," she said.

"Cool," said Imogen. "I'll be back on the floor in a minute. I think they're looking for people willing to start packing books into boxes."

"I'm up for that," said Liv.

Imogen looked over. Her jacket from this morning was still there. Still in a pile.

Liv caught sight of it. She leaned over and picked it up. "This yours?"

Imogen felt her mouth tugging into a smile. "Nah, I don't think anyone wants this jacket anymore. You should take it."

Liv grinned even bigger. She slid into the jacket and asked, "How does it look?"

"Pretty good," said Imogen.

Liv laughed as she said, "Alright, I'll see you inside," before she swooped back into the bookstore.

Imogen smiled at the air for a solid minute. Then she got out her phone. She clicked through, trying to find the app that Jo had recommended. Talk something. Fresh talk. New talk.

Talkspace. That's what it was.

Imogen clicked through and began the sign-up process. It took much longer than she had anticipated. It was frustrating, but she kept going, didn't give up.

She didn't want to give up.

Maybe some piece of her—maybe it was only 3 percent, really—but that sliver hadn't wanted to give up, either. It had held on, tethered her to this place, to these people. It had made her reach out. It was keeping her on task on her phone now. A few more clicks and Imogen had an appointment for the next day. It wasn't perfect, and she didn't know if she'd like the person, but it was a start.

Imogen stood up. She dusted off the gravel from her jeans. She opened the door and moved through the aisles. She stopped just short of the large open space where the chairs were set up.

Ahead, she saw Daniella signing Jordans with a look that was a mix of pride and astonishment across her face. She saw Rinn, enjoying herself. Smiling at what she had done, rather than focusing on what she hadn't quite accomplished.

Imogen smiled. Nothing was perfect. But maybe things could still be all right.

31

A Stately Pleasure-dome

Madame Bettache was about as bossy as Rinn when put in charge of something, and she had run the two of them around the store for the past forty-five minutes. Eventually she was done stating what she could and couldn't store. And Rinn was done arguing what was and wasn't needed to keep the store running in a different space. And then Jo got involved, and they were all arguing and shouting, and for a moment Daniella thought it was going to come to blows again.

But instead they'd all found agreement on what did and did not need to be taken to the new space, wherever that ended up being. Rinn won her argument about the art in the building needing to be preserved.

Daniella had chimed in only once to suggest that they leave all the Clive Cusslers on the antiquated register for Archer as their parting gift to him.

And Jo got to save the inventory she thought would really sell. They made a plan—and a few more customers volunteered, including the Birdman, who had been pestering Rinn all day; the mom who usually read with her kid in the children's section; Myrna, who was told that she could supervise and bring pastries; and the zoologist lady with all those amazing tattoos.

It was all very: *Wild Nights Is Closing; Long Live Wild Nights!*

The Will of the People, and all that.

Which, if she didn't like being such a cynic in public, Daniella might have admitted to out loud. As it was, she could smirk over the fact that in a couple of days, Archer Hunt Junior would come down to close the place and sign over the deed and all the art and all the books would be gone. Except for those Clive Cussler novels.

So Daniella got out a slip of paper from the register. And the Sharpie that was still in her back pocket from all of those signings. In big block letters she wrote out—

THIS IS ALL YOUR FAULT 😛
CARPE DIEM,
THE MANAGEMENT

And then, so there was absolutely no confusion, Rinn left that note for Archer Hunt Junior to find on top of that stack of Clive Cusslers and all his pandering adventures. She set it there along with a copy of Rinn Olivera's written summary that Wild Nights Bookstore had a right to retain Wild Nights' intellectual property, even if the equipment and land were being sold.

The man certainly didn't deserve a phone call or any other valuable use of their time. They all had real work to do saving this store. They weren't going to waste any more of it on him.

Rinn, finally done with all of her orchestrating, signaled Daniella over.

"What's up?" Daniella had practically skipped there, which was embarrassing in and of itself.

"Can you get the microphone from the break room?" Rinn had this serious look of concern on her face.

"Is everything okay?" Daniella watched her, worried.

"It's great," said Rinn with a smile that did nothing to assuage Daniella's worries. "Just go get the microphone, okay?"

Daniella nodded and went off gathering the rest of the employees. Most of the customers were slowly funneling out. They'd had their poetry and their good time and they were ready to get back to their own lives. Daniella saw, for a moment, the kind of community that they could have built had Archer Hunt not kept holding them back. Had he not continued to simply slash prices and pretend to hope for the best. He hadn't been hoping for the best at all; he had simply wanted to say that he'd tried and sold the land back to the purveyors of multiuse space and gentrification.

But there it was, that glimmer of belonging. For the past couple of hours the bookstore had belonged to these people as well. It had been their space, the way it had been Daniella's space and Rinn's space and Imogen's space. Even Eli's and AJ's.

It had been theirs, and they had shared that with the world. And somehow, they all had a slice of it. In the end, they had been too late to save the old girl in her present form, but they had done something big and beautiful, and Daniella wasn't crying, honestly, she just had a sniffle or something from all the dust in the air.

"I know," said Jo, coming up from behind Daniella. "It's kind of magical, isn't it?"

Daniella rolled her eyes, and Jo smiled, like she'd been saying the irritating thing to help keep Daniella from getting too misty-eyed.

"Dance party on the roof?" asked Daniella.

Jo nodded. "Dance party on the roof."

Daniella followed Rinn's instructions and went into the break room and found the PA mic. "Greetings, Wild Nights Bookstore and Emporium—we are now closed. If you could make your way to the exits, that would be a beautiful thing. You're all aces in our book. We couldn't have done what we did today without you. I hate to say that it wasn't enough, because it wasn't. But also, it was everything. So thank you, and maybe don't watch this space in the future, but watch this space, for spaces like this."

Daniella laughed and then said, "Oh, and employees, there's a mandatory meeting of the musical society on the super-terrarium garden annex. I suggest you get there."

That's when Eli poked his head up, out from behind some boxes.

Daniella jumped. "Jesus, you scared the hell out of me, Eli."

"Sorry," he said. And he did look genuinely sorry.

"It's fine," she said. "What's up?"

"I have something to show you."

"Eli," said Daniella. "Can we not do this now? It's cool. I get you're not into me, and that's fine. It's just super weird, and I don't really want to live through this weirdness tonight. Can we save it for tomorrow? Or, like, maybe never. I think never might also be great."

But Eli smirked that goddamned crinkly smile that he had. And then he walked over and turned out the lights so that all across the ceiling were glow stars, as far as the eye could see.

"When did you do this?" Daniella stared at the fake sky in wonder.

"When I was waiting to talk to Jo in the office. Before you came in and got in a fight with the coffee machine."

"It's hideous." And it really was. It was wonky and plastic-looking and the kind of decor value you would expect from an elementary school kid with way too much time on their hands. "I love it."

"Yeah?"

"Yeah." Daniella looked at him; his face was so serious. "Why did you do it?"

"I dunno," he said. "You just seemed so sad, and I wanted to make you smile."

"I wasn't sad," said Daniella. "I was hungover."

They were getting closer and closer together. Like they were pulled together by each other's gravity. By some strange inevitability. So many steps together, so slowly, that it was the most natural thing in the world that they went from across the room from each other to no more than a few inches apart. Daniella didn't even really notice it. Like they'd been moving this way for years and she hadn't noticed it.

"But," said Daniella. "You got so freaked out earlier."

"I know," said Eli. "I'm really sorry. I'm in love with you, too, by the way. I am absolutely terrible at showing it."

"This part isn't so terrible," said Daniella.

"How many more glow-in-the-dark stars do I have to set up before you'll forgive me?"

"A million," said Daniella with a smile.

"A million?" asked Eli. "It's a deal."

And then Daniella threw her arms around Eli's neck, and she pulled him in. Their lips met—soft at first, then playful. It was the kiss of two people who enjoyed sparring with each other. Two people who would never let the other have the upper hand for very long.

Daniella couldn't hold in her smile.

They broke apart when Rinn came crashing into the room with Imogen in tow. "Guys, there's no time for kissing."

And then, unceremonious as she pleased, Rinn grabbed Daniella's hands. She pulled both of the girls up toward the roof, with Eli lagging behind, laughing. Imogen huffed and puffed the entire way, complaining that she didn't exercise for a reason, thank you very much.

When they all arrived at the roof breathless, Rinn began dancing to no rhythm, dancing to no music. Daniella laughed. Imogen came in, rolled her eyes, and then turned on the last playlist that Jo had queued up. AJ found the breaker on the roof and turned on a bunch of old lights. And then the entire staff of Wild Nights Bookstore and Emporium were across the roof, dancing and twirling. Like this really was the end. Like they had fought a good fight, but they'd made their push too late and their effort had not been enough.

But it didn't matter, because they had been enough.

They danced and the world kept going and their bodies kept moving, and they knew that they were all going to be all right.

SUNDAY

SIX WEEKS LATER

NINE HOURS BEFORE BREAKING GROUND ON THE NEW
WEST GARDEN LIVING-DINING-SHOPPING EXPERIENCE

EPILOGUE

A Book of Myths
(In Which Our Names Do Not Appear)

10:00 P.M., Sunday
Eli

There were no rules to watching any of Rinn's videos on her account, but, for some reason, Eli felt like there should be some anyway.

1. Watch the whole live video all the way through. No skipping, no pausing.
2. Get all snacks and beverages ready ahead of time.
3. Don't continuously message hi just to get Danny's attention.

Eli did still miss Jo's weird bag of vape pens. But he was learning to live without it. Learning to live without a few things, ever since Wild Nights Bookstore had closed. Jo was looking for spaces in Pilsen or Bridgeport. She said she'd recently gotten a tip on a spot in Greektown from the old French Tunisian lady who was storing their books. But the live video was about to start, and Eli didn't have time to consider much else. He sat there, waiting for the notification to go up. It wasn't like Eli could have forgotten about the event today, considering Danny had reminded him all week that they were going live at 6:00 P.M. and not to miss the video.

Eli knew she wasn't going to let it slide if he didn't watch.

bookishbruja is going live. The notification pinged his phone right on time.

And there she was. Rinn smiling at the front-facing camera. "Hey, guys, guess what?"

"What?" asked Eli all alone in the room to himself.

Rinn had been gracious enough to pause for a moment, and Eli felt like responding out loud was what he ought to do. It wasn't like he was actually going to type into the feed and pop up along with all of those other mentions, all of them telling Rinn how wonderful and amazing she was.

That was definitely *not* for Eli.

"I am here," said Rinn on an excited, breathless tone, "with two of my friends."

Rinn panned the camera over to Danny, who was smiling, and Imogen, who was, well, not frowning for once. Eli had almost gotten used to Imogen's shaved head. "And we are going to do something we've only ever read about in old books."

"Movies," said Danny, because she couldn't let Rinn get in the last word. "We've watched it in movies."

Rinn stuck her tongue out at Danny.

Imogen gave a playful elbow shove to Rinn. "Don't fight. Tell them."

"We are going to bury a time capsule." Rinn was positively bursting with joy and information. "We're going to do it like— what was the story?"

Danny crossed her arms over her chest. Eli tried to not ogle her. It was a half-hearted effort, and he failed at it, but at least he had *tried*, you know.

"*Now and Then*. We're burying a time capsule like *Now and Then*." Danny tilted her head so her entire pose screamed *disaffected youth* like it was an old album cover. Except her eyes were too bright and her smile was a little too giddy to pull it off.

"That movie doesn't have a time capsule." This was from Imogen.

Danny glared, immediately on the defensive. "Well, it should have."

"Guys." Rinn was keeping the peace this time. "It was a good idea."

And then they all three busted up laughing. At a private joke that nobody really got but everyone had to immediately understand belonged to all of them.

And then Rinn jiggled the camera, and Eli realized she was putting her phone on a tripod and she was setting up a new shot. She looked at the camera, winked, and said, "We'll be right back."

And then they were all walking off, back toward what had once been Wild Nights Bookstore and Emporium. What was now an empty, dug-out pit.

The patron saints of gentrification worked fast.

One day it was a historical building. The next it was a giant hole in the ground—to be turned into a multilevel parking lot attached to a multiuse living-shopping-dining experience extravaganza.

Eli watched as the girls receded from the frame.

Three girls walking out into a construction site and attempting to make it their own. A place that had once been theirs but was now beyond leveled and covered with CAUTION KEEP OUT signs and fencing and all sorts of barriers and cues that told them they no longer belonged.

But instead of staying away, they were burying their secrets on the site. Sure, everyone would know about it, so it wasn't really a great place to bury secrets. But after this video, nobody would be able to access the construction site again for a while. Or, at least, that was how Danny had explained it.

Eli hadn't believed it. But it was still a good shot—the Chicago skyline at dusk behind the silhouette of three girls as they slowly walked toward the sunset.

"Perfect," he said. "Well. Almost perfect."

Three girls, linked arm in arm. The girl in the middle was holding the box filled with whatever it was they wanted to bury there and remember. Whatever they felt had to be essentially itself forever and whatever they felt they might forget if they didn't bury it there in that spot, for the earth to protect it from whatever time would do to it. They had told no one else what was in that box. And then there was a shadow in the background that almost looked like a headless girl wearing roller skates.

Eli laughed—he had been wondering where the roller girl had gone.

That's when a gust of city wind hit the tripod and the phone. The feed wobbled once, then fell from portrait to landscape mode. Rinn's clear, aligned shot had been tipped over.

Everyone in the comments were furious. They were screaming at her, but they were screaming in text, and Rinn didn't have her phone with her anymore so she had no idea. No idea that her perfect shot had been unaligned and that she and Imogen and Danny were no longer on camera or in frame.

That their secret hiding place really would belong to them and them alone.

And then Eli thought about all of Rinn's clever plans and Imogen's love of machinery and Danny's love of math, and the casual blowing over of the camera didn't seem so accidental anymore. It seemed beautifully staged. A different kind of plan. A way for this moment to be shared and, also, theirs alone.

Danny had said it would stay a secret.

"Perfect," he said. And Eli meant it. No conditions, no clauses. Just perfect.

Eli closed down the live feed. It was just a sideways video of a construction site now.

Off camera, three girls were burying their secrets. Maybe one day they'd dig them up. Maybe they wouldn't.

But the city would guard their memories, regardless. Waiting, until they were ready.

ACKNOWLEDGMENTS

This book started with an idea, a very simple one: what if Empire Records was in a bookstore and what if the central characters of the story were the three girls. That was my in. That was my through line. But when you write a book about an independent bookstore, you start to think about all of the little pockets of community that you encounter.

To my editor, Kat, who has gone on this ride with me three times now. Thank you, from the bottom of my heart. Every book with you is work, yes, but it's joyful work and it's purposeful work and I feel like I learn so much about writing, about books, and about myself. This book was so hard for me to get through, but your notes made me feel like it was possible. You're a goddamned hero. Thank you.

To my agent, Lauren, for every time she's found my books a home. You have believed in all of my angry, messy girls from the beginning. You never doubted them for a moment—and for that I will be eternally grateful. Thanks for giving Imogen, Daniella, and Rinn a space to shine. Whenever I see my books stacked in a row, I think of you giving me a shot and taking on my work and I'm just filled with gratitude and wonder.

To my publicist, Morgan Rath, who has worked so hard to get all three of my books out in the world, into the spotlight. Thank you for all of your efforts and thank you for all of your work. I still wish there was a better way to say this other than thank you. But thank you. An enormous thank you goes to the entire team at Feiwel and Friends/Macmillan: Kim Waymer, Jean Feiwel, Alexei Esikoff, Jessica White, and Erica Ferguson.

Liz Dresner—you have given me stunning cover after stunning cover. Your ability to understand my work and translate that understanding into a visual medium always leaves me in awe. Thank you, thank you, thank you. And to Carina Lindmeier—you brought my girls Daniella, Rinn, and Imogen to life. I really did cry when I saw them there, all in a line with their beautiful angst and attitude and come-at-me vibes. Thank you for all your work.

I feel I would be remiss if I did not mention the independent bookstores and the amazing libraries that I have encountered along my journey as an author. Thank you to Rose Brock for being such a champion of young people's literature. Thank you to Emily Aaronson for building your own community at the Studio City Public Library. Thank you to Maryelizabeth and Jackie from Mysterious Galaxy in San Diego. Cathy Berner from Blue Willow Books in Houston. Every member of staff that I've had the privilege to work with at Vroman's Bookstore in Pasadena. Thank you to Mark, Joy, and Cassie at Brazos Bookstore in Houston. Chelsea Maidhof and Bea and Leah Koch at The Ripped Bodice in Los Angeles. It takes an enormous village to get books into the hands of readers and you all ensure that that village is diverse, inclusive, and fun.

To my agency siblings, Jodi and Valerie, who have helped form my first bookish community. Thank you for being there when I needed. Thank you for all of your support.

To Emily, Austin, and Bridget—I'm about to sound a lot like Anne Shirley and say that I feel like I have found kindred spirits who love Jane Austen, Shakespeare, the cheesiest of action flicks, and the bawdiest of humor (see, I avoided saying "dick jokes" like a real lady). Thank you for all of your support as I rewatch *The Mummy* every fortnight. Also, thank you for being the kind of people who feel like home.

To the rest of the Electrics—Bree, Britta, Dana, Farrah, Lisa, Marie, Maura, Somaiya, Ash, Rachel, Tanaz—thank you for building communities across the city of Los Angeles and across the internet. We do such a solitary job and I feel like I have colleagues and community, despite the fact that I spend most of the time working alone. That is no mean feat—thank you so much for all that you are.

To Diya—thank you for reading a key draft of this book and also thank you for sending me Peter Wimsey fan fiction after you read it. It was an internet rabbit hole I never needed to know existed but I'm so glad that I do now. Also thank you for being the recipient of most of the memes that I find. We will always be 2 Fast and 2 Furious.

Brandy Colbert was the first writer to welcome me back to LA. She and I met on the 'gram and when I showed up to a real live book event she claimed she actually knew me to a whole panel full of other writers. You stuck your neck out there for an unknown quantity at the time and I'll never forget it. Thank you, Brandy. To Maux, Sarah, Zan, Morgan, and Elissa—thank you for welcoming me as well when I showed up almost three years ago with a book deal and some stars in my eyes. Y'all are beyond generous with your time and your community. Thank you.

And as always, thank you to Steven, who has been cheer-leading me at this game for the better part of a decade. Thank you for never letting me take the easy way out. Thank you for always being kind. Thank you for every cup of coffee you make in the morning. Thank you for being the person who inspires me to be the best version of myself. You still deserve as many maple-glazed donuts as the universe is willing to send your way.

And thank you to the city of Chicago, for kicking my ass all those years ago. You left an indelible mark.

GO FISH

AMINAH MAE SAFI

What did you want to be when you grew up?
I had no idea. There was a time when I wanted to be a professor. And honestly, I still love teaching. But I wasn't one of those kids who just knew what they wanted to be and knew what they were going to do to get there. I worked hard so that I had options for my future, but I never had a decided plan. I used to really envy people who knew, but now I've just learned to accept that who I am is someone who needed time to find that focus and direction. I had to give myself space to pursue lots of options, which was terrifying when I was younger.

When did you realize you wanted to be a writer?
Is it incredibly nerdy to quote Jane Austen slash Mr. Darcy and say "I cannot fix on the hour, or the spot, or the look, or the words, which laid the foundation. It is too long ago. I was in the middle before I knew that I *had* begun"? Because truly I was in the middle of trying to be a professional writer before I realized I wanted to be a writer.

Writing is this skill that I've honed throughout my life—all throughout school and into my initial working life. I have always been writing. I love storytelling and I always have, so combining those two things—actively using writing as the means by which I tell stories—was something I slowly did throughout my early twenties. It wasn't so much that I ever woke up one day and realized I wanted to be a writer. It was a slow process of building upon the skill set I already had in order to be able to tell the kinds of stories I so desperately wanted to tell.

What's your most embarrassing childhood memory?
I'm really sorry to disappoint, but I am very much like my father and have little to no shame. Lots of embarrassing things have happened to me, but I don't really register them in my long-term memory bank. I think shaking off embarrassing memories might be my superpower.

As a young person, who did you look up to most?
When I was a kid, I was obsessed with Old Hollywood. I think some of it was the glamour, because I love glam and I am super femme. But I loved reading about all of these women who learned to drive their own careers in an age where there was so little they could do and so few other women they could look up to. Mary Pickford started her own production company in the nineteen teens. Marilyn Monroe was the first actor to negotiate their contract to have creative control on their projects over the studio, all during the studio system. I was obsessed with Liz Taylor, full stop.

I also loved reading about female artists and scientists. Marie Curie. Frida Kahlo. Artemisia Gentileschi. Ada Lovelace. I loved seeing and reading and learning about women who made something of themselves, particularly during times when they were supposed to retreat away from the public eye and erase themselves into their homes, their husbands, and their families. I was always drawn to the stories of women who maybe had families and husbands and maybe didn't, but who always found a way to step into the foreground. I'm also Muslim and I loved that the prophet's first wife, Khadija, was older than him, had a successful mercantile business, and proposed to him. That was the kind of woman I wanted to grow up into as a kid.

What was your favorite thing about school?
Is it weird to say everything? I loved learning and I still love learning. I'm also an extrovert, so I loved that when I got to school, I would see everyone I knew. I thrive in group environments and in places where I get to just read and learn intensively. The odd thing I miss most about school is having a built-in cafeteria where I can eat lunch. I also envy Silicon Valley kitchens for this. Being able to just show up and have lunch provided every day is solid gold, and I wish I still had this in my life.

Did you play sports as a kid?
I played soccer for eleven years! Soccer was my first love, but I was lucky enough to be able to try (and honestly be bad at) a ton of other sports. There's a ton of running in soccer, so I ran a lot. I also swam, until swimming required getting up at 5:00 a.m. for practice. (I am not, nor will I ever be, a morning person.) I was also a mediocre field hockey player, a not-quite-good basketball player, and a decidedly terrible tennis player.

I also did a martial art called aikido from ages seven to eighteen. That taught me a lot about discipline and self-control and where my body was in space. I wasn't actually diagnosed until I was in my mid-twenties, but I've got ADHD, so I'm pretty sure all these sports were my way of coping with the sheer enormity of how much excess energy I had. I still need to work out almost every day in order to sit and do my job!

What was your first job, and what was your "worst" job?

First job was selling candied nuts at a market during the holiday season, funnily enough. The market itself helped sponsor the ballet company I danced with, and the stalls were filled with everything people buy specifically for Christmas and Hanukkah and New Year's. I stood around talking to strangers, attempting to get them to try different candied nuts—I kid you not. It was a great job, though. It taught me to talk to tons of strangers, to be absolutely fearless in driving in new customers, and also that I do well in jobs where I'm on my feet all day.

My worst job was actually kind of a dream job at the time. I worked in a museum in the curatorial department, something I thought I really wanted to do. Most of curatorial is actually just a fancy-sounding administration job, especially the roles for anyone right out of college. But the worst part of my job was sending out rejection letters to unsolicited submissions for art. Most museums do this, by the way, and they have listed on their websites that they do not take unsolicited submissions for their collections. But people send them anyway, and I would end up reading about all of these people's art and lives and then draft form letters to crush their dreams all day. I actually got yelled at for trying to make the standard letter slightly more polite. I felt awful every day at that job.

What book is on your nightstand now?

I've just finished *If I'm Being Honest* by Austin Siegemund-Broka and Emily Wibberley, which was such a delight. I'm hoping to dive into *The Revolution of Birdie Randolph* by Brandy Colbert and *Somewhere Only We Know* by Maurene Goo next! I'm also finally getting to this dual biography of

Mary Wollstonecraft and Mary Wollstonecraft Shelley called *Romantic Outlaws*. It's about the parallel lives of mother and daughter, even though Mary Wollstonecraft died giving birth to Mary Shelley. I love any story about legacy, and Mary Shelley definitely felt the weight of her mother's legacy as she grew up.

How did you celebrate publishing your first book?
Went out to a pizza dinner with friends after my launch. I highly recommend it. It was a fantastic and delicious celebration surrounded by the people I love.

Where do you write your books?
Anywhere I can sit with my laptop. My desk, my couch, my bed. A coffee shop. I like variety, and I embrace that I'm able to do that right now in my career!

What challenges do you face in the writing process, and how do you overcome them?
Self-doubt is a big one. I think I just fake it until I make it, on that one. I just decide to keep going, even if I can't quite believe that I'll get there. I've found that continuing to show up and make progress is the only way I can quiet that voice.

What is your favorite word?
Supercalifragilisticexpialidocious.

What was your favorite book when you were a kid? Do you have a favorite book now?
They're mostly the same. *From the Mixed-Up Files of Mrs. Basil E. Frankweiler*. The Harry Potter books. *Pride and Prejudice* was my favorite Jane Austen book when I was growing up, though now I have a soft spot for *Persuasion*

and *Northanger Abbey*. I loved *Harriet the Spy* and the Nancy Drew books and The Baby-Sitters Club. *Bloomability* by Sharon Creech. The Confessions of Georgia Nicolson series by Louise Rennison. *I Capture the Castle* by Dodie Smith. *Their Eyes Were Watching God* by Zora Neale Hurston. *Habibi* by Naomi Shihab Nye.

If you could travel in time, where would you go and what would you do?
Look, I'm a woman of color. I only travel into the future. I love reading history, but participating in courtly intrigue anywhere on this planet is truly not a game I'd like to play if I don't have to. The stakes are way too high. I also like modern dental care and anesthetics.

What's the best advice you have ever received about writing?
Weirdly, it was Natalie Dormer talking about her own acting career. But she said not to envy someone else's career, just learn to appreciate your own, and that has always stuck with me. And by "said," I mean, I think I saw this literally in GIF form. But anyway, accept your career for what it is, and don't worry about anyone else. Staring at their career with jealousy does nothing to further your own. We all get different assets and drawbacks in our careers (and in our lives). Learn to make the most of what you do get and not worry too much about what you don't get. It's out of your hands, anyway.

What advice do you wish someone had given you when you were younger?
You're gonna be all right, kid. Or something of that variety. I was so scared when I was younger that I didn't have my

life mapped out, that I didn't have a plan, that I wasn't sure what I wanted. I'm sure people told me this, but I really wish I had listened. As long as you keep trying, you're gonna be all right.

Do you ever get writer's block? What do you do to get back on track?
I do! Depends on the writer's block. If it's something I'm afraid to write, I have to confront that fear. If I'm feeling burnt out, I have to go outside, go for a walk, or go to a museum and look at other people's beautiful art. If I've written myself into a corner, I have to just delete everything until the last moment I wasn't stuck and start over.

What do you want readers to remember about your books?
The characters. I loved getting to hang out with characters as a reader, and I hope that I get to provide that for my own audience.

What would you do if you ever stopped writing?
Find another way to tell stories, I hope. I think, ultimately, writing is the sharpest tool in my tool kit, but it's not the only one I've got. But I'd love to keep telling stories for as long as I'm able.

If you were a superhero, what would your superpower be?
I think I answered this earlier! Forgetting embarrassing moments! Also making kitchen sink salads and sandwiches. I can almost always take whatever is in my fridge and turn it into a delicious sandwich or salad. Most of my super-powers are of the everyday variety, but they really come in

handy. I just reread this answer and turns out I AM OLD NOW.

What do you consider to be your greatest accomplishment?

Healing from my eating disorder. There were so many days when I wanted to quit, to give up, to let that way of harming myself get the better of me. The recovery was not smooth, nor was it linear. But looking back, I'm so proud of myself for continuing to commit to my recovery. It's made all the difference in my life. I didn't see then all the ways that what I was doing was building toward healing, but I can see it now and it's beautiful.

What would your readers be most surprised to learn about you?

I'm not sure what would surprise them or not, but I did travel to Russia back when it was the USSR. So I've been to a country that no longer exists!

There seems to be no such thing as home in a war.

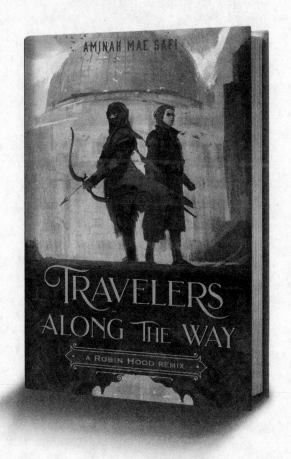

Keep reading for an excerpt.

In the Midst

Earlier, at the fall of Akko

The former dominion of
Yusuf ibn Ayyub, al-Nasir,
sultan of Egypt and Syria
(or, to his enemies, Saladin)
Jumada al-Thani

587 Hijri—
Summer,
AD 1191

CHAPTER ONE

Oo-De-Lally

THE WALLS OF THE CITY OF AKKO ARE NOT HIGH, BUT they're high enough.

I can see that now.

I've still got one handhold on the wall and I watch as my legs swing freely, high in the air. Dizzying, to say the least.

Terrifying, to say the most.

I suppose I should tell you why I'm dangling from the walls of the fallen city, but I haven't much time. Zeena is already halfway down. She likes to remind me that though we've both been climbing date palms since we could walk, she is older and she, therefore, has more experience. Personally, I refuse to admit to her that she's any better than I am.

But the truth is, she's the better climber. I'm better with a bow.

That won't help me here, though.

These city walls were not built for scaling. A statement of the perfectly obvious, I know. But they really, really weren't. The stones were placed precisely in such a way to keep anyone from doing exactly what we are. My arms are sore and my legs are stretched to their limits. Getting from one brick to the next would be difficult even in the daylight, much less with three quarters of a moon as the only source of light. There are campfires not too far in the distance, but those provide little comfort to me—they belong to the very people I don't want to notice me or my sister.

So, when my boot slipped earlier on one of the stones . . . well, now you know why I'm hanging by one arm, scrambling for purchase against the walls.

The scrape of boots against rock, of course, causes Zeena to look up and hiss. I already bit back a curse when I missed the brick, and there's no other way to find my foothold again without a little bit of noise.

But it doesn't matter; Zeena is not reasonable. She cannot possibly resist the urge to silence me, as though I might have missed the stakes in this dangerous game. As though I think we are currently racing down the spine of a palm tree to see who could bring Baba back a fresh date first.

As though her hissing were any less noisy than my one—extremely small—slip-up.

I can hear her warning in my mind: *Silence and invisibility are our one advantage.* Thank you for that sage advice, Zeena. Truly thoughtful and supportive and exactly what I needed this very moment. Could not do this without you, my shining and guiding light. Please, hush me again so that we might draw further notice to our climbing out of a city during a siege in the middle of the night.

My foot, mercifully, finds the next stone. I ignore the burning ache in my limbs as they beg for relief, pleading with me to relax for just one tiny moment. *That* feeling is a lie. Giving in to it would get us caught or killed. Akko fell—is falling—and its walls are not ones that I would dare scale in any other situation.

The Faranji came by the sea; we had to get out the hard way. To be a captive soldier is always a risk, but we did not have the safety of being men. If we were discovered, we would be too far from home for our name or our tribe to mean anything to these strange invaders. The men we fought alongside with for months had told us in no uncertain terms: The Faranji were barbarians. We would not be afforded the honor of being soldiers by *them*.

Zeena had balked at the thought of deserting our comrades, but Omar had ordered us: *Leave now, and do not turn back*. A direct command from our captain. I think he told Zeena to go on and defend Jerusalem, but we knew that part of the order didn't matter as much.

We had to run.

The only thing left in our way is the city's famous walls.

And a Faranji siege.

And, also, the siege of al-Nasir that surrounds that.

And, of course, the invaders who would be reaching the city's port by now, attacking the other side of Akko and potentially breaching the inside and spurring any troops on this side of the wall to approach.

And, not to mention, still surviving this climb.

Simple, right?

A laugh bubbles up in the back of my throat, and I bite my tongue in order to keep it from escaping. Mostly to avoid Zeena's glare again.

Focus.

One handhold and one foothold at a time. Finding the rhythm is always the tricky bit. Doesn't matter if you're scaling trees or walls, you've got to set a pace. Hand to foot to hand to foot. The movement must stay smooth. The movement must be balanced. The movement doesn't have to be fast, just consistent.

I keep moving.

A small thud sounds below me. Zeena's made it down, mashallah.

The rest of my climb is mercifully uneventful. I make it down without thinking further of Zeena's frustration or the expression in Omar's eyes as he ordered us to abandon our company. He was the only one who would look at us; the rest averted their gaze, knowing that this would never have been asked of them. I try not to think of the cast of rage on Zeena's face as I pulled her away from our fellow soldiers.

I try not to think much of anything at all anymore.

As my own feet touch the soft earth, I say a short prayer, in the smallest of whispers. "Allahu Akbar."

"Save it," says Zeena. "We've only just done the easy bit."

I hate her for saying it. Mostly, I hate that she's right. *Again.*

Thank you for reading this Feiwel & Friends book.

The friends who made

This Is All Your Fault

possible are:

Jean Feiwel, Publisher
Liz Szabla, Associate Publisher
Rich Deas, Senior Creative Director
Holly West, Senior Editor
Anna Roberto, Senior Editor
Kat Brzozowski, Senior Editor
Alexei Esikoff, Senior Managing Editor
Kim Waymer, Senior Production Manager
Erin Siu, Associate Editor
Emily Settle, Associate Editor
Rachel Diebel, Assistant Editor
Foyinsi Adegbonmire, Associate Editor
Liz Dresner, Associate Art Director

Follow us on Facebook or visit us online at mackids.com.
Our books are friends for life.